A Legacy of Demons

Pat Molloy

First Impression - 1989

ISBN 0 86383 615 1

© Pat Molloy

Printed in Wales at Gomer Press, Llandysul, Dyfed

CHAPTER ONE

Whichever way you boiled it down, there were only two ways of getting out of the Provisional I.R.A. You could leave in a coffin that was covered by an Irish tricolour, or you could leave in one that was not. You ended up as a dead hero or a dead defector. That was the way it had always been: you were in it for life and there were only two ways out. Until the one known only as *The Soldier* came up with a third.

For him there *had* to be another way. He was the last they would let out without a box around round him. What was more, somebody, somewhere, in yet another internal power-struggle, seemed to be preparing his box already. It was now or never. This was the day on which he would lay the foundations of his exit.

He had never expected it to be easy, but he was surprised at the ferocity of the Chief of Staff's reaction to the first, tentative hints of his idea for a "spectacular" on the British mainland. "Holy Mother of God! Jesus Christ, man, hasn't the Army Council put the block on that kind of thing once and for all? Have you gone off your bloody head entirely? And you above all people?" His face flushing with anger, he made to rise from his chair and the sweep of his arm sent his glass and Guinness bottle spinning across the table.

The Soldier reached over and gripped his chief's wrist. "Just hear me out. I'm offering you the best chance we'll ever have of grabbing the British by the balls and giving them no choice but to get out."

The Chief of Staff swung his body sideways. His chair crashed to the floor. "Grabbing them by the balls is it? Are you mad?"

Footsteps hammered on the farmhouse stairs, the bedroom door burst open, and a stocky young man in combat fatigues was in the doorway, feet apart, arms bent, hands spread, his right hand hovering over the Colt automatic at his hip.

"Leave it, Kieran," snapped the chief, his mouth twitching. "Leave it. Back downstairs. I'll call you if I want you." Kieran hesitated. "Get out, man! I told you to leave it." The gunman turned, closed the door and clumped down the stairs.

The Soldier retained his grasp, for there was no stopping now. Yet his voice was hardly above a whisper: "Would they let it happen? *Would they*?"

"Let me go," said his chief, his eyes blazing.

The Soldier pressed on: "Brave words about standing up to terrorism are all very well, but think about it. Would their people allow it to happen as the price for staying in the Six Counties? Just think about it."

"Jesus, it gets worse."

"Think about it," he rasped, tightening his blood-stopping grip. "If they did allow it to happen there'd be a real pig's arse of a constitutional crisis over there, and they'd know that from the start. Their people would never stand for it in a million years, man."

Though it took perhaps a minute of tense silence for this to sink in, *The Soldier* began to sense, from the slight relaxing of the man's arm muscles and the light in his narrowing green eyes, that he might just be nibbling at his hook after all. He eased his grip. His chief remained passive, so he let go altogether, emptied his whiskey glass at a gulp and refilled it.

The chief picked up his overturned chair, resumed his seat at the table, poured himself another Guinness. And then the two sat staring at each other, jaws set tight, their wills locked in silent combat.

A big man, a powerful man in many ways, *The Soldier* always looked like the one in charge. Except here, in this farmhouse, in these mountains, near that border, where the slightly-built young man opposite looked at him as if he could gobble him up and spit him out in little pieces. For all his own size, strength and supreme self-confidence, *The Soldier* knew only too well that this newly-emergent leader of the Northern 'Young Bloods' had merely to give the word—if he hadn't given it already—and his life wouldn't be worth one devalued Irish penny.

They sipped their drinks in silence, the lithe, black-bearded Ulsterman glowering at his southern subordinate, waiting for him to speak. *The Soldier,* outwardly calm and unhurried, though his heart was beating a tattoo, stretched out his 15-stone, six foot two frame, took off his horn-rimmed spectacles and polished them. "It

6

couldn't be more straightforward. Not *easy*. But straight-forward. And *you* tell *me* if the timing could be better.''

This time his chief heard him out. Then his frown softened and his face shaped itself into a thoughtful smile. He wiped his hand across his forehead and looked up to the ceiling in mock despair. And then he laughed: ''Soldier, you must have gone off your bloody head! If I didn't know you better I'd say it's time we pensioned you off.'' He emptied his glass and took another bottle from the tray. ''Look, you've had a bad time one way and another; we all have, and I know you're under pressure. I know your experience has been worth your weight in gold to us, and God knows what we'd have done without your contacts with Gaddafi and the P.L.O. and all that. It's terrific. But for Christ's sake, hasn't it occurred to you? If I tried to sell them a hare-brained scheme like that you'd be out. And I mean out! Haven't you got enough enemies in the organisation anyway just now? Bide your time a while. Keep your head down and maybe it'll all blow over. You don't need me to tell you that a walking encyclopaedia like you wouldn't last five bloody minutes if they thought you were cracking up. Nobody's *that* indispensable. Come on. Let's forget it. Let's have another drink and I'll sneak off back to Dundalk and not tell a soul about it. No hard feelings ...''

The Soldier left his glass untouched. ''I've done the ground-work,'' he said quietly. ''I can deliver.'' He paused. ''Look, you know and I know that we've pissed about for years and we're no nearer getting the Brits out than we were in '68. Let's face it. So, what about the Big Push? The one to force the issue once and for all? Isn't it time we tried? If we're wrong about the Big Push we're bloody well sunk altogether.''

The Ulsterman's eyes suddenly flashed again, as an unpleasant memory brought the anger flooding into him, and he threw the question back into *The Soldier*'s face: ''Like Brighton? Wouldn't Brighton have done it if your bloody bomber had done his job properly? Didn't the building surveyor who looked at the place after the explosion say that if *he'd* put the same amount of explosive in the *right* place he would have blown half the building away? A building surveyor! Not an explosives expert, a bloody building surveyor! And your feckin' man leaves his finger-prints at the hotel and not only gets himself put into the net, but takes a whole Active

Service Unit and all its kit with him. Life sentences, the whole bloody lot. And we've lost nearly every A.S.U. we've sent to the mainland since. Don't you lecture me on the Big Push, *Soldier.*"

"You're kidding yourself," *The Soldier* shouted, throwing all caution to the winds. "We're all kidding ourselves. Do you really think that if we'd wiped out the whole bloody bunch of them in that hotel, the next Prime Minister, the next Cabinet, would have got the troops out? Do you think the bombs at seaside resorts we'd laid on for that summer, or the bombing campaign we'd planned for the '87 election would have done it either? Have you or any of us learned anything about the Brits? Was Hitler able to bomb the bastards out of the war? What bloody bargaining counter have you got with a bomb anyway? What have you got when its gone off? I'll tell you what you've got. Two and a half thousand bodies, that's what. And what good have *they* done us in the last twenty years?"

"I'm warning you, Soldier . . ."

"You're warning me nothing," he roared, his fists pressing, white-knuckled, on the table as he stood up and leaned over him. "You'll listen me out or you'll shoot me here and now. Look what happened to Cullen, McCann and Shanahan when you sent them over to line up Tom King and the rest. What a bloody shambles that turned out to be. What a bunch of bloody amateurs. Camping like bloody boy scouts in the grounds of the man's house! They stood *no* chance. No wonder they all finished up at Winchester Crown Court. No wonder they're all inside doing twenty-five bloody years. And Clapham! Two years of preparation for blasting them on the 20th Anniversary of the troops being put into the north blown to buggery by a panicky pistol shot at a tuppence-ha'penny car thief. Look, man, there's only one way . . . *intelligence right from the inside.* And can't you see? Can't you see what I'm telling you? Can't you see that if we had our hands on the thing they value most, and with the British people already sick to death of Ulster . . . ?"

The Ulsterman was momentarily reduced to silence as *The Soldier* slowly resumed his seat, lowered his voice, fixed him with his eyes and said in calm, measured tones, "*And what would you say if I told you that the plan includes a swipe at the S.A.S. as well? What if I told you the chances are that we'd get some of the bastards who did for McCann, Farrell and Savage in Gibraltar for good measure?*"

8

That took his chief's breath away . . . for a full five seconds . . . before he collected himself and replied, ''I'd say the chances are that the Army Council just *might* give it the go-ahead. But how in the name of God do you think you could get away with *that*? What can you do that we haven't been able to do all these years?''

''*An Triúir**!'' said *The Soldier*, sitting back in anticipation.

His chief sat up sharply. ''You've been in touch with *An Triúir*? On what authority?''

''On my own authority. Remember? You, your deputy and me? We have the authority to explore the possibilities and the Army Council has the sole authority to launch an *An Triúir*-backed operation. Remember?''

''So?''

''So I've got the real stuff. *An Triúir* say they can give us every little detail. I can give you the rest. It can't miss.''

The Chief of Staff was only just managing to hold down his anger, but his curiosity was now thoroughly aroused. ''How soon?''

''Eight months. August. Bang in the middle of the 20th anniversary of the first deployment of the British army in the North. It's the best anniversary present we could give them.''

''O.K. But how? Where?''

The Soldier told him, and the man was thunderstruck. ''You *are* mad. You're stone bloody mad!''

An hour later, though, he was not so sure. It was certainly unlike anything they had yet conceived. It would be a step beyond terrorism into almost open warfare, but with planning and preparation of a kind never before attempted by the I.R.A. it might just work. And if it did, it would be the Provisional I.R.A.'s 'Big Push' with a vengeance!

*   *   *

It had been an uncomfortable few hours, and *The Soldier* had more than once felt he was helping hammer the nails into his own coffin. But as the time came for them to part he began guardedly congratulating himself. Getting his plan before the Provisional

---

*Pronounced ''An Treer''

9

I.R.A.'s Army Council was his first hurdle. There were many more, but that was the big one and it seemed that he was about to clear it. With luck, they would join their Chief of Staff as unwitting accomplices to his escape plan.

After a final drink and a less than heartfelt handshake, the two men left the strongly-guarded border farmhouse, the Chief of Staff heading east to Dundalk, through the driving sleet of that December day, while *The Soldier* drove south towards Galway, covering his trail by returning a series of hired cars, discarding his false moustache, horn-rimmed spectacles and dark curly hair-piece, gradually dropping his I.R.A. persona and resuming his true identity ... Michael Roche, internationally-respected and widely-travelled personnel executive, a man almost as much at home in the capitals of Europe, in Caracas, Trinidad, Dubai, Teheran, Riyadh and Tripoli as on his home ground, the City of Cork.

*   *   *

On 4th January, and for the following two days, two American morning newspapers—the *Boston Globe* and the *Chicago Tribune* —carried a cryptic message in the personal columns of their small-ads sections:

'And then there were three; Friends, think on Proverbs xxv 25.'

Anyone who had cared to open his Bible and turn to Proverbs xxv 25 would have found the words *'As cold waters to a thirsty soul, so is good news from a far country'*.

An Triúir had no need to check the Bible. They knew that passage by heart. At three o'clock in the morning of 12th January, some-where on the mainland of Britain, a bedside telephone rang. The bedroom light was switched on and the sole occupant of the house, fighting off the sleep that still dragged at his senses, picked up the handset.

The voice addressed him by name, and he answered: "Yes. Speaking. Who is that?"

There was a pause. *"Boru,"* said the caller. *"B-o-r-u,"* he repeated, slowly and deliberately.

The name that had lain dormant in the man since his first moments of understanding sprang back into the forefront of his

10

consciousness, and he was suddenly wide awake. *"Boru,"* he replied, his heart beating wildly.

An Triúir, the I.R.A's mysterious provider, had awakened one of its small army of highly-placed British 'sleepers', and there was no more to be said . . . yet.

CHAPTER TWO

The Day after the activation of *An Triúir*'s 'sleeper', a chance that the British might discover the plot in time died, along with Brigadier Anthony Farrell, O.B.E., M.C. (Retired), on a country road in Hampshire, England.

Outside the Leather Bottle pub, on the A.32 road from Reading to Hook, a dazzling array of red and blue flashing lights stabbed the night sky above a roadway illuminated by floodlights. Policemen scrabbled for clues among the jewel-like shards of windscreen and headlamp glass and the litter of twisted chrome and plastic trim. Camera flashes lit up the faces of the spectators as a police officer photographed the crumpled corpse from every angle. Vehicles crawled past the line of luminous cones, their occupants displaying the neck-stretching curiosity so familiar to those whose trade is death on the road.

In the way that fate can bring the key elements of a drama tantalisingly close to each other and yet let them slip by without touching, Steve Gannon, an officer of the British Secret Intelligence Service, M.I.6, was in that line of vehicles, not three paces from the corpse.

"What's happened?"

"Hit-and-run," said the youthful policeman who had stopped him to allow the other single line of traffic through. "Old chap from the village. Poor devil was crossing the road from the pub. Killed instantly by the look of it. Whoever did it scarpered. We've got road blocks out all over, so you might find yourself being stopped again before you get home."

"Hope you find him," said Gannon, slipping his B.M.W. into gear. "Goodnight, officer."

*   *   *

Steve Gannon arrived home in Maidenhead at sometime after midnight. His wife, Jill, was waiting up for him.

"Sorry I'm late, dear. A hold-up the other side of Reading. Some old fellow staggering out of a pub after closing time was killed in a hit-and-run."

She shuddered, but did not comment. "Scotch, darling?"

"Yes, a nice big one." He flopped down onto the settee and switched off the tail-end of a late-night horror film. "And my slippers. And a cuddle."

They sat talking for about an hour, she filling him in on such earth-shaking events as the phone calls from the children and the the row over the chairmanship of the Women's Institute, he skating lightly over his own day, telling only of friends he had met on one of his occasional visits to the office, and of provisional arrangements for exchanges of social visits. Always *provisional* arrangements. That was one of the drawbacks of working for Her Majesty's Secret Service.

"By the way," he said. "I'm afraid you'll have to give my apologies to the Crowthers next Friday evening. There's a job I've got to do myself. A five-day trip. I'm off on Monday morning. I'll leave the car and catch the train."

Disappointment was disappointment no matter how many years a wife had followed her Royal Marines officer around the world, and no matter how well she understood the uncertainty of the life her man had taken up after returning to 'Civvy Street'. Jill Gannon showed hers in a momentary clouding of her bright eyes. But it was gone in a moment and she was bubbling over as he hurriedly added, "But the Washington job looks as if it's on. Cultural Attaché at the Embassy. I'm hot favourite according to Ben."

She broke from his embrace, sat bolt upright and beamed at him. "Is it really . . .?"

"Just keep those fingers crossed. The post's vacant around August and Ben says an apartment goes with it. I might take you with me if you're good . . ."

She threw her arms around him, planted a kiss on his cheek and then, rising to her feet, took his hands in hers and made as if to pull him up. A provocative glint came into her eye and a wicked smile dimpled her cheeks. "Would a little bribery help?" she laughed, raising her eyes to the ceiling.

He was up like a shot. "Definitely. Works every time."

It was the perfect nightcap to deliver both of them into the soothing arms of slumber. But not for long. Their sleep was shattered at about two in the morning. Screams rent the darkness.

13

The gun ... the heavy, clumsy old Webley thirty-eight ... his fight against aching forearms to put that muzzle into the centre of the sweating forehead between those wild eyes. The blood ... the explosion of blood and tissue ... the voice ... those words. The deafening crack of the revolver that became a scream; the long, piercing scream which tore that recurring nightmare out of Gannon's head and flung and spattered it around the walls of the dark bedroom.

He was still screaming, still holding his arms in the air, his hands locked in a white-knuckled two-handed pistol grip. But this time he was not alone. This time his pounding heart beat against the warm body of the woman who clasped him tight in her arms and tried to soothe him. This time the sobs into which his screams subsided would melt against those soft breasts, the sweat would be wiped tenderly from his face as the bedroom light finally erased that awful picture and the voice that still echoed in his ears, dying away as if its message had been shouted into a steep mountain gorge: *"The strength in our arms ... the strength in ... our arms ... our arms ..."*

*   *   *

She was clearing away the breakfast dishes as he straightened his tie and patted the grey-streaked ginger hair that curled around the nape of his neck and knocked ten years off his age. "Steven, don't you think you should talk to the doctor, love? It's awful you know. Think what it could be doing to you. One of these days ..."

"Don't worry," he said, entirely recovered with a practice born of stern self-discipline, feeling his usual fit self and pressing in his firm stomach over a hearty breakfast. "Don't worry. I might be touching fifty-four, but I'm as fit as a fiddle. The doc passed me A.1 only the other day. It's the old Borneo days coming back, I'm sure. Can happen to anybody." He laughed and pinched her cheek. "Must be my guilty conscience ..."

A final embrace on the platform of Maidenhead railway station and Gannon was away with a crowd of other commuters. In town, the ex-Royal Marines Major, looking every inch the City Gent, walked through the doors of a building near Holborn Viaduct, nodded to the doorman, produced his pass and ran briskly up the broad staircase. There were few formalities and little admin work waiting for him in the office of his small and obscure branch of the government's Central Office of Information, so he was soon out again. Now, though, he was in jeans, sweat-shirt and zipper jacket, and carrying a holdall containing his travelling kit and the passport and other documents that gave him the identity and background to suit the job of the moment. For the next five days, he was *Gordon Colclough*, a free-lance writer whose perambulations around the Irish literary scene provided an ideal cover for his work as an undercover agent-runner in the battle against I.R.A. terrorism.

As for the Holborn branch of the Central Office of Information, it just did not exist. It was a complete fiction; an office without a function, other than to provide cover for the small and highly-specialised branch of the British Secret Intelligence Service to which Gannon had gravitated on leaving the Royal Marines. It was as much a fiction as would be the Washington job if it came his way . . . Cultural Attaché, the cover for anti-I.R.A. intelligence work in the United States.

Unlike James Bond, Steve Gannon had no licence to kill, though he did have the legal right every citizen has to protect his life and others if in mortal danger. If that required two rapid head-shots from a low-velocity .22 pistol, there were few better qualified to administer them. Nor did he have Bond's array of incredible gadgetry. Just the best bits and pieces that money could buy. Little bits and pieces. Bits and pieces that fitted into light baggage and around the body, to supplement a wealth of experience in living the double-life and absorbing, chameleon-like, the colour of whatever environment that double-life pitched him into. And the ability to match any professional actor in applying those simple techniques that can quickly transform a man's appearance with the minimum of effort and make-up.

As to the secret agent's proverbial appetite for women, well, that way, as he had learned time and again from the experience of others, lay disaster, which for an undercover man in the world of terrorism spells death. In any case, there was only one woman for him: the one who did what no one else could do. The only one in the world who could put his demon to flight.

*   *   *

The Inquest jury's verdict of death by misadventure effectively closed the investigation into the death of Brigadier Anthony Farrell, though the file was kept open by the police in the somewhat forlorn hope that something might turn up. The car that had killed him had been found, but it was a stolen car, and the chances of catching the thief or thieves were remote. In practical terms, therefore, it was just one more road accident.

The brigadier was buried by the only family he had—The Parachute Regiment. A chill wind blew a thin but soaking rain through the bare branches of the trees around Rotherwick church-yard and rooks scattered with hoarse cries as six self-loading rifles cracked out in salute over the flag-decked grave. "Ashes to ashes, dust to dust," intoned the Para chaplain, throwing a handful of earth into the grave. "Amen," muttered the mourners. "Firing party . . . Order . . . Arms," snapped the red-bereted Regimental Sergeant Major.

In time-honoured fashion a soldier had been laid to rest. But into the grave with this one had gone a chance that Michael Roche's daring plot against the British Establishment might be discovered in time. Another, though he did not know it, lay with M.I.6 officer Steve Gannon.

*   *   *

One month to the day after he had proposed his plan, *The Soldier* was called to another meeting, behind the same tight security screen and by way of his usual devious approach, but this time on a farm near Carrick-on-Suir in County Tipperary, where his Chief of Staff gave him the Army Council's go-ahead, which he received with quiet satisfaction.

He had good cause to feel satisfied. First and foremost, he had bought time; valuable time, in which to perfect his escape plan. Having got the Army Council behind him, he could now hope to stave off the more extreme efforts to remove him, from wherever they might be coming. He would still need to have eyes in the back of his head, but, for now at least, Phase One of his escape plan was going perfectly. Until his Chief of Staff gave him the rest of the news: "By the way. The Army Council gave the go-ahead only after a lot of thought, and only because, with all the problems we've

16

been having, they've come around to the view that the time might be right for the Big Push. That and the 20th Anniversary of the troops coming in. You nearly lost it all the same. It's chancy. There's a hell of a lot could go wrong and a hell of a lot of damage to us if it did. And you don't need me to tell you there's them that thinks you're burned out anyway.''

The Soldier said nothing, as his chief, his upper lip curling, pointed a menacing finger at him: "So this is the message. It's your operation, Soldier. The whole shoot. You'll be the one who'll run it from start to finish. And I mean finish. In command. On the ground. You're the planner and you're the professional soldier, so it should all come easy, shouldn't it?''

Roche was knocked sideways. Not by the warnings as to the consequences of failure, but by the fact that he was to lead the operation personally, which meant that he would lose all control over events outside it—the events that were indispensable to the full fruition of his plan. A million thoughts were speeding through his brain as his chief's voice bore in on him again out of the fog of confusion that had momentarily enveloped him.

"Any objection?''

"Objection?'' He was quickly back in control of himself. "Objection? Why the hell should there be? It's a winner. Can't fail. Right up my street.'' He held out his hand. "Tell the Army Council I can't thank them enough.''

Whether his chief's response was genuine *The Soldier* could not be sure, but the Ulsterman summoned up a grin and shook his hand strongly. "Well, it's a chance of a lifetime, Soldier, and if anybody can do it, it's you I reckon. When do you plan to go to Libya?''

"In the next couple of weeks. What we need from them will take some time to get together, so the sooner the better.''

They talked on over sandwiches and drinks, going over and over *The Soldier*'s ideas on how the operation was to be conducted, and the nature of the training, weapons and equipment he would be arranging with his contacts in Libya. They parted early in the afternoon and *The Soldier*'s mind was so full of the setback posed by his being given operational command that his sixty-mile drive to Limerick seemed to take no time at all. If he were to be so closely involved in the operation, how the hell could he carry out the rest of his escape plan? No member of an I.R.A. Active Service Unit was allowed to separate from his comrades once an operation had started. Security demanded it. As the man in charge he would be able to extricate himself at the last minute in order to make his get-away, but he couldn't possibly be where he had intended to be, nor do what he had intended to do—the thing that was indispensable to the full fruition of his plan—immediately after his A.S.U. had struck at its target. His girl-friend couldn't possibly do it for him. Apart from anything else, she knew nothing at all about his double life.

There was no way around it. He would have to recruit a helper. The risks involved were enormous and it was the last thing he would have dreamt of doing, but the roundabout was spinning and he would be signing his death warrant for sure if he tried to get off it now.

*   *   *

Maria Carmina Sanchez, Michael Roche's Venezuelan sec-retary, was having a shower when he arrived at Jury's Hotel in Limerick at six that evening. He called to her from the door and she emerged from the bathroom in a pink robe so carelessly drawn around her that her olive skin, her slender legs and her breasts were revealed as she rubbed her long, jet-black hair with a towel. Thrusting his hands inside the robe and feeling the soft curve of her back, Roche drew her to him and the towel dropped to the floor as they kissed passionately. At length she held him away from her and looked up into his face, with the big question in her large brown eyes even before she spoke it. "Well, Michael?"

"Well what?"

"Your business meeting. Have you done it?"

He smiled down at her. "*Señorita*, the deal is done. The contract is signed and I'm off to Europe next week to fix all the details. When it comes off, you and I will fly away like two swallows to tropical climes." He put his finger to his lips. "Only make sure you keep your mouth shut, my lovely, or we'll both finish up in the slammer."

Maria sat down on the bed and pulled her man to her. "Are you sure you can fool the accountants? Is there time?"

"Seven months. We can see it out for that long and I'll have everything set up for us to cut and run with every penny in the company, and more. The assets will disappear so quickly down the computer chain they won't know what's hit them. There's no extradition from where we're going anyway. Happy?''

''Happy as a Princess,'' she trilled, throwing her arms around him. The robe dropped away. There was plenty of time before dinner. As they rolled about the bed in hot embrace, as Maria Carmina Sanchez took every ounce of breath out of her man in her wild ecstasy, she was much too preoccupied to notice that his fire was not burning with its usual intensity. In fact, it was hardly flickering, for his thoughts were not entirely on that lithe, olive-skinned body which seemed so intent on smothering him. Far from it. He was more concerned with the question that had pursued him all the way down from Carrick-on-Suir to Limerick: Who the hell could he trust enough to bring into his plot without double-crossing him, or knowing of his involvement with the I.R.A., or exactly what he was up to? There *had* to be somebody. There was no way he could get off that bloody roundabout now!

CHAPTER THREE

To walk into the Long Hall Bar in George's Street, Dublin, is to step back to the turn of the century. Dark, polished mahogany, shining brass, bevelled mirrors and sparkling chandeliers; white-aproned barmen who might have served the likes of Yeats and Synge and the Abbey Theatre crowd in the days of its founding, and who lovingly tend long rows of pints of stout, scraping off the froth with ivory spatulas yellowed with years of richness, to tease in the Guinness under the hungry gaze of dedicated drinkers.

It was there, towards noon on 31st January, that Michael Hurley, journalist, writer and rabid republican, sipped his pint of Guinness, with one eye on the clock and the other on the ornately-etched glass panel of the door to the street.

Hurley, a dapper thirty-five year old, whose dark curly hair, laughing eyes and tinkling Kerry accent would attract anyone to him in a crowd, had been in the bar for only ten minutes and was already in conversation with a stranger. "What do I do?" he answered, with a modest laugh. "Oh, I write a bit, and I bum around a bit, and I scratch a living."

"Writing what?" asked the stranger.

"Politics mostly. People I meet. Oddities and a bit of poetry. Oh, and I'm interested in the sea and ships and I cover the odd Gaelic athletic event. You might have read the pieces I do in the *Sunday Independent*. You know, interesting people, a touch of politics, a bit of satire. What do you do?"

"Oh, I work in the Castle for some of them bloody politicians you write about . . ."

The street door opened, framing a tall, thin-featured, athletic-looking man with greying ginger hair. He wore jeans, sneakers and a red check shirt, and had a denim jacket slung over his left shoulder. His eyes darted from one end of the mahogany bar to the other, then back to the middle, where he evidently recognised Hurley. He smiled, let go of the door and strode towards him, right hand extended. It was Steve Gannon, in the guise of Gordon Colclough, free-lance writer, often resident in Ireland, otherwise something of a drifter.

Hurley excused himself and walked to meet the newcomer and shake him by the hand. "Hello, Colclough. Nice to see you again."

"Gordon it is . . . Gordon Colclough. Nice to see you too."

"Michael. Michael Theobald Hurley. Michael to you. What'll it be?"

"A pint of the best. What else?"

A barman took the last creamy slice from the top of a waiting glass and with a final burst of stout from the pump, handed Hurley a perfect pint, which he carried over to 'Colclough' at a corner table, as far from the crowded bar counter as it was possible to get.

"*Slainte*," said Hurley.

"And health to you too," said the Englishman.

There was silence for a few seconds, then both spoke at once, Hurley's, "Well, what are you up to these days?" colliding head-on with Gannon's, "Sounds an interesting project, your . . ."

"Sorry," they both said at once.

"Go ahead," said Gannon with a wave of his hand.

"Just wondering what you have on the stocks at the moment . . ."

"Not a lot. A bit quiet really. A couple of manuscripts I'm reading for a publisher. A commission for a history of an old Liverpool shipping line. But that's a long-term thing . . . you know, one of those jobs you can fall back on when nothing more pressing is coming in. I'm in Dublin actually to have a chat with a fellow about doing some literature for some ferry company, but generally, as I say, things are pretty quiet. How about you?"

"Oh, I'm doing pretty good," said Hurley. "I've always got a few steady jobs and in journalism you make your own luck, don't you?"

"I must say, it was a bit of a surprise hearing from you. How long is it now?"

"I remember exactly. A year ago last week. The party at the Shelbourne . . . when Geasons were publishing Tim Brogan's last book. Remember? Brogan got plastered and fell down the stairs."

Gannon laughed.

"I was all right in the Shelbourne," said Hurley, "and I remember us coming over here. I lost it when we went on to the Stag's Head."

"It left me a bit stunned as well, but I do remember you among the crowd." Gannon paused, gathering his memory. "I remember we had a long chat and I seem to remember you getting a bit het up about the I.R.A. To be honest, you frightened me off a bit . . ."

Hurley's eyes twinkled. "It's the whiskey what does it, yer honour," he exclaimed, touching his forelock like a drunken Irish peasant before a resident magistrate in days long ago. He tapped his glass of Guinness. "It's this that puts the spark in an Irishman's tongue, but it's the whiskey that sets light to it."

Gannon laughed again. "Anyway, what have you got for me? What's the project you mentioned in your letter?"

"Oh, yes. Geasons are interested in the idea of a book on the Irish coasting trade in the nineteenth century. More a picture gallery really, with some well-written text. They've come up with a hoard of early photographs and want an authentic vehicle to carry them. I thought of you. I remembered you telling me about your interest in maritime history."

"Sounds interesting. We can talk about it over lunch. Another pint first?"

They lunched at an Italian restaurant alongside the Liffey—a long, lingering lunch, during which it began to dawn on Gannon that the Geason project was not the only thing on Hurley's mind. As conversations do when lunch stretches through wine, port, coffee, brandies and more coffee late into the afternoon, theirs ranged over many loosely-connected topics, but Gannon noticed that his companion always brought it back to politics and the Irish troubles. It was as if, despite the Englishman's obvious shying away from it, that was the main thing on his mind.

During a lull in their conversation, after an over-long examination of the plight of the newspaper industry, Gannon, more certain than ever that there was more to the Irishman's sudden reappearance than met the eye, began to probe. "Well!" he said in one of those exclamations that usually signal that a conversation has run out of steam. "Well, how nice that we should meet again. What a pleasant couple of hours. What a nice surprise."

"Indeed," said Hurley, raising his brandy glass. "An acquaintance renewed and a relationship, I hope, beginning."

Gannon raised his and touched Hurley's. "Sounds promising."

There was silence again. Each filled the void by fussing over his drink and stirring his coffee.

"Wondered how you found me," said Gannon quietly.

"Easy. Well, *fairly* easy. I remembered you telling me you had a cottage on the quayside at Skerries, so I went along there and I think I found it, but if it was yours you'd been away for a while. I found an old biddy who described a fellow like you who had this cottage on the quay. Your name rang a bell with her. Since I didn't know your address over across, I came back down to Dublin and got a girl I know at Geasons to go over their guest list for Brogan's launching party. She gave me your London address." Hurley leaned forward. His brow creased in puzzlement, his green eyes seemed to laugh at Gannon and the sides of his mouth curled into a sly smile. "And then I was in London on a bit of business and I thought I'd call on you."

"And?"

"No such address, would you believe?"

"Strange," murmured Gannon impassively. "But you did find me . . ."

"Yes. I wrote to your non-existent address and, bingo!—you phoned me."

"Evidently you hadn't covered the area well enough on your last visit."

"Evidently," smiled Hurley. The fencing had begun. "And I set to thinking. I set to thinking that nobody at Geason's knew how you'd come to be put on the invitation list, let alone why."

Gannon sipped at his brandy, resting his elbows on the table, cupping the goblet in his hands.

"And I set to thinking a bit more. As to how it was that among all the hundreds of people I know in the newspaper and publishing game—on both sides of the water—many people seemed to know you but few of them could think of anything of any real substance you'd done in the literary line."

"As I said," smiled Gannon, "it's not much of a living. But who knows? One day . . ."

The Irishman was only warming up. "Do you remember we bumped into each other briefly in Belfast just before Christmas? At that bookshop in Donegal Street. Cogan's wasn't it?"

"Oh yes. Now you come to mention it . . ."

"Yes, Cogan's. Firebombed three weeks ago . . ."

"The devil it was!"

". . . . by the I.R.A. Irrefutable proof that the Brits had set it up as a front—a contact point for agents and informers." He grinned broadly. "A nest of vipers you might say. One or two of them got shot in the course of the following week."

"Well, you surprise me. Hard to find good second-hand book-shops. A bit James Bondish though, isn't it?"

"Gordon," said Hurley, "let's cut the crap. I know a lot more about you . . . or rather there's a hell of a lot about you *nobody* can find out. You're a nowhere man. The only places I've been able to tie you down to is that bloody fisherman's cottage at Skerries and a spy shop in Belfast. If you're a writer, I'm a feckin' leprechaun!"

Gannon waited while Hurley turned to a waiter and ordered more coffee. An uncomfortable silence prevailed while the waiter poured. "Anything more, *signor*? More brandy?"

"Yes, two large ones," said Hurley. Then he addressed the Englishman again, and for the first time those merry eyes lost their sparkle. His lips tensed and he spoke as if he had been rehearsing the words for a week: "For my money, Gordon, or whatever your name is, you're a British secret service man." He took another deep breath and the rest of it tumbled out. "With my connections through *An Phoblacht* and other republican rags and working for Sinn Fein I've access to some of the highest levels of the Provisional command, and to some of the most sensitive intelligence that it's possible for a relative outsider to get at. For very personal reasons—don't ask me what they are—I've decided to put all my knowledge and connections at the disposal of the British secret service." He paused. The Englishman did not react. Hurley pressed on: "You're saying nothing, Gordon, but I'm putting everything I've got on my hunch. Believe me. I'm staking my life on it, for God's sake. I want to work against them and I've got a lot to offer. It's all yours."

Gannon's continuing lack of reaction destroyed Hurley's composure altogether. "For Christ's sake!" he exclaimed, keeping his voice down with evident difficulty. "For Christ's sake say something, man." He sank back into his chair, beads of sweat glistening on his upper lip, a strained look narrowing those green

24

eyes of his, the fingers of his right hand nervously drumming the table.

"I'm sorry, Michael," said the M.I.6 man quietly, "but you've got me wrong, old son. If there's one thing I've learned in this beautiful, crazy mixed-up country of yours, it's to steer clear of politics—and even clearer of people who talk about guns. If I wanted to I couldn't even put you in touch with anybody who could help you. I've never met a spy to my knowledge. I wouldn't recognise one if I tripped over him on the way out."

It required an obvious effort for Hurley to pull himself out of the state of nervous exhaustion to which his outburst had reduced him. "Gordon," he said, "I haven't got you wrong. I don't know what the hell you're doing over here, but every instinct tells me I'm right. You're the guy I'm looking for. If you don't tune in you'll want your arse kicking. Don't you know that if I'd fingered you to the boys your life wouldn't be worth that?" He snapped his fingers. "I've had men killed on less. Me. A writer. Not a gunman, a writer. Doesn't that tell you something? Holy Mother of God, man, I don't know how you weren't shot with the rest of the bookshop crowd."

Gannon cast a nervous glance around him. "For God's sake," he whispered. "Won't you listen to me? You're on the wrong bloody horse. If not for your own sake, then for mine, shut up! If this is what you've dragged me here for I'm off."

Hurley reached across the table and gripped his wrist in desperation. "Please. I'm sorry. Just hear me out for half a minute more and then we'll forget it."

The Englishman relaxed under the pressure of the grip as Hurley made his final plea: "I know I've got you right, Gordon. I just know. And it would only take me five minutes to prove to you beyond all doubt that I can deliver..."

As Gannon moved to pull away, Hurley tightened his grip. "All right, all right. Just this. I could be signing my death warrant, but I trust you. Here's my card. You can contact me through the Tara News Agency any time, but always use an Irish name and an Irish rendezvous. Or you can ring me on 75 91 97 in Dublin."

He let go of the wrist, withdrew a card from his breast pocket and pressed it into the pocket of Gannon's red check shirt.

Gannon looked down to his pocket, took out the card and, rising from the table, placed it on Hurley's plate. He took a twenty-pound note from the back pocket of his jeans and placed that, too, on the plate. "My share of the bill. Don't worry, I won't breathe a word about what you've said, but if you've got any sense you won't try it on anybody else. If you're serious about the Geason project, get them to drop me a line." Walking away, he threw a backward glance as he neared the door. "You know the address. Cheers, old son. See you."

Hurley raised a limp hand. And ordered another large brandy.

*   *   *

Detective Superintendent Peter Blake, in charge of the C.I.D. in the east of Hampshire, had not heard of the death of Brigadier Anthony Farrell. After all it was only a road accident, a Traffic Department matter. It is unlikely that he would ever have heard of it had it not been for the facility on the Police National Computer which registers common interest in people circulated as wanted or suspected. At ten o'clock on the morning of Tuesday 24th January, an officer in the fingerprint department at force headquarters came through to him on the telephone. "Trotter here, Guv. Do you know anything about that ex-brigadier who was killed in a hit-and-run at Rotherwick a couple of weeks ago?"

"Hit-and-run?"

"Yes."

"Any crime?"

"No, Guv. Misadventure."

"A traffic job, then."

"Except that it was a stolen car from Hook, abandoned back at Hook."

The Superintendent idly wondered why a matter like that should concern him. "A sub-div C.I.D. job then."

"It is, and I've told them. There was a finger impression on the interior mirror and it's been identified. Sub-div have circulated him as wanted for interview for taking the car without consent."

"So . . .?".

"So there might be a bit more to it, Guv. That's why I'm calling you. He's a guy called James Duggan, thirty-one, born in

Southern Ireland, and he's on the computer as being of interest to Metropolitan Police Special Branch. There's stuff on his record about suspected Provisional I.R.A. activities, but the main thing is he's the subject of a deportation order and he shouldn't have been here. The computer file shows a reference back to D.I. Foster of Met. Special Branch.''

''Who holds our file?''

''D.I. Benson, on sub-div. We've told him and he's put out an all-ports warning on Duggan. He's got no known address and he's probably out of the country again by now anyway.''

Now Blake *was* interested. ''Thanks, Jim. I'll have a word with Foster. And Benson . . . he's in the office with me now.'' He put down the phone and turned to his D.I. ''This brigadier . . . what's his name?''

''Anthony Farrell. Got the O.B.E. and M.C. Ex-Para.'' He gave his superintendent the circumstances of the brigadier's death.

''Doesn't make a lot of sense, does it?'' grunted Blake. ''An experienced Provo nicking a car, doing a circular tour in it and getting involved in a hit-and-run? A guy with a deportation order on him and form for A.S.U. activity on the mainland, coming back into the country and putting himself on the line with a caper like that? Makes no sense at all to me.''

His D.I. agreed.

Blake sat deep in thought for a while, and then, holding up his left hand and counting his fingers, said ''One, he operates under orders. He gave up being a free agent the minute he became a Provo and made his first killing. Right?''

''Right.''

''Two, if he's got back onto the mainland with a deportation order hanging over him, he's come in for something important, under orders. Right?''

''Right.''

''Three, if he's here, he lies low until he's activated, or . . .'' and here Blake formed his right hand into a pistol, putting the fingertip muzzle to his temple—'' . . . it's bang, bang. Right?''

''Right again.''

''And the guy he kills is an ex-Para officer?''

''Coincidence?'' ventured the D.I.

27

Blake snapped back. "I don't believe in it. And if you don't believe in it you'll be wrong a lot of the time, but you'll be bloody well right when it matters! Bring me the file. Pathologist's report, scientific and the lot. I want you to take this one on. I want to know everything there is to know about this Duggan, and the brigadier. Everything. Don't let's miss the bugger if there's anything like a murder here."

CHAPTER FOUR

As the Sealink ferry came abreast of Strumble Head lighthouse at the western tip of Wales, in a light westerly wind on a calm Irish Sea, Michael Hurley was half way down a pint of Guinness in the bar up forward. The loudspeaker came to life: "Ladies and Gentlemen, we shall arrive at Fishguard Harbour in fifteen minutes. Will drivers please proceed to the car deck. Please do not start your engines until you receive the signal to drive off."

Hurley looked at his watch. It was five minutes past noon. Ten minutes later, after another quick pint, he was down on the car deck, and ten minutes after that, to a wave from the car-deck marshal, he started up his engine and followed the line of vehicles up the ramp, along the quay-side road and into the green channel of the Customs Hall. Having passed the customs bench without challenge, he was obliged to spend seven or eight minutes at the police Special Branch check before being allowed to go. He did not drive straight up to Fishguard town, but made several small diversions in order to satisfy himself that he was not being followed. Then he parked his car and strolled into the Royal Oak pub in the Market Square.

He ordered a Guinness and took from his pocket a crumpled piece of paper on which he had scribbled notes as he was taking a telephone call at his home. He read it again:

'Of interest to *An Phoblacht*. Secret documents, Brit Special Branch. Xerox copies. Very damaging. Morning ferry, Rosslare-Fishguard, 7th Feb. Meet Royal Oak (in Fishguard town), 1 p.m. Strictly alone. "Never mind my name".'

And here he was. At twenty to one. No one was taking the least bit of notice of him. He took a seat facing the street door, ordered a second pint and a ham roll, and waited. On the dot of one, the barman asked if there was a Mr. Hurley in the place, and he went over to the bar and identified himself. "There's a phone call for you," he said, placing the set on the counter.

Hurley picked up the receiver. "Hello."

"Hello. Hurley?"

29

"Speaking."

"Change of plan. Follow my instructions and make for the Welsh Guardsman pub in Carmarthen. It's tucked behind the A.40 on the way out of town. You should be there in an hour. You've done all right up to now, but make sure you're on your own. You're being watched." The caller gave him directions and rang off.

It was ten minutes after two when Michael Hurley walked into the Carmarthen pub and he was halfway down a glass of Guinness when in walked the man known to him as Gordon Colclough.

"Well, I'll go to hell!" he exclaimed, grasping Gannon's proffered hand. "You cunning bastard."

Both men laughed as they shook hands heartily.

"Drink up," said Gannon. "Get your kit out of your car. We're travelling in mine."

"Where?" asked Hurley, shaken a little by all the rush.

"You'll see. Let's go."

"Yes, but the documents. Let me see . . ."

Gannon grabbed his arm. "I said, let's go," he said quietly but urgently, steering the Irishman towards the door.

On the car park outside, Hurley transferred a suitcase and a coat from his Datsun to Gannon's B.M.W. He locked his car and, on the Englishman's instructions, placed his keys on top of the front nearside wheel under the wing. "What happens to the car?"

"Don't worry. It'll be looked after. It's all arranged. By the way, your name's McGilligan. Michael McGilligan. Got it? Michael McGilligan."

There was one more precaution. A little way out of Carmarthen, heading east for the M.4 Motorway, Gannon pulled into a lay-by and gave Hurley and his few belongings a thorough going over to ensure that he was not carrying anything in the way of electronic monitoring devices. And off they went, eastwards towards the Severn Bridge.

*   *   *

A little after half past four, after leaving the M.4 at junction 18, sixteen miles on the English side of the River Severn, they turned right off the A.46, about a quarter of a mile short of the village of Sherston in Wiltshire. The car crunched up a gravel drive and turned right again into a car park alongside an ivy-covered Georgian house, the front of which exhibited the palladian charm favoured by its builders, Robert and James Adam. It now housed the Fosse Grange Country Club. In the centre of four delicately-framed twelve-paned sash windows, its fan-topped porticoed entrance led into a circular hall, on each side of which a curved staircase climbed to a landing beneath an ornately embossed ceiling traced with gold through delicate shades of pink, green and cream.

"Mr. Colclough and Mr. McGilligan," said Gannon to the neatly-dressed blonde at reception. "We should have two single rooms . . . four nights."

The receptionist checked her booking list. "Oh yes, sir," she smiled. "Rooms 9 and 10 . . . a nice view over the park and down to the river." She placed two registration forms and two ball pens in front of them. "If you wouldn't mind, sir . . ."

The men signed in. "You've picked a nice time of the year to visit us," said the girl brightly.

"Oh, yes," said Gannon. Remarkable weather for February . . . like an early spring. My friend here is over on business—horse business—so we're having a look at some stables in Malmesbury."

"Have you stayed with us before?"

"No, but you've been highly recommended by a friend of mine, so we know we'll enjoy our stay." He could have added that the 'friend' was the manager of the place—a retired chief inspector of the Metropolitan Police Special Branch, who was always happy to provide the right atmosphere and total discretion for the de-briefing of a potential agent.

Hurley was totally confused. "The documents! That was the message, the documents. What the hell's going on? Have you got them or haven't you."

"Patience, Michael," counselled Gannon. "*You* started the ball rolling, not me, so you'll just have to wait and see."

Hurley shrugged his shoulders and surrendered himself to the flow of events. Half an hour in the sauna and a refreshing dip in the hotel's swimming pool relaxed them and sharpened their appetites for an excellent meal of prawns in aspic, veal Hongroise with cucumber Vichy, and pears Charcot, accompanied by two bottles of Chateau Roc St. Bernard '78. The position of their table—

31

discreetly placed in a corner alongside a scalloped alcove and lit by a single candle—along with the leisurely length of their meal, gave the two men ample opportunity to talk without being overheard.

"Well," said Gannon to a still mightily puzzled Hurley, "here's to that fruitful relationship you talked about in Dublin."

Hurley's glass clinked against his and he nodded. "I'm puzzled," he said. "I suppose I'm right in thinking that there's no bloody secret documents. But I must say that even if you had second thoughts about the proposition I put to you in Dublin, I never expected you to turn up in person. I'd have thought you'd have delegated it to somebody else until you knew it was safe. It's not quite what I expected of the Secret Service."

"Wouldn't it have been obvious anyway? So why beat about the bush, especially since you're going to be here long enough for us to put a few people into the net on your say-so before we really get down to business. And let me tell you this: if you play it straight you'll be very well looked after . . . and well protected. After you've established yourself and done some useful work for us, if at any time you feel your life's in danger you've only to say 'Out' and we'll open the door for you—wide, safely and profitably." Then he leaned forward, with an air of menace. "But if you're here to play silly buggers, then watch out. And I wouldn't try slipping away quietly if I were you. Either way, you're in it up to your neck already and you wouldn't get past the front gate." His eyes flashed, and in that fraction of a second Hurley knew he was looking at a man who could kill. "You've decided off your own bat to deal with some people who can be very nasty if provoked."

Hurley concentrated on his wine glass for a while as if digesting the threat. Then he smiled again. "You know, you haven't given me any proof yet that you really are a secret service man."

Gannon smiled too. "You were sure enough in Dublin, I thought."

"Yes, but it would be nice to see some evidence."

"I'm afraid you'll have to trust that hunch of yours for a while. In the meantime we'll have to see if somebody's setting somebody up, won't we?"

Gannon reached into his inside jacket pocket and brought out a miniature tape recorder. He switched it on and Hurley was astonished to hear his own voice: " . . . . here's my card. You can contact me through the Tara News Agency at any time, but always use an Irish name and an Irish rendezvous. Or you can ring me on 75 91 97 in Dublin . . .'' Gannon switched off the machine. ''Lesson one. Never allow yourself to be recorded without your knowledge.'' He ran the reverse button and played a snatch from an earlier part of the tape: ''. . . . I could be signing my death warrant . . .'' whispered Hurley's voice.

''You could indeed,'' echoed Gannon. ''You could indeed.''

Removing the cassette and replacing it with a fresh one, he connected the machine to a lead under his armpit and put it back into his inside pocket. He tapped his tie pin. ''A mike. Now this is the drill. Over the next few days I'm going to question you in considerable depth and I shall be checking your answers against what we know about you and the Provos. Since we met that day in Dublin I've taken the trouble to find out a hell of a lot more about you, so get it right. Let me repeat, just in case it hasn't sunk in already: you've put your foot in the door, Michael, and there's no going back, so make sure your heart's in it. I want some information—some good stuff—something that will prove your good faith for a start. And then if you stand the test we'll talk about the future. Meantime, you'll be watched, and if there's the slightest sign of a double-cross you don't need me to tell you what will happen.''

Hurley said nothing.

''But first, why? Why put your life on the line? What do you want, money?''

Hurley shook his head. ''You wouldn't understand. Just say I'm doing it for very personal reasons. Don't ask me. Keep your money. Forget it and let's just get on with it.''

Gannon did not press the point. It was important for many reasons that he should know why Hurley was doing this, but he knew that no relationship is more difficult to explain or understand than that between the informer and his clandestine link with the forces of law and order, and that no motive is so unclear as that of the traitor to his cause. There can be a hundred and one motives, and they can operate on men's minds in any number of combinations. If all Hurley wished was to escape into anonymity, he could claim it, at the price of information useful to the security forces. Yet he talked of staying on, in which case he would be treading from one day to the next through a minefield criss-crossed with tripwires waiting to catch the unwary gesture, or movement, or meeting. And if he tripped the mine, death would not come quick and clean, but slowly and painfully, as those he had betrayed tried to wring from him his knowledge of the enemy's methods, their organisation and their people.

Hurley would know all that, so whatever his motive it must be something deep. And yet it might be nothing more than the product of an unlikely bond between two opposites—the informer and his contact. Or the sheer thrill and danger of dicing with death. In such a case even the informer himself will probably not be able to explain his motive. Even to himself.

So, for now at least, Gannon would waste none of his precious time on such esoteric considerations as his man's motive. He would simply set out to prove that his information was genuine and useful, and that he was playing it straight. If he achieved that, Hurley's motive would become of only academic interest. If Hurley were trying to turn himself into a double-agent, then some way would be found of disposing of him—quietly but decisively.

The two men talked on. They talked over after-dinner coffee in a corner of the Louise Quinze lounge and over late-night drinks in the bar, and into the early hours of the morning in Gannon's room. They talked next day as they strolled across the sheep-grazed parkland to see the trout poised beneath the sparkling lazy waters of the river beyond. In the evenings, over more of those splendid gourmet meals and that excellent Claret, they talked again. And on their last night at the Fosse Grange Country Club, in the bar at a small late-night gathering of what, so far as Hurley was concerned, could have been anything from a crowd of happy holidaymakers to a whole cohort of secret service agents, the two practitioners in the deadly game of espionage relaxed, enjoyed the company, talked of nothing in particular, drank their fill, and got their final appetite for sleep.

But there was little sleep for Steve Gannon at the Fosse Grange Country Club. Those same words roared again through his head, battering their way into his brain night after night: "*The truth on our tongues . . . the purity in our hearts . . . the strength in our arms.*" The voice roared on. He clutched the gun. The trembling of his hands made the Webley thirty-eight seem like a ton weight, and all the time those words roared on in his ears like the thunderous voice of

34

doom. He fought to keep his eyes in contact with those of the terror-stricken, screaming man spread-eagled before him, tied to the iron railings of the park, his face distorted, his mouth open in a scream drowned by Gannon's thundering inner voice. Body writhing, hands drained white by the tightness of the cord around them, the pinioned victim saw death in the mouth of the gun barrel rising inches away between his eyes, and died a thousand times in what seemed like an eternity. But whatever happened, however hideous that fear-racked face before him, Gannon had to meet its gaze, had to stare into his victim's eyes, as he struggled to control his two-handed grip on the old service revolver.

The voice roared on: "*The truth on our tongues . . . the purity in our hearts . . . the strength in our arms.*" His heart pounded, his arms ached, his whole mind and body fought with the awful weight of that weapon. And the voice persisted, louder and louder, bruising his brain with those hammer-like words: "*. . . . the strength in our arms.*"

The muzzle was there now, pressing against the forehead, one inch above that wild stare into which Gannon's eyes bored like lasers. The inner voice was like the roar of an express train in a tunnel. The trigger was responding to his pressure. The hammer was coming back with agonising slowness against the protest of his aching forearm muscles. Then the whole terrifying image disintegrated in smoke, blood, skull-bone and brain-tissue. From the deafening crack of the explosion issued a penetrating scream—loud, long, piercing—and for a fraction of a second he saw his blood-covered hands, his revolver, the bullet-punctured mask which was all that remained of his victim's exploded head: a still-frame from a movie picture.

Then it was gone. But the scream remained, piercing the darkness. His own scream, uncontrollable until long after he remembered that it was that recurring nightmare. The relentless message: "*The truth on our tongues . . . the purity in our hearts . . . the strength in our arms.*"

Frantically, night after night, Gannon would switch on the light to drive away the echo, the vivid images. He was bathed in sweat, his heart punching its way out of his rib-cage as he went for the whiskey bottle. Night after night he asked himself, "Is this the crack-up?'' And night after night he drowned the question in deep draughts of scotch.

He would turn off the light, but he would sleep no more. He would lie awake, watching the first traces of dawn touch the blackness of his room to a softening grey from which the shapes of the furniture would begin to emerge, first as blurs and then as solid forms, while the first faint cheeps of awakening birds quickened into the dawn chorus.

At seven o'clock on that last morning, the sun streaming through his bedroom windows across the rolling Wiltshire country-side sent him to an early breakfast with Hurley and to the nine o'clock start that would see them back in West Wales by mid-day. To Hurley's surprise they stopped six miles short of Carmarthen, to collect his car from the car park of a small country pub. When he expressed his surprise at the change of venue, Gannon winked at him. ''Just playing safe, old son. Can't have you setting me up for a follow, can we?'' Just to make sure, he gave his man a few hints as to the precautions he had already taken. As well as speaking for the benefit of his pocket tape recorder at their corner alcove dining table, Gannon told him, he had been facing squarely onto the tiny lens of a closed-circuit television camera (hidden behind a Gainsborough miniature), and while he was sitting in the Regency armchair in Gannon's bedroom, another tiny lens had looked down on him (from the screw hole of a gilded wall-light bracket). What with still pictures taken by a Security Service surveillance team in and around the Welsh Guardsman pub in Carmarthen, and the arrests and arms seizures already made on the information he had given, Michael Hurley was now well and truly in the British pocket.

They shook hands and Gannon watched as the Irishman drove off on the road west, heading for the three o'clock ferry from Fishguard. With a final wave of his hand, he turned his own car eastward for England, switched on the tape recorder, and began to summarise the information Hurley had given him and the impression the Irishman had left on him.

*   *   *

If only half of what Hurley had brought with him were true, Gannon was onto a winner. Names, and a list of murders,

36

bombings and mortar attacks against which to put them; safe houses, weapons stores, projected arms imports, organisation charts. Some arrests had already been made and some of Hurley's other information had already been verified with the M.I.6 computer and the security forces' intelligence files. Gannon summarised the rest of it and gave his preliminary verdict:

"Source evidently well-placed and knowledgeable; motive at present unknown, but obviously something more than mere financial reward.

"Stands up well to deep and devious questioning. Answers consistent over long intervals between questions. If he is a liar, he is an extremely well-rehearsed one and a consummate actor. A likeable character; strong sense of humour, no real signs of tension once our relationship was established. I think he's O.K., but he must be put under intensive surveillance until we are fully assured of his integrity."

It was a promising start anyway, but there were three items of information which, if true, would make Hurley worth his weight in gold to the Secret Intelligence Service:

The first related to bombing and gun attacks on British servicemen in Germany. The Provisionals were finding Holland and Belgium too hot, he had said, and they were going to move their people to France, where they intended setting up a safe house in some village near Paris. They would soon be stepping up their attacks, but, given a month or two, he would be able to locate and identify them.

Second, he had named an I.R.A. group in the United States who had recruited two American electronics experts—one in New York and one in California—to help them design and build radar-guided rockets capable of shooting down British army helicopters.

And, third, what Hurley clearly regarded as the ace in his pack: he had produced from his pocket a crumpled cutting from the *Sunday Times*, which bore the headline '*Britain on terror alert for Libyan arms push*'. He had read from it: "Special Branch detectives now fear that Gaddafi is still willing to sponsor terrorism in Britain, despite recent interceptions at sea and arms finds on both sides of the Irish border. Intelligence analysts especially fear that Republican extremists are looking for heavy automatic weapons and rocket launchers to attack helicopters and disrupt patrols in the border areas, where land mines have made patrolling by vehicles particularly dangerous. Indeed, there appear to be grounds for believing that they already have such weapons and are training for their use. 'The information we have received so far is very worrying,' a senior security source in Ulster said. 'Particularly with the approach of the 20th Anniversary of the first deployment of British troops on the streets of Ulster, which we expect the Provisional I.R.A. to mark with some kind of spectacular act of terrorism. If they continue to receive assistance from Libya it could cost many lives. We have to take what steps we can to stop them.''

Hurley had placed the cutting in front of Gannon. "Every word of that is true," he had said. "And its *The Soldier*. He's your man. He has Gaddafi in the palm of his hand."

"*The Soldier*?" Gannon had asked, without showing a trace of the excitement Hurley's statement had aroused in him. "Do you know him?"

"Do you?" Hurley had asked in return.

"I know of him. Everybody knows of *The Soldier*, but can you put a name to him?"

"Not yet, but I will soon. It's one of the best-kept secrets in the I.R.A."

"You can say that again," Gannon had said, knowing that if Hurley did name *The Soldier* he would be solving a mystery that had baffled the British security forces for more than eighteen years. "How close are you to naming him?"

"Pretty close. I'm very close to a guy who actually works with him. I'm almost there."

What a coup this would be. Since 1970 the indexes of the R.U.C., the *Garda Siochana*, the Northern Ireland H.Q. of the British army and the Security Service in London had been swallowing up hundreds of references to *The Soldier*. Informers and defectors galore had known about him but had never met him. Republican folk lore had woven lurid legends around him, and the evidence derived from many P.I.R.A. 'spectaculars' had consistently pointed to the existence of a planner possessed of highly-developed military skills. That *The Soldier* had maintained his cover so completely over such a long period in the face of everything the security forces could throw at him in terms of special squads, intensive surveillance and top-grade infiltrators, testified to

38

surveillance consciousness of an exceedingly high degree. That he was a renegade ex-member of some *élite* British military unit seemed quite beyond doubt. To identify and neutralise him would be counted as one of the great intelligence coups of the whole anti-I.R.A. campaign.

Hurley had given even more. Something very big was afoot and *The Soldier* was in the thick of it. It was something to which the word *Andrea* related. Did 'Colclough' know about *Andrea*? Yes he did. Well, *Andrea* was being bandied about in high Provisional circles and it seemed to be linked with some very big project of theirs in which *The Soldier*, whoever he was, had some leading part to play. It was being said that when this one broke, everything the I.R.A. had ever done would be eclipsed by its scope and daring.

Hurley had mentioned something else that required urgent attention. It seemed that the Provisional I.R.A. had put out an order for the killing of a senior British army officer, and it had been done. No name, no reason, just 'a senior British army officer', and Hurley's strong belief that it, too, was linked with *Andrea*.

On Gannon's return to his London office, one of the girls did a computer check and gave him the print-out. It showed that *Andrea* had cropped up before from time to time, over many years, as far back as the Second World War, when the I.R.A. had linked itself to the Nazi cause. It had cropped up, then and later, in circumstances which showed that it was the key to a very special and very powerful weapon in the I.R.A.'s armoury. But the computer could identify no pattern and no relationship to events by which its significance could be accurately judged. The girl had also run the word *Andrea* through the computer's synonym file, to try to identify any English word or any in a foreign language which might have the same sound though a different spelling. After all, the word had only ever come up by word of mouth and had never been spelled out as A-N-D-R-E-A. But even that had led nowhere.

As to the killing of a senior British army officer, nothing of the kind seemed to have happened. The Ministry of Defence had carried out a thorough check and it had come back negative, so Gannon had had the information passed to army intelligence for top priority circulation to all its formations just in case Hurley's belief that the assassination had already been carried out had been premature.

39

All in all, then, a promising start, said Gannon's chief, congratulating him on acquiring such a potentially useful agent. Perhaps they might now solve that eighteen-year-old mystery and trap the elusive *Soldier*. Perhaps they might also solve the mystery that went back far beyond the present Irish troubles and far beyond the memories of anyone still serving in the Secret Intelligence Service: the mystery known to them as *Andrea*. Had the M.I.6 computer's synonym file been programmed to scan the Irish language, or had Hurley, Gannon or anyone else on the British side thought of turning to that language for an answer, they might have solved it there and then. They might have recognised *Andrea* for what it was—a phonetic rendering of *An Triúir*, meaning 'The Three People'—and that really would have given the makings of the biggest anti-I.R.A. intelligence breakthrough of all time.

CHAPTER FIVE

On Tuesday 7th February, Michael Roche presented himself at the immigration control desk at Cork airport to board the 7.45 Aer Lingus morning shuttle to Dublin. The officer smiled as he recognised one of his regular customers. "Mr. Roche, sir. Good morning. How are we?"

"Fine, Pat, and yourself?"

"Great. Where are we off to to-day?"

"Oh, Libya, and probably on to Dubai and Teheran. Just a few days. I've got some fellows in the oilfields out there and there's been holy panics over all the trouble in O.P.E.C."

"Thanks be to God the only black stuff we have is the Liffey water," cracked the officer, waving him through.

Once in his window seat on the starboard side of the Boeing 737's 'No Smoking' section, Roche strapped himself in and opened his *Irish Times*. A coffee later they were landing at Dublin; a little over an hour after that, comfortably seated in another Aer Lingus 737, flight EI.652, he was in the air again, en-route for Frankfurt, anticipating a quick lunch with his Libyan host and friend, Salem Ibrahim.

Promptly at 12.20 p.m. the 737 touched down at Frankfurt and within twenty minutes Roche was in the airport bar shaking hands with the Libyan, who, ostensibly the Vice-Chancellor of Tripoli's Al-Fatah University, was better known to the Irishman as Colonel Gaddafi's right-hand man in his country's dealings with the international terror groups who queued up for Libya's deadly bounty.

They sat at a low table, Roche making short work of his Chivas Regal whiskey, Ibrahim sipping half-heartedly at his iced orange juice. They touched on their business over a quick snack, but his companion seemed strangely distant, as if he was having difficulty concentrating on what Roche was saying to him. Or was it just his imagination?

From Frankfurt they travelled to Tripoli by flight LN.173 of Libyan Arab Airlines, and by six o'clock Roche was booking into the Hotel Kasi Libya on the Shari Sidi Asa, near the city centre.

Ibrahim left him there, saying he would send a car for him at nine o'clock next morning. Roche, not fancying the look of the hotel's dinner menu, went foraging in town and dined on grilled sword-fish steak at the Wadi Al-Rabee restaurant, by the Al Shati Beach Hotel on Hay Al-Andalus, before turning-in early and reading himself to sleep with his shopping list. It was a troubled sleep. He couldn't get Ibrahim out of his mind and he could swear there was something different about him.

* * *

Roche's discussions with the team of service officers and government officials—conducted almost wholly in Arabic, in which the Irishman was fluent—occupied the whole of Wednesday. To tease out their approval to the items on his extensive shopping list he hinted at the kind of operations the Provisionals had in mind, not giving any details, but showing the kind of actions envisaged and the material resources that would be needed to carry them out. He persuasively raised the stakes as he did so.

Then he came to the big one: "We have one particular plan in mind which calls for a helicopter." There was silence. "And a cargo ship." More silence. "Just a medium-sized ship," he added defensively. "One modified to carry the helicopter and launch it. For a one-off job. Just transport. We do all the dirty work."

It seemed an age, though it must have been less than half a minute, before Ibrahim broke the silence. He turned to a white-uniformed naval officer. "Possible?"

"Ummm, yes. We would have the ship."

One of the civilians, a top man in the Secretariat for Communi-cations and Maritime Transport, nodded.

A naval officer took up the point: "It would have to be a navy crew of course—at least the officers and petty officers. Perhaps a Somali crew."

"I am thinking of the S-boat we are buying from Greece," said the civilian. "The modifications *could* be done. I would think in Malta. We would have to draw up a specification."

"And the helicopter?" asked Ibrahim of an officer in a light blue uniform.

"We have them. What have you in mind?"

"First," said Roche, "it has to carry the pilot, co-pilot and as

42

many as twenty others, fully equipped, and second it has to look like a British army helicopter.''

The air force officer thought a while. "Aerospatiale SA 330 L," he said. "Two of them were left behind by the French army when our comrades in Chad captured Faya-Largeau. We have them in store for spares. One of those could be made serviceable again. But who would fly it? It is a powerful aircraft.''

"We have a couple of good helicopter pilots of our own and perhaps they could convert to this machine if they haven't flown one before. After all, we are talking about six months from now. How does this French job fit in so far as carrying capacity and similarity to a British machine goes?''

"Perfectly," said the air force colonel. "You see, the SA 330 L is manufactured jointly by Aerospatiale of France and Westland Helicopters of England. The British version of the same machine is the Westland Puma, many of which are in service with the British army. Apart from the pilot and co-pilot it can carry up to twenty fully-equipped troops.''

"Could one of the French machines be made to look like a British Puma?''

"Easily. The right camouflage, British roundels and identification markings and a bit of adjustment here and there. No one would know the difference.''

"So," said Roche, addressing Ibrahim again. "Have we got a deal?''

Ibrahim was thoughtful. "We will talk later about this, Mr. Roche. We must consider its—how shall we say?—political implications. Things have not been going smoothly with our shipments lately, have they? We would need to know more about how the ship and the helicopter are to be used. There would be a need for us to keep our distance, so to speak.''

"I knew it!" said Roche to himself, hiding his disappointment behind a nod and a smile. "The bastard's gone cold on me!''

*　　　　*　　　　*

Picked up next day from the Hotel Kasi Libya by Ibrahim in his Mercedes, Roche was driven to Tripoli airport to board a French-built Super Frelon helicopter of the Libyan army. It flew them to a remote desert village—Wadi Jarif, Colonel Gaddafi's

43

birthplace, thirty miles inland from the port of Sirte, where he occasionally returned to reassert his Bedouin roots. It was there, in his well-guarded desert tent with its incongruous mix of multi-coloured patchwork and oriental rugs with modern office furniture, telephone and T.V. set, that the colonel received the envoy from his fellow-revolutionaries in Ireland.

Michael Roche was relieved to find him in exactly the same frame of mind as at their previous meeting. It seemed that whatever the state of Libya's external relations, the sacred duty of encouraging revolution and arming those fighting for their freedom would always be paramount. Roche was uplifted. There was no limit, said the colonel, to the assistance Libya would give to the Provisional I.R.A., although—and Roche's spirits began to descend again—it must stop short of direct intervention, or any measure by which Libya would be put at a diplomatic disadvantage *vis-à-vis* countries with which it enjoyed normal relations. His heart hit rock-bottom as the colonel added what appeared to be the final blow: that stricture applied even more to Britain now that Libya had set in train—or hoped it had set in train—the process of normalisation.

The Provisional I.R.A. still had Libya's promise of full support, the colonel assured him. Except that it was now a matter for very careful handling, and he had every confidence that his long-time friend, a revolutionary fighter like himself, a man who had such an affinity with the Arab world, would see that Libya's interests were well looked after.

They spoke in Arabic for an hour before Roche was given the news that threatened to sink his project without trace. "I have talked with your people about the helicopter and ship we need for one of our operations . . ." he was saying, when the colonel's smile and upraised hands cut him short.

" . . . That, Mr. Roche, will require a little more thought. We have begun a process designed to reopen diplomatic channels with the British and it may not be quite the best time for us to become so closely involved with your front-line operations. Of course, our arms shipments will receive the highest priority despite recent setbacks. So will the training of your people. But I am sure you will understand the present somewhat delicate nature of our diplomatic moves. After all, a return to normality would help your cause as well as our own.'' Seeing the look of disappointment, even alarm, on Michael Roche's face, he added hastily, "A little more thought, Mr. Roche. Perhaps a modification of your plan, so as to distance Libya from the actual scene of your action . . .?"

"But, Colonel, it is the very essence of our plan. Without it the whole thing will have to be rewritten from scratch, perhaps abandoned . . ."

Colonel Gaddafi rose from his armchair and grasped the Irishman's arms with an affectionate smile. "Patience, Mr. Roche. Patience, please. I am sure we shall find a way.'' It was clear that the meeting was over. He kissed Roche on both cheeks: "God's blessing on your fight, my friend. God's blessing on all our struggles. Your arms shipments will be put in hand at once, and your helicopter and ship . . . well . . . a month . . . two months perhaps? When you come to see us again?''

Roche forced a smile to match his host's. "*Allah Akhba*,'' he said, saluting him.

*   *   *

Having set in motion a temporary solution to his problems in Dubai and Iran, Michael Roche flew back to Frankfurt that afternoon carrying with him all the promises he could wish for in arms shipments. The items that had been approved by the Libyan leader would make their hearts sing when he showed them to his comrades on the planning group who had begun to think that the recent spate of interceptions and seizures might have curbed the Libyans' enthusiasm for the game. But—and Roche cursed his luck that he had somehow missed the boat with the apparent easing of the tension between Britain and Libya—his big plan was slipping away from him. It had almost been in the palm of his hand . . .

Like a parched traveller throwing himself into the muddied water of a Sahara drinking hole, Roche dropped his holdall into a seat and slapped the palms of his hands on the counter of the airport bar at Frankfurt. "Saint Patrick's Eyewater for a dying Irishman!" he said to the startled barman.

"Excuse?"

"A big glass of *that* for a thirsty man,'' said Roche, pointing to the bottle of Chivas Regal whiskey on the bar shelf. He downed it at one go, and then a second, and a third, as he contemplated the difficulties facing him on his return to Ireland. Come hell or high water, his plan *had* to go ahead. But without a ship and helicopter . . .?''

* * *

''Detective Superintendent Blake?''

''Speaking.''

''My name's Gannon. Steve Gannon. Detective Inspector Foster of Met. Special Branch tells me you're looking into the death of Brigadier Farrell and I wonder if I could pop down and have a chat with you.''

''Certainly. What have you in mind?''

''Are you free towards lunchtime to-day?''

''I'm sure I can be. Twelve do?''

Twelve suited the M.I.6 man fine and he arrived at Basingstoke police station right on time. He introduced and identified himself. ''I wouldn't normally make such a direct approach to the police, for obvious reasons, but I know you've been P.V.'d [positively vetted] and I know I can rely on you to keep this meeting absolutely confidential.''

The detective nodded. ''Of course. I'm delighted to meet you. It's about time I found somebody who'll listen. I seem to be the only bugger who thinks it's murder. I suppose Foster told you we found the prints of a top Provo on the car that killed him?''

''He did. That's why I've hot-footed it down here. It has to do with information that the Provos have ordered the killing of a senior British army officer. It's supposed to have been done, and since we can't find anything to fit the bill among active officers, I'm wondering whether it's an ex-officer our source is talking about. Perhaps you could put me in the picture so that I can see if there's anything we can do to help you.''

Blake painted a sad picture of the decline of Brigadier Farrell. Retired on medical grounds, no longer the man remembered by his comrades—erect, six feet three, ramrod-backed veteran of Parachute Regiment campaigns in the Far East, Suez, Northern Ireland, the Falklands and a dozen other battlegrounds—the brigadier had become a round-shouldered, shuffling relic. Hands dug deep in the pockets of his shabby ''British Warm'' greatcoat, head withdrawn turtle-like into its raised collar, he had been given

46

to muttering to himself. He had become a recluse in his seven-teenth-century cottage, but for his regular evening walk along the lane from Rotherwick to the Leather Bottle pub on the main road, half a mile away.

To the customers in a pub used by more than its fair share of retired service officers and colonial types, he was 'The Brigadier', and they would greet him respectfully as he made for his corner seat to down his considerable nightly quota of double whiskies. Only occasionally would he come out of his shell, straighten himself up and adjust his always immaculate regimental tie as his old pride reasserted itself. He would talk of his old regiment; of the Falklands where he had served on the Task Force Commander's staff, and of the fight at Goose Green, in whose aftermath he had stood with head bowed at the edge of the Paras' mass grave. That memory always brought the tears welling up and choked back all further attempts at conversation. So it was only occasionally that he said more than, "Good evening." Mostly he sat in his corner, buried deep within himself.

"What I can't understand," said the detective, "is why the Provos should go to the trouble of killing a poor old bugger like him. After all, whatever it was they had in for him . . . whatever he'd done to the I.R.A. during his time over there . . . they must have had plenty of chances years ago. He's been off the scene for long enough. There's plenty of serving officers around if it was just a matter of having a go at a Para."

"Which would tend to weaken your murder theory, wouldn't it?"

Blake shook his head slowly. "Oh no, not when you look at the bastard who did it. I've said it before and I'll say it again: I don't believe in coincidences like this. A Para officer and a hot-shot Provo come together on a country road in the dark and the officer gets killed? A coincidence? Not on your bloody life." He placed a file in front of the M.I.6 man and opened it. "Have you seen Duggan's record?"

"Yes, I have."

"Well, you tell me if a man like him—a top line I.R.A. assassin, over here in defiance of a deportation order—is going to get involved in a caper like that without good reason."

47

Gannon could not agree more, but the problem was that neither of them could guess what that good reason might be, still less think of how anyone could persuade the Director of Public Prosecutions to change his mind and elevate the case above the level of a bad motoring offence, so that the Irish authorities might consider extraditing him.

They spent the next hour going over the police file and the photograph albums, before deciding to find somewhere for a lunchtime drink and a sandwich, after which they resumed their study of the files, the photographs and the brigadier's possessions and papers, including his voluminous ramblings on Ireland and the Irish. In the middle of the afternoon the detective went off to see his divisional commander downstairs, leaving Gannon to sift through the material on his own. So he was not there when, going through a rather tattered Stationery Office notebook taken from the brigadier's cottage, the M.I.6 man stopped in his tracks with a sick tightening of his stomach.

In a shaky hand, printed large upon the page and framed in interlaced scroll-work that could have passed for Celtic art, though it could equally have passed for inspired doodling, were the words *'The truth on our tongues . . . the purity in our hearts . . . the strength in our arms.'* Gannon's nightmare!

His head swam. All his life he had believed that he was the only one. Blake came back into the room. "Bloody hell, man, you look awful. What's up?"

Gannon got up and wiped the sweat from a forehead the colour of putty. "It's O.K. I'll be all right. It was that bloody pork pie in the pub. I knew it as soon as I took the first bite. A cup of coffee might do the trick. I'll be O.K."

"Jean!" Blake shouted through the open door to his secretary's office. "Two coffees, love, please." He turned back to his guest. "Sure you're all right?"

"Sure. It'll pass."

"Well, any of that rubbish mean anything to you?"

"Not a thing. But he sure had a bee in his bonnet about Ireland. He'd cracked up all right." He paused, his brow creased in thought. "I'm still with you about it being too much of a coincidence that Duggan should be involved, but the D.P.P.'s right. You lack the evidence for anything more than motoring offences."

Blake had to agree. "Pity. I've tried just about everything and I was hoping something might click with you." Then he remembered. "Oh, there's something else that's odd, but nobody will listen to me about that either. I got one of my D.I.s to give the brigadier's background a thorough going over and he came up with a bit of a mystery over his birth certificate. You see, I'd been down to the Parachute Regiment's records office in Exeter and had a look at his record. It showed date of birth as 12th December, 1929, address 22 Hilton Street, in the old Scotland Road area of Liverpool, and his parents as James and Mary Farrell. Father was down as a docks ganger. They're both dead now and the area where they lived has all been demolished and built on. It's the birth certificate that's got me puzzled. The army had obviously seen it, but there isn't one on the file. All the details had been taken from it and the fly-sheet on his file certifies that it was seen on enlistment. The birth was shown as having been registered at Liverpool City Register Office on 16th December. Now the strange thing is that neither the Liverpool Registrar nor the Registrar General in London has any record of it. My man searched well on either side of the birth date recorded by the army, but the result was the same. He could find no record of him, either, in the Catholic Church where he was supposed to have been christened. His parents are on record. They lived and died within half a dozen streets of Scotland Road. Their births, marriage and deaths are recorded in the local and national register offices and in the register of the parish church where they were christened, married and buried. But of Anthony Farrell, not a bloody trace."

"So?" enquired Gannon.

"How the hell should I know. Everybody says it must have been a mistake on the part of some army recruiting clerk back in 1948. Perhaps it was. Anyway, there's no bugger left alive to check it with now."

Only a man like Detective Superintendent Peter Blake would let a thing like that bother him. But the problem was that he had come to the end of the line. It was still, as the D.P.P. had said, only a motoring offence and something the Irish authorities would not even consider for extradition. It was a dead duck. There was nothing for it now but to hope some police officer, somewhere or other on the mainland, would eventually get his hands on

Provisional I.R.A. Volunteer James Duggan, so that he could see for himself what the man was made of.

Gannon had to agree, and began collecting the papers together as if to bring the discussion to a close. But Blake had thought about something else. He picked up two coloured photographic slides and brought a slide viewer out of a desk drawer. "Have a look at these. An odd-looking tattoo under his right arm, near the armpit. Nobody's got a clue what it can be, or even if it means anything. It's just a straight line, an inch and a half long, with a number of smaller straight lines—around a quarter of an inch long—branching off it at right angles at irregular intervals. The Pathologist found it at the P.M. [Post Mortem examination]. See if it means anything to you."

Gannon took the viewer and froze again at this further evidence that the nightmare was not his alone. His chest was tightening, his breathing becoming constricted. He grabbed the back of a chair and lowered himself into it.

"Hold on," said Blake. "I'll get you a doctor."

Gannon put down the viewer and squeezed his fists until the knuckles went white. "No you won't," he said, visibly fighting with himself. "It's indigestion. I know it is. That bloody pork pie."

He emptied his coffee cup as Blake's secretary, having heard the commotion, hurried in brandishing a bottle of Milk of Magnesia tablets. "Works wonders, sir. Take a couple."

Blake was still insisting on a doctor, but Gannon would have none of it and his stubbornness prevailed, especially after he had vomited in the detective's private washroom. As a concession, though, he rang his office and told them he was feeling a little off colour and would go straight home for the day. He rang his wife to say he was coming.

The two men shook hands in the basement car park. "Pity about your indigestion," said the detective. "The pubs are just opening and you could have joined me for a pint. Perhaps it'll pass off before you get home. By the way, what did you make of the brigadier's tattoo? Odd, isn't it?"

"Odd is right. I'd be interested if you ever get anywhere with it. Or if you manage to get your hands on Duggan. See you again, I hope."

CHAPTER SIX

Big Michael Roche was in deep trouble. He had been summoned to another meeting with the Chief of Staff—tomorrow—and he was still without the ship and helicopter that were indispensable to the plan that was to get him out of the Provisional I.R.A. and into clover. He had racked his brain to think of an alternative, after a coded letter he had written to Salem Ibrahim had evoked the same negative response he had received personally from the Libyan leader: "A month . . . two months perhaps?" Time was running out. One of his comrades on the planning group—his intelligence officer, one of the few on whose support he could count in the power struggle—had warned him that things were coming to a head and that he should think twice about going alone to the meeting. But what else could he do?

As if he didn't have enough on his plate, Maria Carmina was once more making impatient noises, while his wife was about to walk out, force the sale of their large country house and bankrupt him. What with the effect of the oil-price collapse on his company's overseas activities and the threats to his bodily health from his enemies in the I.R.A., it was no wonder he took to the bottle that day, and that the evening and the night slipped from his grasp in a haze of whiskey.

Next morning, as he became painfully conscious of the daylight, the barley fever hammered at his head. His brain began to feel its way through confused recollections: a succession of faces, noises, conversations and Cork City bars shuffled around his memory: solicitous friends in the Imperial Hotel, the taxi home, the clothes scattered around the bedroom floor. Then his watery eyes began to take in the clock radio, which showed a few seconds to go before eight o'clock. A shaking hand reached out, found and fumbled with the radio switch . . . *and then, as the sound of the morning news bulletin penetrated his tortured brain, it began to dawn on him that he was saved*:

"At 7 pm local time yesterday, the U.S. 6th Fleet crossed Colonel Gaddafi's self-proclaimed 'line of death' in the Gulf of Sirte, off the Libyan coast . . . Libyan gunboats and shore-based units attacked American ships and aircraft and in the ensuing battle four of the Libyan gunboats were blown out of the water and a number of shore bases are said to have been hit by U.S. missiles. In London last night, the British Prime Minister endorsed the American action, saying that it was a legitimate act of self-defence on the part of ships asserting the right of free navigation in international waters . . .''

God, or the Demon Drink, had answered Roche's prayers. One way or another, this day could see him right back on course!

But—Christ!—it was ten past eight. He should have been at Cork Airport with his wife at 7.45 to board the charter helicopter to Galway, en-route for another series of hire-car changes for his meeting with the Chief of Staff up in Mayo, dropping her off in County Clare to see her sister on the way.

His head swimming, Roche stumbled to his wife's room, then downstairs to the kitchen, where the maid cheerfully announced that Mrs. Roche had gone. He got on to the Airport at once. What story the bitch had spun the pilot, the girl in the Air Charter office did not know, but they had taken off twenty minutes ago.

Pouring down himself every hangover cure known to man, Roche fought to clear his head and work out how to explain his failure to keep his appointment with the Chief of Staff, while making the most of the news from Libya. By ten o'clock he had encoded a message and tapped it out on the telex machine in his study. It was addressed to a contact in Westport, County Mayo, and when de-coded would tell the Chief of Staff and the Army Council that, following those dramatic developments in Libya, he had had an urgent invitation to the Libyan People's Bureau in Paris, where news awaited him from Tripoli. He was sure, said his telex, that his superiors would appreciate his decision to give the Paris trip priority. Their reply told him he was right.

Michael Roche breathed again. Twenty-four hours and a night tucked away in a Paris hotel would at least keep him out of the way of trouble and give him time to think about what to do next.

In fact, he was away and out of touch with Ireland for some thirty-six hours. Which was why he did not find out until his return that his wife was dead. She and the pilot had died instantly when their helicopter crashed into the 1,400 foot summit of Sliabh de Nogla, south of Limerick.

*   *   *

Mrs. Mary Roche and helicopter pilot, Tim O'Rourke, were buried on the same wet morning in the Glasheen Road cemetery in Cork, and Maria Carmina Sanchez stood in mourning black at a discreet distance from the gravesides.

As Roche moved with the crowd towards the cemetery gate he was tapped on the shoulder by Colum Murphy, the owner of the helicopter charter firm. "I can't tell you how sorry I am, Mike. Such a simple thing by the look of it. God knows how it was allowed to happen. I thought our service arrangements were watertight."

"What was it?"

"Preliminary report says hydraulics. Gave him no warning by the look of it. He would have lost all control instantly. Air Traffic Control at Shannon picked up some kind of garbled message but he must have been skimming the top of the mountain when it happened."

Roche stopped and looked grimly at Murphy: "Sabotage?"

"Oh, come on, man. A slip of the screwdriver by the mechanic. He won't have it, of course, but . . . sabotage? I know how you feel and I don't blame you." He put his arm around Roche's shoulder. "The only blessing is that you weren't able to make the flight yourself, although even that thought must be a torment to you. Why not take a break, Mike, and go away quietly somewhere. Before the inquest. The full picture will come out there. A tragedy for all of us, and bloody bad luck altogether."

Bad luck? Roche knew better. Time was *definitely* running out, so he was more determined than ever that his escape plan should come to fruition. Especially after he had spent eleven hours trying to convince a very suspicious Detective Inspector of the *Garda Siochana* that he had not missed the helicopter flight deliberately!

*   *   *

Roche was back in Tripoli by 14th April, having lied to the Army Council that he needed a further three weeks to finalise matters with the Libyans. It seemed a forlorn hope, but the Gulf of Sirte incident made the trip worthwhile anyway. There was just a chance.

"I think Colonel Gaddafi is looking more favourably now on your request for the ship and helicopter, Mr. Roche," said Salem Ibrahim as they sipped coffee in the lounge of the Hotel Kasi Libya. "The support of the British for the American aggression in the Gulf of Sirte, and for Salman Rushdie's insult to Islam, has changed his mind about the restoration of diplomatic relations with them. He wishes to see you at his command post in the Aziziyah Barracks tomorrow morning, and he promises a firm answer to your proposal . . . yes or no."

"I'll drink to that," said Roche, tiredly raising his coffee cup.

They parted early and Roche was in bed by ten, though with all his problems he slept fitfully. Until one o'clock, that is, when sleep was knocked out of him by the sounds of small arms fire and explosions. He leapt out of his bed, raised the Venetian blinds, and gasped at the display of tracer shells arcing through the black sky like fiery necklaces. There was a hell of a fire-fight going on somewhere and it lasted for a couple of hours before silence and a darkness tinged by the glow of burning buildings enveloped the Libyan capital.

The next four days were full of confusion and rumour as Roche tried to find out what had happened. Many parts of the city were blocked off by armed troops and the telephone system had either been put out of action in the fighting or been deliberately interrupted to deny communications to what one rumour alleged were dissidents trying to foment a counter-revolution. He got his answer on the Tuesday morning, three hours before he was due to fly out to Rome, when an army staff car rushed him to Aziziyah Barracks, where a grim-faced Colonel Gaddafi embraced him, thanked Allah for his friendship, and vowed vengeance on the British for conspiring with Israeli intelligence in an attempt to overthrow him.

The British, said the colonel, had been threatening unspecified measures against Libya for supplying arms and explosives to the Provisional I.R.A. and for supporting Ayatollah Khomeini's sentence of death on Salman Rushdie. According to his own intelligence service, they had connived with Israel's Mossad intelligence agency to have him assassinated and the Libyan

54

revolutionary government overthrown . . . hence the gunfire. The Libyans' most direct avenue of retaliation against the British lay, it seemed, through their co-revolutionaries in Ireland, so Roche's helicopter was even now being made serviceable and his cargo ship would be ready well in time. It was clear to him, said the colonel, that his friend had in mind a very important operation, and he was sure its magnitude would also reflect the anger of the Libyan people over the violent attack on them by the British and their Israeli co-conspirators. He did not expect to be given the details of the operation; all he asked—and he was sure his friend would see to it—was that his country's enemies would not be able to produce evidence, as distinct from suspicion, of Libyan involvement.

A sentry appeared at the entrance to the tent. The colonel nodded to him and he turned to usher in a man in naval officer's uniform, whom the colonel embraced in what Roche felt was a somewhat emotional fashion. Then the officer turned to him. ''Captain Qasim al Maqhur, Libyan Navy,'' he said in excellent English. ''I am to command the ship which is to be put at your disposal.'' He brushed a wet spot from the corner of an eye and quickly explained: ''You will please excuse me, Mr. Roche, but I have suffered a great loss. My only son, a naval officer, was wounded in the American air attack on our naval forces in the Gulf of Sirte. He died early this morning.''

''I'm so sorry,'' said Roche. ''May God rest him.''

The captain visibly recovered his bearing. ''It is God's will, Mr. Roche. And so is my duty to you. I am at your service.''

CHAPTER SEVEN

To-day, for a change, Steve Gannon was Steve Gannon. For a further change, he was wearing his suit and Royal Marines tie, and he was off, not to Ireland, but to the Holiday Inn by Heathrow Airport to answer a rather intriguing invitation from a man he had not seen for years, who said he had something to discuss which he was sure would interest a man with Gannon's talents.

Of course, no secret service man would dream of taking up an invitation like that without a few preliminary enquiries and a recce of the meeting place. That had already been done for him and his man had been pronounced 'clean', so the appointment was kept, with a Security Service surveillance team discreetly in the background.

It was Thursday 20th April. Gannon arrived first. He was standing by the counter in the hotel bar sipping a whiskey, when his man walked in, looked around, then walked up to the end of the counter without seeming to recognise him. But Gannon recognised him. *Ex-Sergeant Major Michael Roche, Royal Marines Special Boat Squadron, the big, genial Irishman from Cork, had hardly changed a bit!*

"Roche," said Gannon, carrying his glass over to join him. "Michael Roche, by God. How are you, man?"

Roche grabbed his hand and shook it hard, staring at his one-time boss as if trying to penetrate his disguise. "Well, Holy Mother of God, sir, it's yourself. But where's the moustache?"

"Long gone. When I chucked the Marines."

"How long?"

"Early '71. Remember? 41 Commando had done a spell in Northern Ireland. The kids were growing up and I decided I couldn't keep dodging bullets as well as doing my domestic bit. So here I am. How's the world been treating you since . . . when was it?"

"Norway, '68. S.B.S. Never seen you since, though I've met the odd buddy from time to time and heard you'd left the Corps."

"How'd you find me?"

"Through the Corps Association. At least I got your old address from them and took it from there."

As they sat down to a table, Gannon said, "Well, you're looking prosperous enough. What are you up to these days?"

Roche stretched back in his seat, clasped his hands across his striped blue shirt and Royal Cork Yacht Club tie, and looked very satisfied with life. "Personnel. Applying the old man-management techniques. I put my lump sum into a little agency in Cork just when the oil boom was on and the business took off. Just like that." He snapped his fingers. "Big money, low overheads—almost a one-man show. The old Arabic course helped—remember, Dhofar, '66? We're pretty big in the Middle East now. We've got branches out there, and in London and Frankfurt." He paused. "And yourself?"

"Civil Servant. Desk job. Central Office of Information, in town. Far cry from cutting up bandits in the Gulf and sneaking boats up jungle rivers in Borneo, but secure enough. Nobody shoots at you anyhow."

"Oh, come on," teased Roche. "'Ginger' Gannon, toughest officer in the S.B.S. gone soft? I don't believe it. The guy who could go roaring into a jungle village and shoot the bloody place up like a one-man commando? In a desk job? Pull the other one!" Gannon sipped his scotch, smiled and nodded.

Roche put down his own glass and his forehead creased enquiringly. His grey-sideburned, heavy jowls, his somewhat rubbery lips and the slight lisp in his rapid, Cork-accented speech suddenly reminded Gannon of Broderick Crawford in the old-time T.V. 'Highway Patrol' series. By God, he thought, with the weight he'd put on he was his double.

"*But what about Mad Mike and the Seychelles caper*?" lisped Roche, who seemed to find Seychelles a bit of a tongue-twister.

He had hit Gannon straight between the eyes. The M.I.6 man's brain raced for a fraction of a second before he could reply without betraying his shock. "And what about Mad Mike and the Seychelles?"

Roche grinned slyly. "I have my contacts. In fact, Mad Mike approached me when he was putting his team together. Told me he'd contracted with Gerard Hoarau to throw out Albert Rene's government and put Mancham back in charge. What a cock-up. I noticed you weren't put on trial with the rest of them after it failed.

I know you were there, Major. Did they give you leave from the office?'' he asked with more than a hint of sarcasm.

How much did Roche know? Did he know Gannon was with M.I.6? Did he know he had been planted in Major 'Mad Mike' Hoare's team of mercenaries specifically to frustrate the November 1981 coup and put Hoare and his men into the hands of the Seychelles government forces? If so, Gannon's cover was blown for sure. And by an Irishman! If the Provisional I.R.A. ever blew his cover—and how could he know that Roche wasn't one of them?— his whole network of agents north and south of the border would be dead meat. He decided to test the ground. ''I don't know where you heard that, but you're on the wrong horse, old son.''

But then a waiter arrived and the conversation lapsed while more drinks were ordered. It was a moment for regaining one's balance.

Roche reached into his briefcase, extracted a dozen half-plate black and white photographs and spread them out on the table. ''Let me see,'' he said. ''You went out from Heathrow to Swaziland with three others.'' He touched his forehead with his left forefinger and narrowed his eyes as if reaching into a mental filing system. ''. . . Thompson, Calvert and Hughes, if I remember right.'' He pointed to each of them in the photographs. ''Isn't that you, Major, between Calvert and Hughes? And weren't you the guy who was to lead the assault on the control tower at Pointe La Rue airport, but it all went haywire? A bunch of them got back to South Africa in a stolen plane and were arrested and put on trial by the South African authorities. If I remember right, four were unaccounted for and you were one of them. No doubt the old S.B.S. survival training came in useful . . .'' He looked at Gannon with a glint of triumph in his eyes as he returned the photographs to his briefcase.

Gannon threw back his whiskey and laughed. ''Well, let's say it seemed a good idea at the time. The money would have been good. The down payment wasn't bad anyway, so I'm not grumbling.''

Roche laughed with him. ''So what's all this bull about a civil service desk job?''

''Oh, yes. Cross my heart and swear to die. Mind you . . .,'' and he winked, ''. . . I get six weeks annual leave, and the rota's a bit flexible. And the Civil Service doesn't pay all that much.''

"And other capers?"

"Here and there," said Gannon, shrugging his shoulders. "Gets the old adrenalin up now and then. Old habits die hard, I reckon."

"Fancy bubbling up the old adrenalin again?"

Gannon looked up at the ceiling and down again. And then he motioned to the waiter. "Try me," he said.

"O.K.," replied the Irishman, breaking off to tell the waiter to keep filling up their glasses as they emptied them. "O.K.," he said. "How's your free-falling these days?"

Gannon smiled. "Getting on a bit for that, aren't I?"

"Rubbish. You look as fit as a fiddle, man. Done any jumps lately?"

"Now and again. I'm still in a club in Oxfordshire. But free-falling . . . not for a while. As a matter of fact, I thought I'd done my last."

"Well how does one more grab you? For eighty grand, Sterling."

Gannon was impressed. "What kind of a drop?"

"2,000 metres free fall, open at 200. Into water . . . in darkness . . . wet suit and one-man dinghy, with homing transmitter. 45 kilogram payload. When they pick you up you've just got to see the delivery through, to my man in . . ." He smiled. ". . . wherever."

"Where?"

"A long way from here. Doesn't matter where for now. There'll be a friendly reception, dry kit and an escort back to civilisation."

Gannon sipped his drink thoughtfully. "What's the pay-load? I'd have nothing to do with drugs or . . ."

". . . or nothing. Don't you worry about that. No drugs, nor arms . . . nothing you need have any moral qualms about at all. Just something very valuable to me personally."

"Must be," said Gannon with scepticism written all over his face. He thought some more. "Hostile territory?"

"Only just. A bit of a jungle trek. It would only be a very short exposure before you're picked up and escorted, and your kit would include an Ingram MAC II [sub-machine gun] and a Browning nine mil [semi-automatic pistol]. There's risk, of course, but that's why I've come to you and why the money's so good."

Gannon said nothing for a while. And then, almost to himself, "It's got to be worth more than eighty."

"A hundred, top weight. All expenses covered. Twenty down and the rest waiting for you in a mail drop when you get back."

Gannon was still not sure. "Christ, man, you're nearly ten years younger than me, and you're as good a free-fall man as I ever jumped with. Why not do it yourself and save the money?"

The rubbery features rolled themselves into a worried look. "I trust you, Steve, so I'll give you the lot. I'll put all my cards on the table."

Gannon leaned forward and cupped his glass in his hand as Roche lowered his voice. "The good times are over," said the Irishman quietly. "Recession, and the drop in oil prices, have played hell with the business. We haven't diversified as we should and we're heading for big trouble. I want to cut and run. I can strip the business and have plenty to start up again far, far away. That's where you come in."

"And your family? Have you any family? What happens to them?"

"That's the other half of my problem. No kids, and my wife was killed in an accident recently . . ."

"I'm sorry."

Roche shrugged his shoulders. "I've got this lady in tow and she's putting the pressure on me. I'll be taking her with me."

"To where?"

"To never-you-mind where," said Roche sharply. "It's a need-to-know job and your brief doesn't include where. Not yet, anyway. Nobody's going to know, not even you." He laughed. "I love you, Steve. You saved my skin a time or two, but I don't trust even you that much."

"Did your wife have any idea? Does the bird?"

"Neither of them. But my wife knew about the other woman, and I'm pretty certain she put a contract out on me. *Some* bastard's trying to do me in, that's for sure. As for doing it myself, I can't split till the last minute. Believe me, if I thought I could save a hundred grand . . ."

"OK. When does it happen?"

"Four months from now. Next August. I'll see you nearer the time to spell out the details. All the logistics will have been worked out for you and all you have to do is like I told you. Just a good drop and recovery. Right up your street. All I want off you now are passport photographs so that I can provide you with a passport and other documentation and brief the people on the other side. You'll send me your passport photos within the next two weeks. O.K?''

"Fair enough. Except ..."

"Except what?"

"Except it doesn't sound like a one-man job to me."

"It isn't. There'd be a team on the ground ..."

".... who I don't know and can't vouch for." Gannon's manner had changed to the one familiar to Roche ... the *Major's* manner ... all the old military training and tactical instincts: "Would you have dropped blind? On your own? Into water, for a jungle trek with native guides you couldn't vouch for?"

"For a hundred grand, yes."

"Not for a million. It's a team job. What went in Borneo goes here. A team job."

Roche's blunder stared him in the face. He had shown his hand and the bloody man had snatched the initiative away from him! He insisted in return that the risk matched the price, but the inescapable logic of Gannon's argument left him with no choice. Short of backing out and turning his secret loose with Gannon, he had to bend. "What's your bottom line?"

"Three. Two dinghies and three sets of gear. 'Unit' chutes, and we pack our own before take-off, so you'll have to build in sufficient time on the airfield. Now," he said crisply, "who finds the other two, you or me?"

"Three? Three? You can do this standing on your bloody head, Major, and you know it. You on your own and a hundred grand. Take it or leave it."

"Then I'll leave it." Gannon rose from his seat, straightened his tie and said, "Goodbye, Mick. Nice to have seen you again."

Roche's expression said it all. Gannon hesitated and the Irishman got up and put his hand on his shoulder. "You win. I should have known better." He was stumped. There was nowhere else he could turn.

"I know just the chaps," said Gannon. "A couple of the boys who were on the Seychelles job with me. Make it a hundred and fifty grand and its as good as done. The expenses are down to you. O.K?''

It had been a long time since anyone had seen big Michael Roche on the defensive, but it lasted only a moment. His brain clicked back into gear as he saw the soundness of Gannon's plan. ''Done. A hundred and fifty grand. The split between the three of you is your affair. Give me three sets of passport photos and I'll provide everything else you need.'' His eyes narrowed and he looked every bit the killer again: ''*But don't you do a bloody Mike Hoare on me,*'' he said grimly.

Gannon laughed. ''Any shooting?''

''Shouldn't be. Not if everybody plays it straight and there's no double-cross. There'd be plenty of shooting if there was. And you'd be in the line of fire for sure, Major.''

Gannon waved a dismissive hand. ''No need for threats, old man. I'd be boxing in your ring and under your rules. You needn't worry about me or the others. A hundred and fifty grand sounds fine to me. Let's just talk about that, shall we?''

''Cash,'' said Roche. ''Fifty thousand down, the rest on completion . . . as soon as you and the package come out of the water and I'm satisfied the delivery has been made. Fair enough?''

''Fair enough.''

The deal was sealed over lunch in the Holday Inn's Tudor Restaurant, and the two ex-marines separated with a handshake. Roche flew back to Cork that afternoon, while Gannon went straight to his office to put out some more feelers and, with luck, find out what the hell he was up to.

An uncomfortable feeling was creeping up on him. This was the second 'out-of-the-blue' approach from an Irishman in three months. Coincidence? Or a concerted attempt to crack M.I.6's Irish agent network? And what about *The Soldier*? First, Hurley had intimated that he might eventually finger *The Soldier*, and now Gannon had been brought face-to-face with a man who had all the qualifications British intelligence had been ascribing to that legendary figure for the past eighteen years. He had been a highly-skilled member of an *élite* British military formation, the Special Boat Squadron; he was an Irishman with fingers in clandestine, if not political, pies, and he had left the British forces when *The Soldier* first appeared on the scene—1970, the year when Northern

Ireland's current campaign of terrorist violence had really begun to get into its stride.

And what about Roche's knowledge of Gannon's involvement with the attempted coup in the Seychelles? Given M.I.6's certainty that the Libyans were behind the murder in London of Gerard Hoarau, the man who organised it, and given Roche's Middle-eastern connections, the possibilities were endless.

But was it possible that a man with the undoubted profess-ionalism of *The Soldier* would break cover like this and risk compromising the water-tight cover he had so painstakingly perfected over so many years? Something was afoot, and Steve Gannon was beginning to feel very uncomfortable indeed.

*   *   *

The briefing took place in the conference room in the spurious Central Office of Information building near Holborn Viaduct. The briefing officers were two senior men of the Security Service's (M.I.5's) surveillance unit, assisted by Steve Gannon, to whom the three young men and three young women of the unit had been assigned for a particularly delicate operation.

Gannon darkened the room and switched on a video recorder. "Ladies and Gentlemen ..." He pointed to the screen with a shortened billiard cue as he froze a frame, "... this is Michael Roche. He lives in Cork and is to all appearances a prosperous, hard-working and well-respected business man, but I have reason to believe he is not what he seems to be. Your job will be to tell me if I am right or wrong about him. The delicacy of your operation lies in the fact that your surveillance of Roche will be conducted on Irish sovereign soil, without the knowledge of either the Irish government or its security forces. The reasons for this are two-fold: first, Roche moves in high places over there and we are satisfied beyond any reasonable doubt that he would know of our intentions within an hour of our making an approach to Dublin. Second, Roche is a personal friend of a very senior officer in the Cork Division of the *Garda Siochana*, with whom he regularly plays golf. We know, of course, that the co-operation we normally get from our friends on the Emerald Isle is total, but in this case ... after all, blood is thicker than water. Need I say more?"

The nods and murmurs from his audience told him he need not.

63

"Mr. Hancock and Mr. Adams here will brief you on the operational details. My task is to tell you what our preliminary look at your target has told us about him."

The video recorder whirred into action again and the screen showed Roche outside his office near the Imperial Hotel in Cork's South Mall, then getting into and out of his car at his home in Douglas down the river, then one or two of him chatting to people in various streets and open spaces in Cork. Gannon's word-picture came from the darkness to the right of the screen, beginning at another freeze-frame, which showed a younger Roche in uniform. "This is Michael Roche in 1970. 4335672 Warrant Officer First Class Roche, M., Royal Marines. He served under me and I knew him as a first-class marine—big, tough, loyal, a good leader of men, tactically very sound and an expert in counter-insurgency, under-cover work and small arms."

The machine whirred again and a picture of Roche's service record appeared on the screen. Gannon picked out the relevant parts with the point of his billiard cue and filled them out with his commentary: "Born in Cobh, Cork Harbour, in 1938. His father was a clerk with the local council and his mother a hotel waitress. He was one of five children. At the age of fifteen he went to work as a clerk with the Cork Harbour Board, but at seventeen went to seek his fortune in London. In 1957, while he was working as a barman, he signed on with the Royal Marines."

Gannon skipped through the section listing Roche's promotions and the courses he had attended, including one in Arabic and Islamic studies, undertaken shortly before he went with the Marines *élite* S.B.S. to the Persian Gulf. He went through an impressive list of places where Roche and the Marines had been engaged in counter-insurgency warfare and mentioned one campaign in which the Irishman had particularly distinguished himself: "Borneo, '63 to '65. Mentioned in Dispatches for gallantry in action against Indonesian guerillas. And a hairy one it was. I was there. Roche got in behind an intended ambush, sank a boat and killed five of them single-handed. As I've said, he was a fine tactician and a highly-skilled man with a gun. Not a nerve in his body. One of the best warrant officers in the Corps. In fact, he did a couple of tours with our training wing. I was sorry to see him leave us."

A voice came from the audience: "He'd be a bit of an asset to the Provos, wouldn't he?"

"That's just it. Neither we in the north nor the *Garda* Special Branch in the south have got even a whisper against him. We've done that little bit through an inside contact there. On the face of it, he's as clean as a whistle. Except ..." Gannon leafed through his file of papers. "... Except that a Detective Inspector of the *Garda Siochana* in Cork suspects him of murdering his wife by getting somebody to sabotage the helicopter she was travelling in. He's interrogated him at some length, but doesn't seem to have any real evidence. His superiors and the Irish prosecuting authorities are blowing cool on it, but the D.I.'s got his teeth into it and won't let go. He's determined to prove the chopper was sabotaged, and he seems to be getting some support in that from an inspector with the Irish Civil Aviation Department. If that leads anywhere, and given the fact that Roche has no satisfactory explanation for missing the flight, he could well land up in the dock charged with murder."

The surveillance team began to chatter among themselves, but Gannon cut in and stilled it. "I said *if* he's right. We'll have to wait and see. In the meantime we'll have a look at his current status and see what *we* can make of him. When he left the Corps he went back to Cork and bought himself into what was then a small employment agency, and he hit it at the right time. What with the oil boom and the boom in civil engineering in the Middle East, and his knowledge of the area and the lingo, it was just his drop. Now he has the biggest agency in Ireland for the recruitment of technicians, navvies and the rest of it. I suspect that on the side he's not averse to bringing a few mercenaries together if the price is right, but I'd be surprised if he got involved himself. He does a hell of a lot of travelling, all over the Middle East, Europe, the States and South America. We know he's been to Libya a few times, which might or might not mean something. He seems to be big with the Libyan National Oil Corporation."

Gannon ended with a caution: "I really don't know what this guy's up to. He may be genuine; he may be involved in something criminal, or he may be a terrorist. If he turns out to be a Provo, we need to know very quickly, because he could be poised to do us a tremendous amount of damage. You don't need me to remind you just how delicate this mission is going to be. *Don't get sussed*! If there's the remotest chance that you have been, get the hell out. Abort. Understand?''

They did.

"O.K. I'll pass you over to Mr. Hancock.''

"The usual headings, ladies and gents,'' said Hancock. "Personnel, Cover, Objective, Method, Equipment, Communications and Admin.'' He rattled off six names and paired them, male and female. "I think you've all worked together at some time or other?'' They had.

"Cover,'' said the surveillance officer. "I think you've all done this before, too. That's why you've been picked anyway. This time its Corvus Films, Wardour Street. Background shots of Ireland for an advertising series—our own ad. agency, of course, as usual. You'll be booked into an out-of-town hotel as your base, but you'll be on the loose, going wherever he takes you.'' He singled out one of the six in his audience: "Freeman, you're the senior man, you're in charge. I'll see you afterwards.''

It took Hancock over an hour to do his briefing and to take questions from the floor. And then his round-up. "Two days should do for orientation, and you, Freeman, can get the surveillance underway when you're satisfied the team is ready. All six of you know your way around Dublin already—you covered that man Hurley for Major Gannon. What about Cork?''

Three of the six had operated in Cork before, so half the orientation problem was already solved.

"When do we report back, sir?'' asked Freeman.

"Any time you have something you think might be significant. You'll have your contact points, codes and reporting-in times, so keep in touch. *And if in doubt, abort!*''

CHAPTER EIGHT

Joseph Zammitt's second-floor office window, tucked away in a corner of the Marsa, commanded a splendid view across the southern end of Malta's Grand Harbour to the high limestone battlements of Floriana, which gleamed like the desert sand in the morning sunshine. The window also looked down on a scene of noisy activity, where men swarmed and oxy-acetylene burners flashed and sparked all over a ship tied up at the Marsa Engineering Company's repair berth. It was Wednesday 3rd May.

As the senior design consultant for the company, Joseph Zammitt was interviewing a delegation from Libya led by Mr. Ibrahim al-Faqih Hijazi, of the Libyan General Maritime Transport Organisation, and Captain Qasim al-Maqhur, of the Libyan navy. Spread out before them on the table beneath the window was a large working drawing of the cargo ship *Thessalonika*, owned and registered in the Greek port of Piraeus. The 12,000 ton *Thessalonika* was shortly to join Libya's sixteen-vessel merchant fleet, to be re-named and re-registered at her new home port of Tripoli.

Of a type known as the B-430, or, more popularly, the S-boat, and built in 1973 at the Stocznia Szczecinska (the Stettin Shipyard) in Poland, she had been about a bit and was past her prime. Before going into service with the Libyan fleet, therefore, she was to be smartened up. She was also to have some relatively minor, if unusual, modifications made to her superstructure.

Zammitt's right forefinger traced over the lines of the side elevation drawing of *Thessalonika*'s superstructure aft of the accommodation and over the poop deck. "Briefly, Mr. Hijazi, your specification calls for an extension of the accommodation, aft of the boat deck, to provide a storage space the full width of the ship with a minimum height of six metres. And then, behind that, provision for the erection of a prefabricated platform over the poop deck. Am I right?"

"You are," said the Libyan.

Over the next six hours, with a break for lunch, the Libyans and the Marsa Engineering team went over the details of the alterations

and various other jobs listed in the specification, and at about five
o'clock in the afternoon the Libyans withdrew for private
discussions. In an adjoining office they pored over the drawings,
checked and re-checked them with their specification and returned
to Zammitt's office where Mr. Hijazi delivered their verdict.
"That will suit us admirably, Mr. Zammitt. If you can give us
satisfactory starting and completion dates and, of course, an
agreeable price, the Libyan government will be happy to sign a
contract and do business with you."

Joseph Zammitt consulted his repair yard manager and came up
with June 12th as the starting date and June 23rd as the completion
date.

The Libyans flew back to Tripoli that evening by executive jet.
Within a week, a price in U.S. dollars had been agreed and before
May was out the contract had been signed. By June 26th the
Thessalonika was on her new berth in Tripoli with all the work done.
On June 27th her registration was transferred from Piraeus to
Tripoli. She became the *Ghadames*.

*   *   *

Neatly bearded, his tanned face creased around merry,
sparkling blue eyes, Thomas 'Tug' Wilson looked every inch the
retired captain that he was. His forty-odd years in the Royal Navy
had seen the golden years of Malta's Grand Harbour and, now a
sprightly seventy-seven, he was one of the many old salts who had
lost all but their emotional ties with the old country and looked to
the sunshine for their old age. Living in a comfortable flat above
the old Custom House on the heights of Valletta, with the Grand
Harbour spread before him, he could still get out his binoculars
and take a critical look at the ships moving about the harbour and
those who navigated them.

'Tug' Wilson was a regular correspondent with a branch of his
old service—the office of the Director of Naval Intelligence in
London. The way he saw it, you never knew what was going on in
a place like Malta, the Mediterranean cross-roads, with a
government that didn't always seem to care who it consorted with.

On 30th June, his latest offering was received in London and
'actioned' out to the officer on the Mediterranean desk in the

68

D.N.I.'s department at the Ministry of Defence. He had watched *Thessalonika* undergoing her somewhat unusual change of shape and had photographed her as she passed down the Grand Harbour and headed out to sea. He had tried to work it out, but apart from ascertaining from men working on her at the Marsa repair berth that she was being bought by the Libyans, he could discover nothing. Perhaps there was nothing worth discovering. But perhaps—and it was a big 'perhaps'—the extra accommodation and the poop deck platform had a sinister purpose. Who could know, he asked the D.N.I., with a man like Gaddaffi behind it?

His letter and photographs were noted, indexed and filed. They were not acknowledged, for that was his arrangement with his patient listeners in London. 'Tug' Wilson did not regard himself as a spy, just an old sea dog enjoying his last years in sunshine, genial companionship and familiar surroundings; one who liked to feel he could still do his duty by the old country. But he had no wish for a Maltese postman to know that he was corresponding with the Royal Navy. After all, these bloody Maltese were all related to each other; all in each other's pocket . . .

*   *   *

At 6.10 p.m. on Thursday 22nd June, British Airways Concorde flight BA.002 from New York landed at Heathrow Airport. One of its passengers, the elderly president of a Chicago-based multi-national electronics corporation named Daniel Twomey, took a cab to the Sheraton-Heathrow and went up to the suite booked for him.

Early next morning, Twomey made a telephone call and then took a cab to Beaconsfield in Buckinghamshire, where, at the Bellhouse Hotel, he picked up a man who had stayed the night there and was booked in for a second night—a man who was not a little surprised to be whisked away from the hotel immediately. In a fresh cab—pre-booked by Twomey in the name of Priestman—the pair travelled to Hampstead in north London, to the Clive Hotel in Primrose Hill Road, where, again in the name of Priestman, Twomey had booked a room. Having travelled by a circuitous route through the quiet roads of Buckinghamshire and Hertfordshire, Twomey knew they had not been followed, but when they arrived in the hotel room he still went through an elaborate identification and searching ritual to make sure the man was genuine and 'clean', and, no less important, to identify himself to him.

The American opened his companion's briefcase, took out all the papers, spread them out on the coffee table, and ran an electronic scanning device over the briefcase to make sure that it, too, was 'clean'.

For the next six hours, and through the lunch brought to their room, the two men went through every detail of the papers. Twomey made copious notes, annotated a number of sketches made by the Britisher on a drawing pad, and tape-recorded the entire conversation. Finally, he took from his wallet what appeared to be a slimline pocket calculator. That it was really a miniature camera became apparent when he proceeded to photograph each page of the bulky file. It was then time for dinner, he said, and he called a cab to take them to the Thatched Barn restaurant in Boreham Wood, north west of London, where they had a well-earned five-course dinner at a pre-booked table.

At around 9.30, Twomey excused himself. He was going to the toilet, he said. His British contact never saw him again. Promptly at 9.40—ten minutes after Twomey's disappearance in the direction of the toilet—his dining companion heard his own name called from the bar. "The taxi you ordered is at the door, sir," said the barman, to his surprise. He went outside. "You want to go to the Bellhouse Hotel, Beaconsfield," said the taxi driver. "You ordered me for 9.40." The meeting was over. His work was done.

*   *   *

The 10.30 a.m. Concorde from Heathrow next day had Daniel Twomey, his microfilms, sketches, tape recordings and notes back in New York by 9.20 a.m. local time. By the 10.45 a.m. United Airlines DC.10 transfer from John F. Kennedy to O'Hare, he was back in Chicago just after noon, and his chauffeur-driven limousine took him from O'Hare airport to his home in fashionable Lincoln Avenue, on Chicago's aptly-nicknamed 'Gold Coast'.

It had been a whirlwind trip for an old man like Twomey, but it had been an immensely profitable one, for *An Triúir* was now poised to provide Big Michael Roche and the Provisional I.R.A. with the key to the most ambitious plan they had ever conceived.

*   *   *

The surveillance operation on Michael Roche, begun early in May, was completed at the end of June and a case conference was called in the M.I.6 base at Holborn Viaduct. It was chaired by Steve Gannon's immediate boss, Ben Craig, and it opened with a presentation of the surveillance log by Freeman, the leader of the team.

Freeman's first comment was that Roche had employed enough basic counter-surveillance tactics to show that it was always on his mind. Not surprising, perhaps, in view of his having served in the British S.B.S., and especially now that he was involved in some nefarious scheme or other. Otherwise it was the usual surveillance picture: most of it repetitive, undramatic and without any particular interest, covering Roche's social life, business meetings, daily routine, and his love affair with his secretary, the black-haired beauty from Venezuela, whom he had first met on a visit to her country's oilfields.

All very routine, then, except for the fact of the continuing interest of the Cork City detective inspector in the death of Roche's wife, which had resulted in several more inconclusive interrogations. And the fact that Roche had visited Geneva, Zurich, Frankfurt, Brussels and Paris, where other British agents had taken up surveillance on him and tailed him to his branch offices and an impressive number of banks. From Frankfurt he had taken a four-day trip to Libya, beyond the reach of the British secret servicemen. But agents in the Bahamas had followed him to several more banks, in Nassau, before he had flown on to Caracas, Venezuela, apparently to do business with an oil company.

If nothing else, these visits, allied to the suspicion that Roche had engineered his wife's death as a prelude to an elopement with his Venezuelan girl-friend, could be said to corroborate the scenario he had painted for Gannon at their Heathrow meeting.

Was there anything in the surveillance log to indicate that he might also be the renegade ex-British serviceman mentioned to

71

Gannon by his new under-cover agent, Michael Hurley? Could Roche be the legendary *Soldier*?

The video recorder clicked and whirred into life. O'Connell Street, Dublin. Roche and his secretary entering the Shelbourne Hotel. Roche leaving alone and walking down O'Connell Street, over the Liffey Bridge, to an office in D'Olier Street. The name plate on the wall: Integrity International Inc.

"A security company based in New York, with branches in Dublin, London, Paris, Brussels, Geneva and Rome," said the surveillance officer. "Genuine top-class outfit ... V.I.P. protection, building and cash security, industrial counter-espionage, employee vetting and so on."

A series of rapid shots from a motorised surveillance camera, showing Roche and two others leaving the building to go to lunch. Close-ups and a run-down on each: "Conrad Geraghty," said Freeman. "Known as 'Con'. A big fellow he is too—all of six feet three and heavy with it. Ex-detective inspector of the *Garda Siochana*. Father was a policeman too. Con Geraghty left the force under a cloud in 1970 in the aftermath of the alleged I.R.A. gun-running conspiracy which was said to have involved top politicians. Geraghty was in there somewhere. Nobody was convicted, but one or two—including a future Irish prime minister—bit the dust and he was one of them. Somebody must have looked after him, though. He's now the boss of the Irish end of Integrity International and has acquired a big reputation in the security world. Does counter-terrorist work for big industrialists, Arab sheikhs and the like. Attends security seminars all over the world and is seen as one of the top men in his field. You know the old story, anything legal, anywhere, any time. Does vetting work for Roche's company. So far as the *Garda* are concerned he's clean. Whatever political connections he may have had when he was serving in the force seem to have been dropped. They find him very co-operative and his links with the force are regarded as mutually beneficial in matters of crime prevention and such things as fraud investigation."

The video recorder whirred on: "Tom Cotter," said the commentator, pointing to a slim, thin-faced, dark-haired man. "Well educated this one. Was a lecturer at Trinity ... International Relations ... pretty well-travelled, too. Chucked it all up

72

six years ago and runs the family import-export company on the North Wall. He also has a travel agency with branches in Dublin, Cork, Limerick, Waterford, Londonderry and Belfast. Does a lot of travel arrangements for Roche's clients going on overseas contracts. It may be a coincidence that *Garda* S.B. think he might have been on the fringes of a couple of gun-running stunts that went wrong some years ago. Their surveillance teams have spent a lot of time on him and they've had his phone tapped this long time. Makes interesting contacts now and again, but nothing definite. If he *is* active he certainly keeps a low profile. One theory is that he was drawn into it unknowingly because of his shipping connections. It's not for the want of trying, but they've never been able to pin anything on him or even harden their suspicions to anything approaching certainty. Roche's legitimate business connections with him are clear enough, as they are with Geraghty and Integrity International.''

The video show ended. ''By the way,'' said Craig, ''how did you leave Roche at the end of your operation?''

''We didn't. *He* left *us*. We followed him—with his secretary—from his office. They headed for the airport and we assumed they were going to catch the morning shuttle to Dublin. John and Anne were going to board with them and tail them like we'd done before. But just this side of the terminal building they suddenly turned into the airport maintenance gate, drove up to a charter helicopter and hopped aboard. They headed off north, back over the City, and that was the last we saw of them.''

''Didn't you have any idea where they might have gone to?''

Another of the surveillance team spoke up: ''Well, I popped into the charter office on the pretext of talking about chopper hire for our film crew, and it came out casually in conversation with the girl. The pilot had filed a flight-plan for Tipperary, Dublin, Longford, Galway and Shannon, and the order in which they would fly to those places all depended on how Roche's business developed during the course of the day. Short of a police check on the pilot's log, that's as far as anybody could take it. They could have gone anywhere.''

It was the end of the de-briefing. The surveillance team departed, and Craig and Gannon were left alone. ''Well, there they are,'' said Craig. ''An ex-cop who left the force under the shadow of an alleged gun-running conspiracy, an ex-college lecturer who might have been on the fringes of gun-running, and an Arabic-speaking ex-Royal Marine Sergeant Major who visits Libya and whose expertise in field tactics, counter-insurgency and small arms would be an asset to any terrorist organisation. But what the hell is it all about? Is it conceiveable that if Roche were *The Soldier*, the man with the tightest cover in their whole organisation, he'd go outside for whatever he's planning—to a man he hasn't seen for years and whose loyalty he'd presumably have to take on trust?''

"Unlikely, I agree," Gannon replied. "I suppose he *could* have been telling the truth about planning to cut and run from his business and take his woman off to a new start somewhere far away. I suppose his wife's death *could* have been the first step in the plan. But it's too damned chancy. Even if the possibility that he's a Provo is as much as a million-to-one shot, we've got to take it seriously. We daren't take any chances with our Irish network. So what if we're wrong and Roche was being straight with me? What have we lost?''

That was it. The safest option. The possible 'set-up'. So the decision was taken, at the highest level. For the time being, at least, the Irish authorities would not be told about M.I.6's interest in Roche, in view of his influential connections in the Republic, murder investigation or no. The diplomatic stakes were high enough, but the risks attendant on failure to pre-empt a possible blow at M.I.6's Irish network were far higher. The surveillance operation would continue.

CHAPTER NINE

"Twelve thirty," said Roche. "Twelve thirty in the bar at the Holiday Inn. Like last time. O.K.?"

"O.K."

"Don't bring anyone with you, Steve. You'll be watched. I hope you haven't ..."

"... haven't what?"

"Mentioned it to anybody ..."

"Don't you bloody threaten me, Roche. Do you want to meet or not? Any more of that and you can get stuffed?"

"Sorry. Getting jumpy, I guess. Forget it, Steve. Come on over."

Gannon put down the phone and went to Heathrow, preceded by a four-man surveillance team. He and Roche had only one drink in the bar before going up to a room where a drinks trolley and a cold lunch were waiting.

Roche took a black brief case from the wardrobe and threw it on the bed. "It's the Bahamas," he said. "You board a boat in Nassau. The package is already on board. You boat it to Norman's Cay Island, sixty miles to the south-east, and fly from there to Central America. You fly over the southern edge of Nicaragua and drop with the package into Lake Nicaragua. You'll only be a mile or so from the southern edge of the lake, the border with Costa Rica. You extend your aerial and switch on. My friends home-in on you. The code word is *Carlos*. They escort you through the forest into the hills, to a village where you'll meet a man who will identify himself to you as Carlos. He'll have a letter from me and a photo of me and him together. You hand the package to him. From there it's back to Nassau. Your hundred grand will be at a prearranged mail drop ... provided the package is intact. If it isn't, all you get is a bullet in the brain. I have to say it, O.K.?"

"O.K.," said Gannon quietly, shrugging his shoulders.

Roche unlocked the brief case, opened it and tossed out several bundles of Bank of England notes. Gannon picked up a couple and rippled through them. "Fifty thousand," said Roche. "A hundred to come."

Gannon grinned.

Roche took several documents from the case and tossed them onto the bed: "British passport ... Richard Bentley, born Nottingham 10th October '32, insurance rep. Don't worry, it's a hundred percent. Bentley's six feet under in the Nottingham Municipal Cemetery. So are the guys on the other two passports. When you meet my man in Costa Rica the passports will be stamped to show you leaving Nassau and arriving in San José, so all three of you can leave the country legitimately."

Gannon picked up the passports and other documents as Roche introduced them to him: "Airline tickets—return—British Airways, Heathrow-Nassau, flight BA.265, Sunday afternoon 13th August. Three seven-night reservations at the New Olympia Hotel, Nassau."

"What about the meet in Nassau?"

"Be at the East Bay Yacht Basin for 14.30 hours local time on the Monday. You'll be looking for a 42-foot cruiser, the *Arabella* of Miami, owned and crewed by two brothers named Carillo. The package will be on board, and the drop container for you to pack yourself, and all your other gear. The Carillo brothers will have a Gulf Stream Commander jet prop aircraft waiting on a disused runway on Norman's Cay Island. You take off not later than 17.00 hours. You have about a 6 hour flight and your drop window is the fifteen minutes either side of midnight local time. Free-fall from 2,000 metres, open at 200, and once you're through the forest and in the village to make the meet with Carlos, you're home and dry. Your Nassau hotel reservations will still be current when you get back, and you're booked on the following Sunday afternoon's flight back to Heathrow."

Gannon spent a few minutes skimming through the documents.

"How about your side?" asked Roche. "All geared up? Who're the other guys?"

Gannon looked up from his papers, smiled, and tapped his nose twice with his left index finger. "Need-to-know. Remember?"

Roche nodded. "Everything's O.K., then?"

"Fine," said Gannon, piling the cash and all the documents back into the briefcase, locking it and pocketing the key. "I'll be there on time, no sweat." He paused for a second or two. "Oh, by

76

the way. The co-ordinates. And the wavelength for the homing transmitter. You haven't mentioned them.''

It was Roche's turn to smile. "Oh, no." The smile spread over his flabby jowls like a ripple over a water bed. "But I haven't forgotten." He withdrew an envelope from his pocket and handed it to Gannon. "At any time after noon on the Friday before you fly to Nassau, you can go to the Nederlandse Centraal Bank in Amsterdam and with this key and this authorisation you can get them from a safe deposit box. Not a minute before twelve, because they won't talk to you."

Gannon took the envelope without comment. Then he appeared to have an afterthought. "Hold on. Isn't there a bloody civil war in Nicaragua?''

"Not really. It's almost petered out now. In any case, what fighting there is would be on the northern border with Honduras. The Contras are operating out of there. You're only skirting the southern border anyway. You'll be as good as in Costa Rica from the minute you hit the water."

Gannon muttered something to himself and shrugged his shoulders resignedly.

"I told you," said Roche. "You'll be well equipped to deal with trouble in the unlikely event of any coming your way. There'll be Ingram MAC IIs in your weapons kit, and Browning nine mils, and a variety of grenades—fragmentation, phosphorous . . . you know the old 80 WP and the XFS. You'll feel right at home, Major; like the old days. It'll just be Borneo all over again. A piece of cake, as you used to say."

The two men spent an hour over lunch and drinks, talking over old times and old comrades. Their paths would never cross again, so, whichever way it went, however edgy each felt in the presence of the other and whatever misgivings Roche had about sharing even a small part of his secret, there was no altering the past. No altering the fact that in other times and at other places each had had cause to be grateful to the other for saving his life. When they parted for the last time, that Wednesday afternoon, the 5th of July, all else was for the moment forgotten; they shook hands like blood brothers. Which didn't stop a young man and woman of the Security Service's surveillance unit boarding the Cork plane with Roche and following him home. Nor the agent in charge of the

77

F.B.I. Field Office in Miami, Florida, forming a special unit to mount surveillance on the Carillo brothers. Nor the British Foreign Office arranging with the U.S. State Department to have an AWACS plane standing by to mount a radar sweep of the Caribbean during Gannon's flight to Nicaragua, and the C.I.A. on the ground in Costa Rica to mount a shadowing operation between the drop zone and the village in the mountains where the British Secret Service man had his rendezvous with 'Carlos'.

*   *   *

Maria Carmina Sanchez was not the ideal secretary. Her shorthand was a joke, her typing a two-fingered travesty, and her English would have been better suited to serving American sailors in the Maracaibo bar where Roche had met her. But as an ornament to an executive's office she was a stunner. She was also shrewd and calculating when it came to the material things of life. On what was to be their last day together in their office in Cork, she was learning the intricacies of her employer's computer-linked secure communications system and the importance of split-second timing in the execution of his complex plan for—as he told her— getting themselves and the company's assets to their Costa Rican hideaway.

Holding an instruction card prepared by Roche, she went over the drill for the last time.

"Are you sure you've got it now?"

"Yes, Michael. Only . . ."

"Only what?"

"Only I'm not sure what I am doing."

"Now that's something you needn't worry your little head over. Just go through the drill again so that I can see you've got it right."

She pouted and looked as if she was going into a sulk.

"Oh, all right. They're instructions for the banks . . . the transfers . . . bank to bank, company to company . . . that sort of thing. I've laid it all on, but now the timing's important and that's down to you. Come on, sweetheart, let's see it once more. Sure you've got it now?"

She nodded vigorously.

"O.K. then. When we leave this office to-day the equipment

78

will be switched to 'Satellite', which means that it's simply a link in a telex and telephone line from the Bahamas—where you will be—through here, and through an identical remote unit somewhere else, to where the messages are going. So, when you do the business in Nassau it will get through to the people who matter. It'll all happen in a matter of seconds and they won't have a cat in hell's chance of tracing the calls. Now, my lovely, start by telling me what you will be doing on Sunday 13th August.''

Maria went to the safe and withdrew an envelope, which she emptied onto the desk. It contained her passport and airline tickets. ''I am in Nassau. I have left Cork with you in the helicopter and you have dropped me at Shannon. I fly home to Caracas. From there I fly to Miami and Nassau and I am there on Sunday. 21.30 Bahamas time . . .''

''. . . half past four in the afternoon in the U.K.''

''Yes. At 21.30 Bahamas time I am in the office you have rented on Shirley Street.'' She walked over to the telecommunications console. ''Power is on. I switch to telex.'' She pressed a button. ''I load the disc. I key in the number and the date and time for despatch. I press the 'Auto-call' key.'' She went through the motions. ''I watch for the red light at exactly 21.30 hours.'' She waited. ''Red light . . . now. Watch for green light to indicate message sent and arrival authenticated.'' She waited. ''Green light . . . on. I press the 'Stop' key. I press the 'Eject' key, remove the disc, disconnect the power. I put the disc in my handbag to throw away.''

''Great. Can you imagine? Between the red light and the green one . . . twelve seconds, no more . . . that telex message, with my instructions to the banks, will have been whipped through to where it matters, and they won't have a clue where it came from.'' He allowed himself a moment of self-admiration, then suddenly snapped back to earth. ''O.K. Next move.''

She consulted the card again. ''Two and a half hours later. It is five minutes to midnight the same day. Power is on. Change to audio communication.'' She pressed the key marked 'Phone'. ''I load the disc.'' She went through the card again, to the point where, the voice message having been sent, she would remove the disc and destroy it.

Roche nodded approvingly. ''Fine. Now what?''

Carefully finding her place on the instruction card and then holding it behind her back to show that she could do it from memory, she continued: "It is now thirty-seven hours later; 13.00 Bahamas time on the Tuesday . . ."

" . . . Eight o'clock in the morning U.K. time."

Maria nodded. "The power is on. I am waiting for a telex to come through from my brother, Ricardo, in San José. It comes. Quote: '*Consignment arrived intact, repeat intact. Signed Carlos, repeat Carlos*,' unquote."

"And then?"

"And then, at 14.55 I prepare to send the last message . . . another voice message."

Roche nodded.

Maria again went through all the procedures for loading the audio disc, keying in the telephone number, setting the timer for automatic despatch, authenticating the receipt of the message and the removal and disposal of the disc. She paused expectantly.

Roche kissed her on the forehead. "Full marks, sweetheart. What's next?"

She picked up the documents from the desk, replaced them in the envelope and identified them to him as she did so: "Passport. Airline tickets, Nassau-Miami-Caracas-San José; U.S. dollars; Costa Rican currency. I wait in San José for you to come to me." She beamed at Roche. "*Muy bueno?*"

"*Muy bueno*, my lovely. Except. . ."

Her face dropped. "Except?"

"Except you forgot that when you go into the Bahamas from Venezuela to do the business, you go in as Victoria Angelica Valdez—on that other bloody passport!"

She put her hands to her head. "*Madre de Dios!*" she cried.

"*Madre de* bloody *Dios* is right. We'd have the whole bloody British army, navy and air forces on our necks, wouldn't we?"

Maria was puzzled. "*Que?*"

"Oh, never mind," said Roche, hurriedly covering his slip of the tongue. "Let's go over it all again." And they did. Until she had it word and action perfect.

It was a complicated plan. Much more complicated than Roche would have wished. But the Army Council had tied his hands by giving him operational command. He had no choice. At least he could comfort himself that in Steve Gannon he had picked a professional to do the rest of the job for him. He could only hope now that the computerised communications system would not prove too much for Maria Carmina Sanchez.

*   *   *

It was a testament to the skill of the British surveillance team— still on Irish soil without that government's knowledge—that Michael Roche never gave them the slightest cause to believe that he even suspected they were following him. So it may not have been specifically for their benefit that, after his secretary's rehearsal of her role in his escape plan, he resorted to the final burst of evasion that got him out of Cork and on his way to Libya under their very noses. It may have been just his way.

They had followed him from his home in Douglas to his office in South Mall at eight o'clock that morning. They had watched his office while he was inside with his secretary. They had followed him around the corner to the General Post Office, where they saw him make a call from a public call box without being able to make out who he was calling or why. They followed him and his secretary to Mallow, twenty-two miles north of Cork, and they followed them into the race-course car park. They stood close to Roche when he placed a bet in the ring. But they stood helplessly on the ground, holding onto their hats in the down-draught, when he and the woman suddenly hopped into a helicopter on the car park and were whisked away over the hills.

They never saw them again.

*   *   *

In that week, beginning 10th July, in groups of two and three, twenty-three Provisional I.R.A. volunteers, from both sides of the border, received orders to go to different addresses in Dublin. Their orders were verbal and brief: 'Be prepared to travel. Report in casual clothing with a holdall containing the clothing and toilet requisites you would need for a week's holiday. Slip away quietly so that your absence from the scene is not immediately noticed.'

81

As some of the best and most experienced street-fighters the Provisional I.R.A. possessed, they carried out their instructions to the letter, and when they arrived in Dublin in their carefully separated groups, they received their briefings and were supplied with air tickets, false passports and foreign currency. They were variously directed to Dublin, Shannon and Cork airports to board flights for Frankfurt, Rome, Zurich, Paris, Marseilles, Madrid and Amsterdam, where they would be met and receive further orders. None would go unaccompanied anywhere, not even to the lavatory, and each small group travelled in ignorance of the fact that there were others.

At their various European destinations they were met by unidentified couriers who conducted them directly to transfer airports or, where it was necessary for them to stay overnight, to small hotels. And then, without knowing where they were bound until they arrived at the transfer airport, they boarded Libyan Arab Airline flights to Tripoli.

At Tripoli airport, each group was ushered by a security policeman into a room adjoining the airport police suite in the new terminal building. There, a Libyan security officer solemnly stamped their passports with the 'official' immigration service rubber stamp of any of half a dozen Mediterranean holiday resorts. On paper, at least, they were on holiday anywhere but in Libya.

From the 'air-side' of the terminal building, an airport bus took them around the perimeter to the army's airport security base, where they were loaded onto Soviet-made GAZ-66 personnel carriers. Within an hour they were in a barrack room at the heavily-guarded Nahar-El-Barad training camp, just outside Tripoli. They did not know it because all the signs about the place were in Arabic, but they had just arrived in the main guerilla training camp in Libya of the P.L.O.'s fanatical splinter-group, *Abu Nidal*.

The man they would know only as *The Soldier* was already there and he saw each group as it arrived, and, later, when they assembled as a unit for their first briefing. For this he was accompanied by two Libyan army officers and a man who turned out to be a Palestinian guerilla fighter with an extraordinary catalogue of spectacular missions behind him, including the hijacking of the cruise liner *Achille Lauro*, the holocaust of the

Egyptian air-liner hi-jacking at Malta's Luqa airport and the 1985 Christmas massacres at Rome and Vienna airports. He was to be their chief weapons instructor.

As for *The Soldier*, the tall, greying, smart-suited personnel executive had reverted to type: a black beret, camouflaged smock and trousers, and jump boots. Roche was a hard professional soldier again. He even held in his right hand something that looked suspiciously like a British officer's leather-sheathed cane.

He called them sharply to attention. His eyes bored into theirs. He tapped his cane menacingly on his trouser seams. Tap, tap, tap. Not a word for a whole, long minute, but when he did speak he rammed home a hard message. "Well, boys and girls. I have news for you. This place is called Nahar-El-Barad. It has turned out some of the finest guerilla fighters the world has ever known. Hard, ruthless and totally dedicated fighters, who knew how to die for their cause. And now Nahar-El-Barad is going to turn its full attention on you. This is going to be the most punishing two weeks of your entire lives!"

They would, he told them, endure harsh physical training and the rigours of a devilish army assault course. They would spend hours of every day and every night poring over maps, aerial photographs and scale models of their objectives, learning by heart all the distances, movements and timings that were to make this the most complex and demanding mission the I.R.A. had ever undertaken. They would leap into and out of helicopters and they would handle weapons they had never even heard of. The amount of ammunition they would expend would make a Belfast P.I.R.A. quartermaster weep.

They would get to know their objectives like the backs of their hands. They would know to a centimetre how to set their weapon sights. But there were two things they would not know until the very last moment— the aim of the exercise and the name of the place where it was all going to happen. "Until then," said *The Soldier*, "the only man in the whole of Africa who knows that is me. Suffice it to say that the nature of this operation demands the very best the Provisional I.R.A. can call upon, and you can take pride in knowing that that means you."

Then the warning: "But the key to the success of this operation is secrecy. God help any man or woman who makes the slightest suspicious or undisciplined move, from first to last. It'll be Goodnight and God Bless you, make no mistake about that. We'll be divided into three groups. I'll be in overall command, with Gerry McMahon as my number two. Tom O'Donnell, you'll command No. 2 group and Jimmy Duggan, you'll run No. 3. I shall be with the main group, No. 1." He called forward the three men and handed them sheets of paper listing the names of those assigned to their groups.

Then he turned on his heel and stamped briskly out of the room.

CHAPTER TEN

After five months of communicating through dead-letter drops, coded writings, pay-phone to pay-phone conversations and occasional brief meetings in Irish pubs, Steve Gannon journeyed to Scotland for his second detailed de-briefing of Michael Hurley. They met at the Douglas Arms Hotel in the small Kirkudbrightshire town of Castle Douglas.

It was Wednesday 12th July ... the day on which two of Hurley's five month long intelligence-gathering efforts had come to fruition, the first with the arrest by the F.B.I. of the group engaged in the American plot to provide the I.R.A. with radar-guided surface-to-air missiles, and the second with the arrest by the Irish police of two members of an I.R.A. Active Service Unit as they stepped from the Cherbourg ferry at Rosslare.

The Irish arrests were to be the first in a series aimed at the I.R.A. organisation engaged in attacks on British forces in Germany, and this meeting was meant to up-date the information on which French counter-terrorist officers planned to pick up the remainder of the team on the French/German border in two days time, but, as they sipped their first whiskey, Hurley greeted Gannon with a whispered bombshell: *"The Soldier. I know who he is."*

"Who?" asked Gannon with studied nonchalance.

"Michael Roche. A businessman from Cork. He's the Provos' Director of Strategic Operational Planning."

Gannon experienced that strange feeling of emptiness in the lower part of his spine; that feeling of floating a couple of inches off the floor that comes with the revelation that you have won a million pounds on the football pools. Very fleetingly it paralysed his brain. He looked thoughtful, his eyes narrowed in concentration and he slowly inclined his head towards the ceiling as if consulting his memory.

"Know him?" asked Hurley.

"No. Should I?"

"Well, somebody should. He's *The Soldier* all right. No doubt about it."

Hurley had the journalist's bottomless filing system in that inside jacket pocket of his and he was always pulling out crumpled pieces of paper, despite Gannon's warnings that one day it would be the death of him. He pulled out yet another, smoothed it on the bar, and turned it around so that Gannon could read it. It was Michael Roche all right: name, rank, service number, complete background and all. And his Libyan connections, and a list of his exploits in the service of the Provisional I.R.A.. Hurley had done his homework with commendable thoroughness and Gannon did not need his department's computer to verify this. *The Soldier's* record was burned into the brain of every British intelligence officer working on the Irish scene. *Michael Roche was The Soldier all right!*

"What's he up to at this moment?" asked Gannon, trying desperately to remember the latest situation report from the surveillance section.

"Missing. Gone off the scene. Last I heard he was heading for Paris." He fetched out another piece of paper. "Aer Lingus from Dublin . . . last Tuesday afternoon. I hope to God he hasn't got wind of what's going on and gone to take the team out of St. Menehauld. Are the French ready to move?"

"Yes, they are, and Roche can't do us any damage there anyway. The French and the Germans have got them under tight surveillance. They're going to pick them up as they re-cross the border into France."

Hurley relaxed. "Perhaps he's heading for England, then . . . via the continent. Not many immigration checks that way."

"Why bother? Isn't he supposed to have watertight cover?"

Hurley thought that one out. "Hmm, yes. Well, what about Libya, then? Some of the boys are supposed to have been out there training. For that big operation I've been telling you about. You know—*Andrea*."

"Like who?"

"Like Tom O'Donnell from Derry, Gerry McMahon from Newry and Jimmy Duggan from Anagassan. Bloody good street fighters, them. The Provos' best, I'd say. Haven't you noticed how quiet things have gone lately in the north? You were having a pasting last year and the first half of this, weren't you?"

"You can say that again."

"Well, haven't you noticed how it's only bombings and mortar attacks you're getting in the last couple of months? That's because they've laid off all their best gunmen for the big one—the one they've gone off to Libya to train for."

"Any idea yet what it is?"

Hurley shook his head. "None at all. They're really keeping it under wraps. All I hear is it's a big one. The biggest yet. The only ones I've heard of being involved is gunmen, so it might be an assassination job. I haven't heard of any bombers with them." He suddenly thought of something else. "Oh, by the way, did you get anywhere with that officer? The one I told you had been put up for assassination?"

Gannon side-stepped. "We checked with the army, but nothing of the kind has happened since you told me. They haven't had one officer killed or attacked since last autumn, well before you first told me about it."

"Well, a bloody smart outfit you are for sure," laughed Hurley. "It *did* happen." He pulled yet another piece of paper from his inside jacket pocket, read it and looked up again. "It happened on the main road between Reading and Basingstoke on the 13th of January. It was made to look like an accident. Like a man hit by a stolen car."

"That should be easy to check out."

"It doesn't bloody look like it. Anyway—and here's the important bit—the Provo who did it was Jimmy Duggan. You know, the one I just mentioned—gone to Libya with O'Donnell and McMahon for the big job. He had orders to make quite sure the man was dead because he's been working for the I.R.A. somehow or other and had to be killed because he'd become unreliable."

Gannon nodded thoughtfully as he made a quick check on his miniature tape-recorder to make sure he had plenty of tape left in the cassette. Hurley was still speaking: "And there's another contract out. *Andrea* again. It's a guy who works for some government information service in London—a civil servant— another accident job by the sound of it . . ."

Gannon froze. For an age that was only seconds to his companion, he did not answer. There was a roaring in his ears as the words he had seen in the brigadier's written ramblings

87

thundered anew through his brain: '*The truth on our tongues . . . the purity in our hearts . . . the strength in our arms.*' The brigadier's tattoo seemed to be woven through the pattern of the wallpaper, the carpet, the moulded ceiling . . . everywhere he looked, as he felt the bar closing in around him. The room swam, the inner voice thundered; it required every ounce of his will-power to break his mind clear. "Hold on," he heard himself saying. "A British army officer . . . ?" The storm was passing.

"No, a civil servant. The guy killed with the stolen car was the army officer."

Gannon was stuck for words again. He threw back his large whiskey and motioned to the waiter for another round. "Are you sure of this?"

"Certain. I hope your bloody outfit does better with this one than you did with the army officer. I don't think it's happened yet."

"Is Duggan going to do it?"

"Don't think so. He's gone off now on this big assignment. That has something to do with *Andrea* as well, and *The Soldier*'s running it. They're probably in position on the mainland right now, ready for the off."

Gannon had recovered his full composure. He went out and made a long telephone call before returning to the dining room, where, over a five-course dinner, they talked more of terrorism and Gannon filled more cassettes with doings on the Irish terrorist scene. They retired late, but there was no sleep for Gannon. His nightmare, aroused again by that remark of Hurley's, pursued him through the night, succumbing only to scotch and daylight, leaving its victim exhausted, more certain than ever that his demon was about to catch up with him.

They parted next morning with a handshake and the promise to keep in closer touch than ever. Hurley left for Stranraer and the Larne ferry, telling Gannon he was optimistic that he would make the breakthrough on the big mission before long, and— "Please God," as he said—stop them taking more innocent lives.

CHAPTER ELEVEN

Thursday 3rd August. 11 a.m., Libyan time. Forty-five minutes to go before the *Ghadames* was due to depart Tripoli's fine Italian-built harbour. Her official orders were to proceed in ballast to Dunkirk and there take on a full general cargo for her home port. But she already had a cargo: twenty-one Irish 'Freedom Fighters' and two Irish helicopter pilots, en-route for an operation on the mainland of Britain. Dunkirk, the Libyans hoped, would come later.

Libyan Navy Captain Qasim al-Maqhur had been given temporary command of the *Ghadames* and had been allowed to choose his own crew—naval officers and petty officers, with Somali deck hands. He also had on board a small navy helicopter-handling crew for the helicopter that had been craned aboard at night under tarpaulins and now stood concealed, main rotors folded, behind the locked double-doors of its Maltese-built deck hangar.

Stowed away in number four hold lay the H-beam supports and frame and the timbers that would form the ship's *ad-hoc* helicopter pad on the poop deck. Hidden behind the stacked timbers and beams, in cramped quarters which they would swap for more comfortable accommodation only when they were well out to sea, was the Provisional I.R.A. Active Service Unit with all its weapons and equipment.

Before leaving the Nahar-Al-Barad training camp, the Irish men and women had had their passports returned, complete with the entry and exit stamps of the immigration services of the various Mediterranean holiday countries they were supposed to have visited, and post-dated Irish immigration service stamps showing that they had legally re-entered their home country. They had also received various slips of paper and documents such as would be found in the pocket or handbag of anyone recently returned from holiday—authentic hotel bills, restaurant receipts, bus tickets and the like. The Mediterranean tan they had already.

Smuggled aboard under cover of darkness behind a tight security screen, the Irish terrorists were raring to go. The only thing on their minds now was that in forty-five minutes they would be on their way to mount the most spectacular operation ever conceived by their masters. Spectacular and also highly dangerous. Dead or alive, somebody in Ireland would be writing a patriotic song about them before this month was out.

*   *   *

At 11.40 a.m. the last mooring rope was cast off, the *Ghadames'* engines throbbed louder. Her propellor turning slowly, and with a tug pulling her by the bow, she moved gently away from the quay, and with increased engine revs began to head for open water, where she slipped her tug's towline. Captain al-Maqhur nudged his ship ahead, correcting course, teasing out the engine revs and watching the buoys and land markers for the harbour exit. At seven minutes after noon he was free of Tripoli harbour and into the Mediterranean. "Course 341," he called to the Officer of the Watch. "Full ahead."

The *Ghadames'* speed edged up until she was at fifteen knots. "Steady ahead," called her captain, and she was on course for Tunisia's Cape Bon, the first landmark on her track to the British coast, two thousand two hundred and fifty nautical miles, and six and a half days' steaming, from Tripoli.

*   *   *

The *Ghadames* had been at sea for six days. It was 2.58 on Wednesday afternoon, 9th August. She was thirty miles off Land's End and she was in deep trouble. Since Gibraltar, an over-heated propeller shaft had led to a progressive reduction in engine revs and sea speed, which had already knocked fifteen hours off the twenty-four allowed for delays. Now there was another temperature alarm. This time her chief engineer did not have to say a word. The choice lay with the captain: turn back and be in Falmouth in just under nine hours or, with only a slight change of course, make for Milford Haven on the south west tip of Wales.

The advantage of Milford Haven was clear enough. Once the rogue bearing had been replaced and the vessel was able to proceed at her maximum speed of seventeen knots, Milford Haven would be only about three hours from her rendezvous. Falmouth would be twenty-one. But would the prop-shaft stand it? Would it stand a hundred and fifty revs a minute, nearly nine thousand an hour, on a worn bearing, for the twelve hours it would take to get to Milford, and emerge from the ordeal without being scored to such a degree as would put the *Ghadames* in dock for a month?

Captain al-Maqhur weighed his options again. Divert to Falmouth and they might just about get there, but the operation would be off and he would have to get rid of the Irishmen, their helicopter and all their weapons and equipment well before entering the harbour. Try to carry on northwards and, if his chief engineer were right and the prop-shaft seized up completely, the *Ghadames* would be left helplessly adrift and he would still have the problem of disposing of her incriminating cargo.

He studied his charts again. His chief engineer pleaded with him, but none of his navigating officers uttered a word. He picked up his telephone: "Please ask *The Soldier* to come to the bridge."

When Roche arrived, his heart fell. He saw everything falling apart again as the captain explained the stark choice facing him. "Well, what is it to be, captain?" he asked.

Captain al-Maqhur stared silently through the bridge window and beyond the ship's bows. Roche thought he saw his eyes glistening, as if a tear was close. He was right. In his mind's eye, the captain was gazing at a boy in white naval uniform . . . a pale-faced boy whose cheeks were streaked with blood . . . a boy he would never see in life again but who beckoned him on, northward.

He swung around. "Milford Haven," he said, to the horror and astonishment of his engineer officers. He turned to the Officer of the Watch and asked him for a course and distance.

The officer made a quick calculation: "118 degrees, a hundred and nine miles. E.T.A. 0300."

"Alter course 118 degrees," said Captain al-Maqhur. The Officer of the Watch adjusted the auto-pilot and received his next order: "Require Milford Haven to provide an anchorage as a port of refuge. Estimated repair time twenty-four hours. Request tug to stand by in case of total engine failure."

There was nothing more to be said. Roche nodded, muttered a "Thank you" to the captain, and left the bridge.

The *Ghadames* steamed on, all eyes watching the shaft temperature gauge, and with frantic efforts on her poop deck to erect the helicopter deck in record time against the possibility of complete breakdown and the need to evacuate the Irishmen and everything belonging to them.

*   *   *

At five o'clock that afternoon, as the *Ghadames* limped towards Milford Haven, an immigration officer was on board another new arrival there, a Russian tanker, in from the Middle East with a cargo of crude oil for one of the refineries. The immigration officer was collecting and checking the ship's crew list—and enjoying the liquid hospitality dispensed by her captain.

Half a mile away, standing on a cliff-top, David Prothero, a local photographer who 'did a little bit now and again' for Naval Intelligence, took several photographs of the Russian ship, on the principle that everything the Russians do abroad has at least some element of espionage associated with it. At home that evening, he received a telephone call: "Dai, there's a Libyan ship coming in for repairs. They're putting her on a mooring by the old Esso terminal. She'll be in at about three in the morning. She's in ballast on her way to Liverpool to load. Thought you might be interested."

He was. He had not actually been told to photograph Libyan ships, but one never knew . . .

*   *   *

At 2.58 that Thursday morning, three miles out from The Heads, the one and a half mile wide entrance to one of the world's finest natural deep-water harbours, the Milford Haven pilot launch closed with the *Ghadames*. The Pilot and the Port Health Officer clambered up the rope ladder.

"Welcome aboard, Mister . . .?" began the captain.

"Davies . . . David Davies, sir. Pilot."

"And I'm Stanley Miles," said the Port Health Officer.

"Welcome aboard, gentlemen. I am Captain al-Maqhur."

They shook hands.

"Steady as she goes . . ." said the pilot, taking control of the ship and lining up the land-markers in his practised eye. "Steady as she goes."

By the time the *Ghadames* had anchored off the jetty, the Port Health Officer had collected the inoculation certificate from Captain al-Maqhur and had received his assurance that there was no illness—or, more to the point, no contagious diseases—on his ship. The ship's engineers were already at work on the propellor shaft's bearing box.

At 3.20 a.m. the pilot launch pulled away. At 8 a.m. another arrived, carrying an immigration officer and two customs officers. The former was happy enough just to scrutinise the crew list and to receive an assurance from the captain that no one would attempt to leave his ship and no one would be allowed on board.

The customs officers seemed bent on an equally brief encounter. They went over the inventory and sealed the ship's stores. "Thank you, captain," said the senior of the two.

"Thank you, gentlemen," said Captain al-Maqhur, preparing to bid them farewell.

"Oh, if you don't mind, captain, we'll just have a stroll around." And off they went, down to the boat deck to wander through the officers' and crew's quarters, while the captain thanked Allah that he had had the foresight to dismantle the helicopter pad and clear the Irishmen and everything they possessed out of the accommodation. Everything, that is, but their helicopter.

"What's in here?" asked the senior customs officer of the ship's third officer as they emerged from the rear of the officers' accommodation into the passage connecting with the space immediately above the hidden helicopter.

"Our gymnasium, sir."

The customs man grasped the lever and tried to open the door. It held firm.

"We keep it locked, sir."

There was a moment's pause. "If you would be good enough to unlock it . . ."

The third officer did so—and the two customs men were most impressed by the quality and variety of equipment with which it was furnished. As they observed admiringly, whoever had been responsible for equipping the gymnasium had done a remarkably good job within the limited space available. The Libyan agreed.

Had the customs officers given the same attention to the accommodation immediately below the gymnasium they would have been even more impressed. But they did not, for there was no access to the narrow helicopter hangar save through the double doors facing the stern, and it somehow escaped their normally eagle-eyed attention that there was more than a bulkhead at the after end of the crew's accommodation.

So they went for a stroll forward, along the *Ghadames*' foredeck and past the cargo holds, the forward of which contained twenty-three extremely apprehensive Irish terrorists and enough fire-power to fight off a company of infantry.

The Libyan officer allowed himself to be left farther and farther behind, his heart pounding as the customs officers neared what would undoubtedly be their deaths if their curiosity got the better of them.

The captain and his officers could only look down from the bridge in horror. They saw the two Britons stop abreast of the forward hold. They were talking fairly animatedly, but whether arguing or even whether talking about the ship or about something entirely different, no one could tell. For five minutes they talked. To those on the bridge, and to the shaking third officer by number two hold, it seemed like five hours.

Then one of them produced a cigarette packet and offered a cigarette to his companion. They were laughing as they turned away from the bow and walked back to their guide. He could have kissed them. But he contented himself with a wave as they mounted the rope ladder and climbed down with the immigration officer to the harbour launch.

CHAPTER TWELVE

Steve Gannon, had been conscious of the follow since Paddington. He couldn't be sure if they had been on the train from Maidenhead, but they had certainly pushed their way to the front of the queue as he boarded his taxi, and they were now in the one behind. Thank God they were amateurs. Only two. Both men. And both in one bloody taxi.

Gannon leaned forward. "Driver, I know this sounds like a put-on, but I have a feeling someone is trying to follow us. Take a couple of turns around Marble Arch, would you? No dramatics, mind. Just a couple of gentle turns."

No professional would have fallen for it. There would have been a mobile team ready to drop in behind his taxi as it eventually made its exit from Marble Arch. The ones immediately behind him would never have taken the two turns with him. Pure basics. Never follow your man around a corner or a roundabout. Hand 'eyeball' over to your next in line at every deviation.

Gannon had seen enough. "Drop me at the nearest phone box in Oxford Street please, driver."

Amateurs. They were getting out of their taxi fifty yards along Oxford Street as Gannon made his call. They fitted in all right, with their jeans, sneakers and bomber jackets—him with his beard and him with his sun glasses—but so far as surveillance techniques went, Humphrey Bogart would have made a better job of it in trench coat and snap-brimmed trilby!

He was through to his department's answering service. "I'm running a little short of time and I think I'll go direct to Heathrow instead of coming into the office. That is unless you have anything special for me."

There was a short pause. "No, nothing for you, sir."

"O.K. I'll phone in when I get to the Embassy in The Hague."

They followed him to the Bond Street tube station, weaving in and out of the crowd, each alternately taking the lead and dropping back. Bound to show out, though, without a second and third team to share the exposure. Avoiding the ticket machine, which would have given some clue to his destination, Gannon booked at the window. "Heathrow. One." His shadows were too far back to hear him. They were in some difficulty and he smiled when he saw them go to the machine with the dearest tickets just to make sure.

Down he went to the platform for the Central Line, eastbound, using his well-trained peripheral vision to the utmost. They were closing up on him now that the rush-hour swarm made it safe to do so. The platform was packed, but they managed to close right up as he pushed himself forward to the platform edge at about the halfway mark. One of them was right at his back, and he sensed that the other was standing close enough to support his partner.

It was going to be a one-man job. He could feel the guy behind him. Nothing definite yet, but there was no disguising his nervousness. He fidgetted. This was it. They were going to push him under the train. Hurley was right. There *was* a contract out on 'a man from the Government Information Service'!

The first faint rumble could have come from any direction, but he felt his man react. Louder it came. Then a rush of air from the tunnel to his left. With a roar, the train entered the platform and hurtled towards him. Two hands touched his back. Too late. Gannon was already spinning around to his left, while the back of his left arm, aided by the swinging weight of his brief case, hurled the bearded one forward. His scream rose above the roar of the tube train, but before anyone except Gannon and his other shadow had realised what had happened, his limbless body was a bloody heap of flesh under the front wheels.

Gannon, oblivious of the yelling panic around him, had eyes only for the other one, who was paralysed with horror for another split second, his unbelieving eyes fixed on the spot where his comrade had been struck by the train driver's cab. Then he was off, yelling and fighting his way through the crowd towards the 'Way Out' sign.

Gannon paused, then made his way quickly away from the chaos on the Circle Line eastbound platform. On the westbound platform he beat the sliding doors of a departing train and headed for Notting Hill Gate, Earls Court and Heathrow.

*   *   *

Captain al-Maqhur glanced at the clock on the bridge of the *Ghadames*. It was 9.30 p.m. They had been in Milford Haven throughout that Thursday and his chief engineer had just reported that the installation and testing of the replacement shaft-bearing would be completed in one hour's time . . . two and a half hours ahead of his best estimate. The captain was delighted, and the Officer of the Watch conveyed his instruction to the radio room: "Message for Milford Haven signal station. Repairs near completion. Request pilot and clearance to leave as soon as possible after ten."

A message to *The Soldier* and his people hiding in number one hold sent their spirits soaring. They were eight hours late already for their original rendezvous, but there was still just about time to rearrange it and set about their mission.

A second message delivered twenty minutes afterwards dashed their hopes again. There was no pilot available. The 220,000 ton tanker, *Texaco Caracas*, was about to enter the Haven and it would take at least four tugs and several hours to bring her in and manoeuvre her onto her refinery jetty berth. The arrival of two other ships—a smaller tanker and a gas carrier—was also imminent and there were not enough pilots to go round.

In short, Captain al-Maqhur could not have a pilot until eight in the morning.

The Soldier made a final revision of their E.T.A., and made a radio-phone call from the *Ghadames* to a number in Cork City. Thank God, he said to himself, they had built in twenty-four hours for delays. It looked as if they were going to make it by the skin of their teeth.

*　　　*　　　*

With Milford Haven sixty miles astern, the *Ghadames* hove to at 11.26 a.m. on Friday 11th August, on a mirror-like Irish Sea in the narrowest part of St. George's Channel, between Ireland's Tusker Rock and Wales's St. David's Head. Fifty yards off her port side lay the twenty-nine foot Fairline Mirage II motor cruiser, *Slievenamon*, of Dungarvan. A fifteen foot Gemini inflatable ferried between them.

The *Slievenamon*'s skipper—alone on the boat—was joined by six passengers from the *Ghadames*. James Duggan, killer of Brigadier Anthony Farrell and now commander of the seaborne element of the I.R.A. operation, had brought with him two other

Irishmen and three dark-haired young women, all dressed in holiday attire. Several rucksacks and sports holdalls went with them and, when all were aboard her, the *Slievenamon* was just one of the hundreds of holiday craft plying the Irish Sea in the high summer of August.

The transfer effected, the inflatable moved slowly around the bows of the motor cruiser as Duggan placed adhesive sheets of printed plastic over her name. Finally he moved to the stern and affixed a much larger rectangular sheet. For the next couple of days, the *Slievenamon* of Dungarvan would be the *Spalpeen* of Dun Laoghaire, the port of Dublin. The real *Spalpeen*, with her innocent skipper and his family, was cruising the blue waters of the Mediterranean, oblivious of the diabolical slur about to be cast upon her.

With a final wave to the departing inflatable, the *Spalpeen*'s skipper pushed forward the throttle levers and his craft sped off towards the Welsh coast, her twin Volvo 145 horse-power engines punching her to her top speed of twenty-eight knots as she rounded the bows of the *Ghadames*. Her heading was 167 degrees and her destination Cardigan Bay.

CHAPTER THIRTEEN

At precisely three o'clock, as the bogus *Spalpeen* sped towards Cardigan Bay and the cargo ship *Ghadames* steamed on up the Irish Sea, the Royal Train pulled into the University town of Aberystwyth on the West Wales coast. On the station platform, the Heir to the British Throne was introduced to a line-up of local dignitaries and then walked out into the forecourt to a tumultuous welcome. All eyes were on him, but only the knowledgeable noticed the five smartly-suited, keen-eyed men around him, four of whom moved along at a discreet distance, boxing him in, their eyes darting continually over their four separate quadrants, their hands hanging loosely at their sides, ready to draw and fire the revolvers tucked into their hidden holsters.

Outside the close-protection box, placed inconspicuously around, moving along with the royal party and deployed flexibly enough to respond to any situation and to throw an armed cordon around the scene of any attack, were enough armed police officers to ensure that a close-quarter attack on their Prince would be an attempt at suicide.

Right at the centre, inside the close-protection box, the Prince's personal detective stuck close enough to his charge to receive any bullets meant for him. The use of his revolver would be a secondary consideration.

It was a level of protection based on a high-profile but general alert put out as the result of current intelligence pooled by the Metropolitan Police Special Branch, M.I.5 and M.I.6. In other words, nothing specific to this visit but the knowledge that university students could be expected to stage their usual boisterous demonstration, yet enough of a general terrorist threat, given the twentieth anniversary of the deployment of British troops in Ulster, to call not only for additional police firearms cover, but also for greater than usual emphasis on crowd control and crush barriers, on the searching of every culvert, bridge and manhole on the royal route, on tight convoy drill, on the manning of strategic rooftops by keen-eyed observers and police sharp-shooters, and on aerial observation from the helicopter hired by the local police for the occasion.

The great wide street in front of Aberystwyth railway station was a mass of colour—Union flags and Welsh Dragon flags, cheering crowds of colourfully-dressed local people and holiday-makers. The shouts of a handful of protesting students were lost amid the tumult and their protest banners went unnoticed as, grasping hands stretched out over the crush barriers and giving a final wave to the welcoming crowd, the Prince stepped into the rear seat of his stately old Rolls Royce. The shining maroon coach-work of this forty-year-old doyen of the Royal Mews sparkled in the sunshine and the Royal Standard on the apex of its silver radiator stirred only slightly in the breathless air as the car moved away at a snail's pace.

The crowds cheered on, the flags waved wildly and the police motor cycle outrider moved slowly out of the station forecourt. He was followed by a gleaming black limousine carrying the Chief Constable, his chauffeur and two of his senior officers. Next, the Royal Rolls, with the Prince's personal detective sitting in front, alongside the Royal Mews driver. In the rear, the Prince and the County's Lord Lieutenant.

Almost bumper-to-bumper behind the Rolls, in an overtaking position ready to charge down any attempt to intercept or obstruct its progress, sat the souped-up Rover protection car. The armed police driver—trained to racing track standard—was accompanied by three other armed plain-clothes officers who, hands on door handles, were prepared to spring out at the least sign of trouble. Sandwiched tightly in the back seat, his shoulders hunched to give his armed companions as much space as possible for an emergency exit, sat the local Detective Chief Superintendent. The tension in that car was electric.

Half a dozen other cars followed, snaking between crush barriers behind which the crowds acclaimed the royal progress. The Prince's *aide-de-camp* was there, and then the worthies of the town and university in civilian cars. There followed the police car containing the radio control unit which gave the convoy its self-contained communications system and—right at the rear, six vehicles back from the Rolls—a minibus carrying the accredited press corps.

Eight hundred feet above the town and to one side of the area occupied by the crowds and the royal procession sat a Bell 47 helicopter. Inside its perspex bubble, alongside the civilian pilot, sat a police inspector armed with binoculars. He also had a knee pad holding a copy of the programme and timetable, and a personal radio linked into the convoy's radio net. A trained aerial observer, his brief was to observe and report on anything of interest or concern taking place out of the view of those protecting the convoy on the ground.

At 3.09 p.m. the procession began to clear the northern edge of the town and headed up the hill to the university. The crowds were thinner there, but just as enthusiastic in their welcome, which, every few yards on the still slow progress, was acknowledged by a wave of the royal hand.

3.11 p.m. A right-angled turn from the main road into the university's main entrance. A brief flurry of activity as some students broke the uniformed police cordon and tried to shout something into the rear window of the royal car. The protection car's engine revved sharply, its driver swung his wheel and began to shoot along the offside of the Rolls. Its doors began to open. But the uniformed men had pursued the group of protestors and held them off. The convoy moved on, the shouts of the students drowned by the cheers.

The long broad flight of steps at which the Rolls came to a stop was the next potential hazard and the protection men were out of their Rover while it was still moving. They boxed in their royal charge, scanned the three hundred and sixty degrees around him and hung their arms in that loose and ready manner characteristic of armed bodyguards. The steps were lined by uniformed police officers and, above them, plain clothes men had already marked the half dozen who looked like protestors. The royal progress was unimpeded; another brief flurry of protest went all but unnoticed.

At last they were through the swing doors of the glass-fronted entrance to the Great Hall and everyone relaxed. Searched in every nook and cranny over several days and protected by police officers continuously since, with every visitor carefully scrutinised, that building was as safe as anywhere on earth.

A line-up of college principals and heads of departments in full academic regalia received the royal handshake, each being introduced by the University Principal. Then, after donning his own robes in a robing room on the ground floor, the Heir to the Throne, as Chancellor of the University of Wales, ascended the staircase to the concourse, to take his place at the centre of the Great Hall's stage, and chair the meeting of the University Court.

*   *   *

It was just half past three. The *Ghadames* was reducing to dead slow in Cardigan Bay, fifty-three miles west of Aberystwyth. The sea was still smooth and the high pressure area lying over West Wales still giving the light airs and clear skies which would prevail for the next three days at least.

In the interval since her rendezvous with the *Spalpeen*, the *Ghadames'* crew had gone faultlessly and in record time through their well-drilled routine of constructing the fifty-eight square metre platform above the poop deck, aft of the addition to the ship's superstructure. And now they unlocked and opened up the two steel doors of the accommodation and rolled out the steel plates that brought its floor flush with the platform.

The underfloor fuel tanks of the SA 330 L, now reborn as a British army Puma, were filled to the brim with 1,500 litres of aviation fuel, enough to give the helicopter a range of three hundred and forty miles at its cruising speed of a hundred and sixty miles per hour.

Slowly the aircraft was wheeled from its hangar as its ground-crew unfolded its forty-nine foot diameter main rotors. The pilot and co-pilot took their seats and the helicopter's two Turbomeca Turmo turbines whined into life. Behind the crew, sixteen men climbed aboard. They were dressed in the combat gear and Royal Irish Rangers Tam O'Shanters which would mark them as soldiers of the British army. Their equipment went in with them: British army camouflaged tents, field rations, radios, weapons and satchels of explosives.

To all outward appearances this was a squad of British infantry-men carried in a British army helicopter. But in separate holdalls packed in the equipment bay they carried enough jeans, T-shirts, sneakers, windcheaters and rucksacks to clothe themselves as hikers, holidaymakers or lorry drivers when the time came to drop their cover.

The helicopter's rotors began to turn. As they accelerated, the crew retreated from the tremendous down-draught, and then, at ten minutes to four exactly, she lifted, swung her tail to the west and, rising to two hundred feet, put her nose down and headed off at a hundred and twenty miles an hour, for the Welsh coast.

The helicopter pad was quickly dismantled and stowed away. Not an Irishman was left aboard, nor any trace of their presence.

*   *   *

It was eleven o'clock in the morning on the eastern seaboard of the United States of America. Thomas Patrick Brennan was being interred at Boston's Catholic Cemetery. A solitary police patrolman, far from attempting to interfere, stood to attention and saluted as six men fired three pistol volleys over a coffin draped with the Irish tricolour and surrounded by a huge mound of wreaths in which green, white and gold predominated.

Of all the floral tributes, the massive Irish harp, constructed in roses, carnations and laurel, attracted the most attention, and its enigmatic Irish language dedication, *O na bheirte* ('From the Two'), the most comment and curiosity. For most of the hundreds of Irish-American mourners filing past Brennan's grave after the singing of the Irish National Anthem, that dedication would remain an enigma. But before the day was out, one man among them would be admitted to its secret in circumstances which would change his life. That man's name was Seamus McDonagh.

McDonagh, short, stocky, with the face and physique of a boxer and a cigar clamped in the corner of his mouth, was sixty-seven, an American citizen of forty years standing, and his business, which had made him a millionaire several times over, was investment banking. As he drifted with the crowd towards the long line of waiting limousines, McDonagh received a tap on the shoulder.

"Martin Burke," said the elderly stranger, proferring a hand.

"Seamus McDonagh," replied the banker, gripping it.

"I know. I take it you're going to the wake at The Plough?" He was.

"Well, look, I'd like you to come over to my place afterwards— over on Commonwealth Avenue." He handed McDonagh his card. "There's something I'd like to talk over with you."

"Fine," said McDonagh.

They separated with a smile and each climbed into the back of his chauffeur-driven car to make his way across the Charles River to that favourite haunt of Boston Irishmen, The Plough and the Stars on Massachusetts Avenue.

*   *   *

Steve Gannon had picked up the envelope from the deposit box at Amsterdam's Nederlandse Centraal Bank, but as he sat in the British Embassy in The Hague there was something else in the forefront of his mind. Thirty hours ago, somebody had tried to kill him.

His main concern was the possibility that his 'Central Office of Information' cover—perhaps even the organisation itself—had been blown. Yet the periodic checks on Gannon and his family by the security service's highly proficient counter-surveillance branch continued to indicate that his cover was watertight. The latest routine checks, completed only a matter of days ago, seemed to show that the bulkhead between his aliases and his real identity was as secure as ever, and M.I.6's cover seemed not to have been penetrated either.

Yet somebody had tried to kill him, not, apparently, as 'Gordon Colclough' the Irish-based freelance writer, but, presumably, as Steven Gannon, a civil servant on his way to a mundane job in a London office. He knew from last night's London paper that the railway police were treating the death of the man on the London underground as an accident and that he had not yet been identified. Or had there *really* been an attempt to kill him? Had he become over-sensitive, imagined it, reacted to the man at his back with instinct not reason? The more he tried to talk himself out of it, the more certain he was that Hurley had been right, and that it would not be the last attempt on his life. Somebody, somewhere, intended that Steven Gannon should be disposed of in the same way as Brigadier Anthony Farrell—a man he had never met and whose existence had been unknown to him until he was given the tip-off by the Metropolitan Police Special Branch.

For reasons of his own, Gannon was telling no-one of his brush with death, and nothing had come up in his telephone conversation with his boss, Ben Craig, to suggest that he felt he was in anything more than the usual danger associated with his work, or that he had seen anything out of the ordinary in Gannon's decision to skip his intended visit to the office and come straight to Holland. Now that he was out of London and had enough work to keep him away for a while, Gannon felt reasonably safe, but he had to protect his wife, so he telephoned her to tell her that he had made arrangements for her to fly out first thing next morning to Florence for a week or two with her sister. Jill Gannon was surprised and touched that he had remembered her sister's birthday and had planned such a nice surprise for her.

At 3.15 that Friday afternoon, he was suddenly pitched from one dilemma to another by a phone call from M.I.6's London answering service. Within two hours he was out of Holland, on Aer Lingus flight EI.609 from Schipol. At 7.35 he was in Dublin.

It was the word '*Birthday*' that had sent him off at such speed. ''Tell Gordon I'm looking forward to having a drink with him in the usual place on my birthday.'' *Birthday* denoted a rare but highly significant departure from normal routines of communication between himself and an agent. It meant that his man in touch with top Provisional I.R.A. sources had some life-or-death information. Michael Hurley would be expecting to see him as soon as possible, and 'The usual place' was the Stag's Head pub in Dame Court, around the corner from Dublin Castle. From the moment he had left that message, Hurley would be expecting a rendezvous. Ten in the morning or ten in the evening. He would cover the pub at both those times until his Secret Service contact showed up.

Gannon's mind was in a turmoil as he headed out over the North Sea. Was it a coincidence that within thirty hours of an attempt on his life he was being called to Dublin in circumstances that admitted of no delay or question? Was he heading for a second encounter with death? Ben Craig had advised him to contact his agent through the more usual channels. Would he not at least take a back-up team with him? But Gannon had a pressing reason for brushing aside such advice. A reason big enough for him to cast all his fears aside, regain his well-honed, ice-cool professionalism, and put his head once more into the noose. He had to know. He had to know if the demon that had pursued him for most of his life was now about to catch up with him. Anyway, he told Craig, there was no time to fix a back-up team.

*   *   *

Hurley was already in the bar when Gannon walked in at ten that evening. He joined him at a small corner table that gave a clear view of the street doors of that classic, untouched Victorian bar of dark mahogany, shining brass and white-aproned barmen.

"Gordon, I've cracked *Andrea*."

Gannon stiffened. "You have?"

"Yes. I've cracked it. It's a codeword for sleepers planted high up in the British tree."

"How high up?"

"Bloody high. High enough to set up the Royal Family. And I mean set them up!"

"How?"

Hurley swilled a deep draught of his Guinness, then stroked his chin for a while. "I'm not sure. There's something happening, but I just can't exactly put my finger on it."

"What *have* you got?"

"This," said Hurley. "First, there was the senior army officer I told you about—the brigadier, the one the A.S.U. had been ordered to kill. He was one of the sleepers. Second, they've had some people in Libya for training for this big operation on the mainland. The next in line to the Throne is the target . . ."

"Not the Prince . . ."

"The very man. It can't fail because one of their plants— somebody right on the inside—has set him up. It's all connected with *Andrea*. It's run from America, but that's as far as I've got on *Andrea* itself."

"How has he been set up? What's the plan?"

"I don't know exactly, but *The Soldier*'s with them. In command of the A.S.U. And . . .," Hurley paused. "It's incredible. Incredible. It seems they're going to bump *The Soldier* off when it's all over."

Gannon managed somehow to appear calm. "Bump him off? What kind of sense is that supposed to make?"

"How the hell should I know? That's what *you're* supposed to be good at. All I know is that they tried to get him not long ago, by sabotaging a helicopter he was supposed to be travelling in, but they got his wife by mistake. And they must have a bloody good reason for wanting to get rid of him, because there's a hell of a panic on just now in the Army Council."

"My God. Are you sure of all this?"

"I'm a hundred percent certain they've targeted the Prince, and I'd put it at ninety-to-one that it's right about *The Soldier*, with what I know about his helicopter crash."

For a while Gannon sat still, rubbing his finger around the rim of his empty whiskey glass to make it hum softly. "The Prince," he said quietly. "An inside set-up." He looked up. The barman arrived with more drinks and he waited until he had gone out of earshot. "When?"

"It's either to-day or tomorrow. I can't be sure which. We're probably too bloody late now, anyway."

Gannon looked at his digital watch. It was 22.43. Friday 11th August. "I've got to go," he said, rising abruptly from his bench seat. "Tomorrow morning, O.K.?"

"O.K."

"Let's make it the Shamrock, shall we? Ten o'clock?"

"Fine."

They left the Stag's Head as they always did, separately and in different directions. With a wave to each other they parted. Hurley walked off towards Merchant's Quay. Gannon watched him for a moment, then turned and hurried along Dame Court towards O'Connell Street Bridge.

*   *   *

The meeting of the Welsh University Court at Aberystwyth had ended at six o'clock that Friday evening and the royal programme had taken its carefully-timed pre-determined course: dinner in the University Hall of Residence, a visit to a *son et lumiére* performance of a Welsh tale of fairies, dragons and magic in the grounds of the castle ruins on the sea front, and then a night's sleep at the home of an old friend three miles out of town.

The last traces of daylight were still in the sky when the doors of the house closed for the night, leaving a night shift of armed police officers to protect the outside. Those inside sipped their nightcaps and congratulated each other on the end to a perfect day, another faultless protection operation.

*   *   *

While Aberystwyth slept, the Provisional I.R.A.'s 'Puma' helicopter, in British army camouflage, roundels and identification markings, was sitting on a mountain top eighteen miles away. It sat in a hollow close to Carn Saith Wraig (the Rock of the Seven Wives), two and a half miles from the nearest sheep farmer's cottage. At 4.35 that afternoon, after its forty-five minute flight from the *Ghadames*, it had lowered its tricycle undercarriage and touched down precisely at map reference SN 771528. Now, its pilot, co-pilot and passengers were settling down in their British army camouflaged tents to a satisfying supper of British army field rations, cooked in their self-heating cans and served in army mess tins. Two of the men sat on guard, their British army SA80 rifles cradled between their knees.

Men like them, in the camouflaged combat gear and the green Tam O'Shanters of the Royal Irish Rangers were a familiar sight in those mountains, as were their helicopters, for large parts of central Wales serve as military training areas and the farmers and shepherds who encounter them never raise an eyebrow, but merely pass the time of day. Occasionally they will share a cup of that thick, sweet, stand-your-spoon-up tea that only the British army knows how to make.

The chances that the Irishmen would have their cover blown on their mountain-top hideaway were as remote as human ingenuity could calculate. They had rehearsed their cover stories well . . . but their fingers were on the safety-catches of their British army weapons, just in case.

CHAPTER FOURTEEN

After leaving the wake for Thomas Patrick Brennan, Seamus McDonagh was driven back over the Charles River and reached the gates of Martin Burke's house on Commonwealth Avenue at around half past seven. His chauffeur announced their arrival through the grille of the inter-com, and the elaborately-wrought, remotely-controlled iron gates slid silently aside to admit them. Closed-circuit TV cameras covered their progress up the drive to the pseudo-colonial mansion where, bathed in light on the colon-naded porch, Martin Burke was waiting. Alongside him stood a silver-haired man, also in his seventies, who introduced himself as Dan Twomey.

By the time McDonagh, Burke and Twomey had gone through the great hallway, with its crystal chandelier and broad, sweeping staircase, and settled themselves into deep velvet-covered armchairs, it was evident, from the size and shape of the men on Burke's domestic staff, that they were in a very well-guarded house. A glance at the equipment-packed room on the first floor, where all the electronic surveillance devices were monitored, would have suggested a well-protected bank.

Drinks were served, the butler left the room and the three Irish-Americans were alone. They raised their brandy glasses to the toast *Erin go bragh*!

The conversation was opened by Twomey. "Let's begin by telling you what we know about you, Seamus, and then we'll come to the point."

McDonagh crossed his legs, sank back into the depths of the vast armchair and blew a great cloud of cigar smoke towards the ornately-moulded ceiling. "Go ahead," he said, tapping his cigar over the onyx ashtray on the table beside him.

"Born Macroom, November 20th, 1921," said Twomey. "Your father took part in the I.R.A. ambush of Michael Collins at Bealnablath, County Cork, and was himself shot and wounded by the Free Staters at Clonankilty three weeks later and put in prison. He died in Macroom in February, 1935. His older brother—your uncle Christy—died in 1916 in Clandouglas House during the

Easter Rising while beating back a battalion of the Sherwood Foresters from Mount Street Bridge. You and your brother were sent to Philadelphia on 28th April, 1929, to join your uncle, Patrick McDonagh, whose surname you both took after your mother's death. You graduated from Harvard Business School, entered your uncle's banking business and rose to the top of the tree. You and your younger brother, Patrick, served in the U.S. army during the war and he was killed in action. You were sworn in as an American citizen on 12th April, 1946. Married three years later to Una Murphy, a second-generation Irish-American, who died two years ago. Active in Philadelphia politics as a Republican. For your work for the Catholic Church and its charities, you were invested by the Pope with the *Pro Ecclesia*. You were a leading member of *Clann na Gael* and are an active supporter of Noraid. Republican pedigree impeccable.''

McDonagh interrupted, removing his cigar from between his teeth and waving it with a flourish. He laughed. ''What's this, a citation?''

''In a way. In a way.''

He swirled his brandy glass, emptied it and took another puff at his cigar.

''Our assessment of you,'' Twomey continued, ''built up from a very close study of you over many more years than you might think, is that you are a man who would die for the cause.''

''What? Now?''

''Never. Unless . . .''

''Unless what?'' McDonagh suddenly stiffened and moved to the edge of his chair. ''Unless what? What is this? Blackmail or something?''

It was an uncomfortable moment and Burke intervened to calm it. ''Nothing of the kind. But I think we'd better put our cards on the table, Dan.''

''Be my guest,'' snapped McDonagh, still on his guard.

''What we're saying,'' said Twomey, ''is that the proposition we want to put to you—an invitation to be part of the biggest thing in Irish-American solidarity to-day—is so hot that any mention of what we are about to say to you will be the death of you. Swift and certain. If we tell it to you, we shall have put a time bomb under you. Savvy?''

McDonagh savvied. The atmosphere relaxed. Burke refilled their brandy glasses and they drank again to *Erin go bragh*. "Trust?" he asked. "If there's any doubt at all in your mind, say so now and we'll forget it. It'll be too late once we've told you."

"Trust," replied McDonagh, and the three shook hands and settled down again in their armchairs.

Twomey took up where Burke had left off. "To-day you attended the funeral of Thomas Patrick Brennan, didn't you?"

"I did."

"Well, *I* know, and *he* knows [pointing to Burke], and now *you* are going to know what nobody else in the world knows. That the man we buried was not Thomas Patrick Brennan but George Kennedy."

"So?"

"Kennedy. George Kennedy ... Northumberland Road ... Mount Street Bridge ... the Easter Rising ... the Sherwood Foresters ..."

McDonagh sat bolt upright. "But Kennedy was killed, along with my Uncle Christy and most of the others."

"Kennedy's body was never found," said Twomey quietly, "and the only first-hand evidence that he was still there when the troops burst in with their hand grenades and killed nearly everybody came from one of his comrades who had tended his thigh wound. As you probably know, that man, along with several others, *did* get out of the burning building and *did* break through the British cordon in the confusion. I mean, everybody knows that, don't they? What nobody but us knows is that George Kennedy got out with them. He was semi-conscious and he had a tourniquet around his groin, but he got out all right."

McDonagh was staggered.

Twomey took some pictures and papers from his table and handed them to him. The photographs of a younger 'Brennan' in swimming trunks by his private pool showed a long, ugly scar on the outside of his left thigh. The photocopy of his medical records showed the fictitious entry that his 5 inch scar was the relic of 'an accidental gun-shot wound from a thirty-thirty sporting rifle'.

"But this is incredible," said McDonagh. "One of our greatest heroes survived and no one ever knew it?"

"No-one but us. They smuggled him out of Dublin to County Carlow—to Hacketstown—and by the time he had recovered enough to know what was going on, fourteen of his comrades had been shot by General Maxwell's firing squads. Kennedy knew it was all over and that if he should be found they'd shoot him, too, for what he had done to the British soldiers on Mount Street Bridge. Half the British casualties in the whole rising were inflicted there."

"How did he finish up over here?"

"Six months later he signed on as a deck-hand on a cargo ship at Dun Laoghaire—the *Inchigeela*—and jumped ship in Boston. From then on it reads like a penny romance: a job at illegal immigrant wages in a lamp factory; catches eye of owner's daughter, takes ill, daughter goes in search and finds him dying in a garret, nurses him back to health; works his way up in company, marries boss's daughter . . ."

"There's one small thing I don't understand. The civil war. Others went back home from here to fight the Free Staters . . ."

"Have another glance at the medical record."

McDonagh did. And he understood. The late Thomas Patrick Brennan, otherwise Section Commander George Kennedy, C Company of the Irish Volunteers, had been permanently disabled by his thigh wound and other bullet and shrapnel injuries and had walked with a stick for the rest of his long life. "But," Burke interjected, "he remained a soldier for the Republic until his last breath, and the things he accomplished for the cause will stand comparison with anything achieved by men in the field."

In the thoughtful silence that followed, another bottle of brandy was brought in by the butler, with a silver tray of sandwiches, snacks and coffee. The colonial grandfather clock struck nine. The silence was eventually broken by McDonagh: "Fascinating. But how does this affect me? What's so secret now, anyway?"

Martin Burke told him. "Have you ever heard of *An Triúir*?"

"No. Should I?"

"It's Irish. It means *The Three People*. Kennedy was one of the original three. Dan here and I replaced the other two when they died in 1940 and 1941. Those few people who have ever heard the words *An Triúir* have no idea what they mean; whether there really are three people or whether it's just a symbol of something—you know, like the Holy Trinity for example. But you are looking at two of them now.''

McDonagh was riveted. ''Of course. The funeral wreath, *O na Bheirte*. From the Two People.''

''You've got it. Dan and me. It all goes back to 1923. George Kennedy and two other Irish exiles who survived the Rising and the civil war swore an oath by mingling their blood on a copy of the 1916 proclamation of the Irish Republic.'' He handed the fading document—a handbill—to McDonagh, who could see some small dark stains above the name of the first signatory, Thomas Clarke. ''They swore to exact retribution from the English for so long as three could be found to take the same oath.''

McDonagh was stirred, but still somewhat puzzled. ''But surely, isn't that what all of us have sworn, and isn't that what every true Irishman stands for?''

''Sure,'' said Twomey, taking up the story, ''but the route they chose was a special one, complementary, if you like, to the fight in the field. Their way was to mount a highly secret operation of their own; just the three of them. They set out to put a worm right in the middle of the English apple and to feed it, encourage its growth and development, and then, when the time was right, to put that worm to work, right where it mattered.''

''For example?''

''For example, we have people seemingly English to the tips of their fingers, in key positions in the highest reaches of the British government, their civil service, their armed forces and their police. Not many, but whenever we see fit to call in our marker—and they owe everything they have to us—it will be met in full. They would even kill for the cause.''

''You're telling me,'' asked McDonagh, ''that you have sleepers right on the inside—right at the centre? And you're telling me that you have only to snap your fingers, and they'll break out? And kill if they have to?''

''Yes,'' said Twomey coolly.

''How? How can you be so sure after you've left them inactive for years?''

''We *can* be sure. We've done it. Believe me.''

Martin Burke came in again: ''The only reason people don't ask the same question about Philby, Burgess, McLean and Blunt—

spies in the British Secret Service itself—is because they *did* deliver, even after twenty or thirty years. Just look at Blunt: knighted by the Queen, keeper of her art treasures, personal contact with her . . . and all the time a Russian agent. If an Englishman can be persuaded by a foreign country to devote his entire life to a foreign cause, what price an Irishman for Ireland? It's *belief*, Seamus. Belief that over-rides everything . . . self, family and every other loyalty but that to the cause you believe in above all others. If communism can do it . . .'' His voice rose with his emotion, ''. . . why not Irish republicanism?''

It only remained for Burke and Twomey to fill in the details of *An Triúir*'s sixty-odd years history, and by the time they had had a short sleep, and breakfast was served on the terrace overlooking the swimming pool and the parkland beyond, McDonagh had been taken through the whole set-up. He had learned, for instance, of the secret writings found among the papers of Padraig Pearse after his execution for leading the 1916 Easter Rising—papers whose existence was known only to *An Triúir*.

Pearse, the first President of Ireland's ill-fated first Republic, had not only been a soldier, he had been a scholar; a prolific writer on the Gaelic legends and pre-history which had been the inspiration for what he saw as the inevitability of a blood sacrifice in the search for a free Ireland. It had been the spur to his own search for death or glory, which had ended before a firing squad. ''Pearse expected all along to die, of course,'' Twomey told him. ''Looking to the future, he had expounded his dream of what should follow, in writings which came into the hands of Kennedy and his two fellow exiles. They took up his dream of an Ireland returned to the heroic and romantic purity of its ancient Gaelic customs and culture, and especially those aspects of it in which they found the inspiration for the means by which the worm could be injected into the apple.''

''Fostering,'' said Burke, taking up the thread. ''The tradition of fostering the sons of Ireland's ancient heroes. If you've ever read the legend of Finn McCumail . . .'' McDonagh shook his head. ''Well, if you had, you'd remember how the *Fianna*, his band of spartan warriors, cut all ties with family and home. There were initiation rites and harsh training, but at the end of it all they were an *élite*—an heroic band fighting for justice and defending their land to the death against invaders. And the *Tain Bo Cualuge* . . .?''

McDonagh shook his head again.

''The ancient Irish chronicle. The tradition that the sons of fighting men were sent at an early age to live with foster parents, with whom they forged even stronger ties than with their blood relations. They were given everything in the way of care and education, and they had an eternal and over-riding obligation to give whatever aid was required of them in return. These princes received their first weapons and were trained in the arts of war from the age of seven. War was their paramount duty and to die on the battlefield was to be assured of a glorious reincarnation.''

McDonagh lit another cigar. ''I'm with you, but it doesn't sound so easy to me.''

''It wasn't easy, at least not until the right kind of money became available and communications across the Atlantic improved, but it worked. By God it worked. They arranged for a small number of the sons of what you might call twentieth-century Irish heroes— men who had fought and perhaps died in the war of independence and the civil war—to be grafted onto the families of second and third generation Irish extraction, who lived in England but still had well-rooted and uncompromising republican sympathies. *An Triúir* funded and managed the whole scheme, and saw that the boys were guided into positions from which, when the marker was called in, they could strike a blow for the cause. Their English accents and the remoteness of the foster family's Irish connections allowed them to blend into the scene completely.''

Then Twomey answered the question which McDonagh was about to ask: ''There was always the chance, of course, that the boy might not make it high enough to be really useful, but *An Triúir* believed—and rightly so as it turned out—that if they launched enough of them, enough would hit the target to make it all worthwhile . . .''

McDonagh puffed quietly at his cigar for a while, and then, ''Three questions,'' he said. ''First, identity. If these kids were born in Ireland and yet were supposed to have been born in England, how about birth certificates?''

''Easy,'' said Twomey. ''Stolen by sympathisers in registry offices in various parts of England and forged by them. Of course,

115

there'd be no corresponding entries in the registers there, or in the central office in London, but if a certificate is produced have you ever known anyone to take the trouble to check back? They certainly haven't for the past fifty-odd years with us anyway, and if the boys ever need a replacement . . .'' He tapped a box on the table beside him ''. . . they know where to come.''

"O.K. Second question: what hold do you have on the guy and how do you monitor him?''

''There's the knowledge that he's the son of a hero, groomed for heroic deeds himself, and the more practical reason for loyalty, that he's sworn to secrecy on pain of death. Plus the fact that as a youth he was required to kill for the cause to prove himself. In fact, that was the final act of his initiation—a cool, close-quarter killing on orders that carried no explanation and had to be obeyed without question. Not just a quick shot and away. *The* ultimate test. He had to get his man first, secure him so that he was helpless, and let him know exactly what was coming to him. Then he had to do it face-to-face, looking into his eyes as he blew his brains out with a revolver shot in the forehead. The supreme test of nerve. And just in case, even after all that, he should show any sign of wavering, the evidence to prove that he'd killed for *An Triúir* was securely stored away. *And he knows it's there.*''

''And then there's the tattoo,'' explained Burke, looking up from a file of papers on his lap. ''When it was felt that he was ready, the newly-graduated warrior as you might call him was tattooed to identify him to *An Triúir* for ever more.''

''We have it too,'' added Twomey, taking off his jacket and rolling up his shirt sleeve, ''so that there can be no doubt about who we are on the rare occasions we need to meet face-to-face.''

McDonagh examined Twomey's tattoo, which was on the inside of his right upper arm, below the armpit, and took the shape of a small straight stem line, from which tiny straight lines branched at right angles at irregular intervals along its length. ''*Ogam* writing,'' said Twomey. ''Only a Celtic scholar would recognise this, and only he would be able to decipher it: *Boru*; Brian Boru, the last High King of All Ireland, the man who freed Ireland from the Norse invader.''

''A bit melodramatic isn't it?'' exclaimed McDonagh. ''A

tattoo? There's no hiding a tattoo, is there, if somebody gets suspicious?''

"Isn't it all melodramatic? Isn't the whole idea? That's how they were in the old days. If we were doing it to-day . . .''

Burke came in again: "If we were doing it now there's a lot of things we'd do different. You're right. The tattoo could be dangerous. It's a good I.D. that nobody could duplicate, but you're right. It could be *very* dangerous.''

"You can say we've been lucky," said Twomey. "Sure the tattoo was a crazy idea, but, hell, I guess the whole damned thing was crazy in the first place. But it's worked. It's got its weaknesses. It's crazy, but by hell it's worked.''

"And secure enough?''

"Almost one hundred percent. In virtually every case the relationship has held firm. Its greatest proof against infiltration or leakage is this: each of our boys, and his foster parents, think they are the only ones. It's the keystone of our security; a cellular system. Each worm in the apple believes he's unique—even though he might be working alongside another!''

"Third question," said McDonagh. "Have any ever turned?''

"Very, very few. On only three occasions have we had to ask the I.R.A. to kill any of our people. Incidentally, they do it without a quibble. In that respect *our* word is *their* command. When we say Kill, they Kill, and no questions asked. They've done it twice recently, as a matter of fact, and one of them wasn't *consciously* betraying us. He'd cracked mentally and there was a real danger that someone in British intelligence might put the pieces together. He was killed by a Provisional I.R.A. team in a way which avoided any suspicion of homicide. Hit by a stolen car as he walked out of an English country pub late at night.''

McDonagh failed to grasp the point: "That's a hell of a way to go about it. Why not just shoot the guy straight out? Surely there was a danger that it would all go wrong. Why not shoot him clean?''

"Because we couldn't afford a homicide investigation. We couldn't afford it being handled by a detective instead of a traffic cop. Believe me, Seamus. Don't you remember what I said about the tattoo under his right arm? Isn't that why the idea of tattooing them was crazy? It might have been a million-to-one shot, but

117

there was always the possibility that a detective might stumble across the answer and blow the whole damned thing. No. It just had to be a hit-and-run. It just had to be a case for a traffic cop.''

"O.K. So who was the guy?''

"Do you remember Bloody Sunday . . . 1971 . . . the shooting of thirteen unarmed civilians by British Paras in Derry . . . and the official enquiry finding that it had happened through a breakdown in discipline among the soldiers?''

McDonagh, like every other Irish republican, remembered it only too well.

"I don't need to tell you of the propaganda value that affair had, and still has, for the cause, do I, Seamus?''

"You're damned right.''

"Would you believe that it was brought about by our man in the Paras, just when the I.R.A. was running low and needed a big propaganda boost? Wasn't that a stroke and a half?''

"And Warren Point,'' said Burke, coming in again. "Eighteen Paras ambushed and killed at Warren Point. The same officer. Can you think of any stronger test of one of our boys than asking him to sacrifice men alongside whom he'd worked and lived and fought for years? And there's a lot more he's done for us.''

McDonagh was stunned. "I can't believe I'm hearing this.''

"We can show the evidence,'' said his two hosts together.

"How come he cracked?''

"Goose Green. The Falklands,'' said Burke tersely. "He must have developed a conscience.''

"And the other guy? You said there were two recently . . .''

"Oh, yes. An ex-marines officer. A guy named Steven Gannon. For years we monitored him while he served in the Royal Marines, and since he came out we've been monitoring him while he's been a civil servant in the British government's information service. We knew he was in Ulster with the Marines, but we couldn't understand why we couldn't manage to activate him. We thought it was just a communication problem until, after he'd left the Marines, somebody in the I.R.A. stumbled on the fact that while he was serving with one of their special units he'd operated under cover in the north with a squad that had killed a lot of our boys out of hand and got information out of others under torture. His unit, along with the S.A.S., was acting on secret orders to shoot on sight, and they played hell with our boys north and south of the border, so even though he was out of the fighting line, even though he was in a civilian office job where he couldn't do us any direct harm, we decided we couldn't take any chances. He'd betrayed us already anyway, and we were pretty sure he was working for British intelligence in some way. Better safe than sorry."

"Another accident?"

"Yes."

"The tattoo again?"

"The bloody tattoo again," said Twomey. "We're still waiting to hear."

McDonagh asked what other achievements could be ascribed to *An Triúir*, and Twomey and Burke rose from their armchairs. They crossed the room and swung aside a broad-framed oil painting hinged to the wall, revealing a small control panel. Twomey touched a switch and a red light illuminated. They took from their pockets three bunches of keys and inserted a key into each of three ignition switches, extinguishing the red light and illuminating a green one. Twomey lifted a hinged cover from a square button, which he pressed. With a gentle humming sound the marble hearth of the fireplace slid aside, to reveal the steel cover of what turned out to be a strong-box. Three other keys released the cover, and, raising it, Twomey removed three two-inch ring files and several bundles of documents from the cavity beneath.

He turned to McDonagh. "This strong-box contains our only records and it can only be opened by three sets of keys kept separately by the three members of *An Triúir*. If that green indicator isn't switched on, any attempt to open it will activate an incinerating device inside." He handed the files to McDonagh. "Skim through these. Start with Dieppe."

"*Dieppe*?"

"Yes. 19th August, 1942; five thousand British troops landed there. Three and a half thousand of them were killed or wounded. The Germans were waiting in full force and almost wiped them out on the beaches. There have been many theories about who tipped them off and why."

"What had that to do with uniting Ireland?" asked McDonagh, once again non-plussed by the twists and turns of *An Triúir*'s role in the struggle.

"Don't you remember the I.R.A.'s part in the war? England's difficulty, Ireland's opportunity . . . the old cry from 1916 . . . the I.R.A.'s collaboration with the Germans? Don't you remember the German spies who landed in Ireland and worked with the I.R.A.—Herman Goertz and the others? And the boys who went out to Germany to train with the *Abwehr* in sabotage and such?"

McDonagh said he had heard such stories, but he evidently did not know the whole of it. "In May, 1940," said Twomey, "the I.R.A.'s Chief of Staff, Sean Russell, went to Berlin and met Foreign Minister Ribbentrop. Two days later he was on a bomb-making and sabotage course with another I.R.A. man who had arrived separately in Germany from Spain. Three months later a top-level German intelligence and foreign affairs committee sanctioned an operation in Ireland and provided them with a U-boat to take them from Wilhelmshaven to Galway. Unfortunately, Russell took ill and died and he was buried at sea wrapped in the German flag, with full military honours."

"Oh, yes, I heard something about that."

"Well, the operation was called off and the U-boat turned back to Germany. It was from there, early in 1941, that the other guy contacted *An Triúir*."

"And then . . ."

"And then George Kennedy, Martin here, and I, activated one of our men in England and eighteen months later he gave us our chance to strike a blow at British preparations to invade occupied France. Through my business contacts in Spain I passed the plans for the Dieppe raid to the *Abwehr*'s man in Madrid." Twomey paused, his eyes lighting up with the memory. "Wasn't it natural that the I.R.A. should follow its old tradition? England's difficulty . . . Ireland's opportunity?"

"So you had a man somewhere who gave you the tip-off."

"Yes. On the British army's planning team."

"What happened to him afterwards?"

"Posted to Egypt. He followed General Montgomery, who was posted from the planning team to take over the 8th Army in North Africa, just before the Dieppe operation was launched. After the war our man went into politics, in a prime spot eventually. We've made use of him since."

McDonagh sat deep in thought for a full minute. "Dieppe," he

120

said quietly, almost to himself. "Jesus, what a scam." And then he slowly leafed through the remainder of the three bulky files. For a while there was silence, save for the slow ticking of the grandfather clock, the soft rustle of paper and the occasional whistles of astonishment from McDonagh. "Negotiations between the British government and the Provisionals in 1972?" he asked with some surprise, stopping part-way through volume two.

"Oh, yes," said Twomey. "Whoever would have thought *that* would happen? Do you know, Adams and O'Connell had actually got the Brits to agree to cease operations, to give the I.R.A. freedom of movement on the streets while bearing arms, and to end their searches of cars, houses and people on the streets?"

"The hell they had!"

"The hell they *had*. *And* what seemed to be a commitment to a withdrawal!"

McDonagh was dumbfounded.

"They actually met face-to-face, at the home of a government minister in London, and the Northern Ireland Secretary agreed to virtually every condition the I.R.A. put to him, just to get an end to the fighting. Then the Prods found out and all hell was let loose. Even the army commander had been kept in the dark and he went berserk!"

"And that was the end of it . . .?"

"It was. But just think of it. Who would ever have thought the British government would sit down and talk with the I.R.A? Didn't our man in the British government almost pull it off? And wasn't he the same guy who gave us Dieppe on a plate?"

"Jesus!" exclaimed McDonagh, returning almost incredulously to the last of the three volumes. A moment later he looked up again, wide-eyed. "*And* Mountbatten?"

"*And* Mountbatten." Twomey shrugged his shoulders. "But that went off the rails. That's why we had to get the I.R.A. to blow up the Dublin ambassador's car."

McDonagh read on in silence, and when he had turned the last page he looked up again and laid the volume aside. "Well, guys, you sure have something to boast about. It's incredible." He paused. "One last question: how do you call in your marker?"

"We lift the phone," said Twomey, "and we simply say *Boru*. He'll understand."

"Brian Boru," Burke interjected. "Padraig Pearse's hero. Threw out the foreign invader, killed his brother for the kingship. The end always justifying the means. Pearse wrote and said it time and time again, proved it by his own sacrifice in the Easter Rising. *Boru*. That's the magic word. None of them has ever heard of *An Triúir* by name. *Boru* is their call-sign. We never saw any need to let them get closer to us than that."

It was two o'clock in the morning. "Time for bed," said Burke.

The butler filled their champagne glasses and an enthusiastic toast was drunk to *An Triúir*. But then Burke leaned forward, his face clouded. "What's wrong?" asked McDonagh.

He sighed deeply. "We're getting old, Seamus. Dan's seventy-nine, I'm eighty, you're . . .?"

"Sixty seven."

". . . . and all our people planted over the water are still in their fifties and sixties."

"So?"

"So we can't keep it up much longer at this rate." The problem, he explained, was that when it had all begun, Irish immigrants into America numbered tens of thousands a year. Young men, fresh from the struggle in the old country, were still coming over to join relatives in families well-established over the years since the Famine had begun to empty Ireland—families that had prospered in the great free-for-all rough and tumble of nineteenth century American capitalism. There had been all the youth, the fire and the money needed for a great heroic crusade. Now, in the 1980s, Irish immigration had all but ceased. Irish freedom-fighters would be stopped and turned back at any airport immigration desk and they wouldn't have a bean between them anyway. It was getting more and more difficult to identify anyone who could really be trusted and didn't have one foot in the grave.

"Look at me," said Twomey disconsolately. "Eighty years old and doing London and back in a day by Concorde to make the contacts for our latest job. It's a young man's work, Seamus. The torch will soon be passed to you if you join us. But who will you pass it on to?"

"Come on, boys, for God's sake," said McDonagh. "Drink up. *An Triúir*'s safe with me. Always will be. I've had a great night so far. Don't give up on me now."

122

The atmosphere cleared as quickly as it had darkened. Twomey slapped Burke on the shoulder. "Cheer up, Martin. You're not dead yet, you bloody old rebel."

"It's right you are, Dan," said Burke, laughing with him. "Come on, boys, a chorus of *The Holy Ground* ..."

And there they sat, three ageing rebels, glasses in the air, singing of 'The Holy Ground, and the girls that we adore ...' Three ageing rebels, singing the old songs, telling the old stories, and carrying their torch through a dark tunnel with no end.

CHAPTER FIFTEEN

In West Wales, at 6.30 a.m. on Saturday 12th August, the Prince's protection team took over from the night shift, as everyone rose and prepared for the day's programme: an hour and a half in the University for the presentation of honorary degrees; a slow drive to the centre of the town; a walkabout in crowded North Parade and Dark Gate Street, and a drive down the coast road to Aberaeron, sixteen miles to the south. There, a fifteen minute walkabout in the main street, followed by a school-children's concert in the adjoining park, then into the cars again for the eighteen mile drive to the R.A.F. airfield at Aberporth, where an HS.146 executive jet of the Queen's Flight would be waiting. It would then be back to R.A.F. Northolt, en-route for Windsor and an afternoon's polo in the Great Park.

*   *   *

At 10.20 a.m., with the degree ceremony in full swing, a hired Ford twelve-seater minibus travelling west along the Abergwesyn mountain road, eighteen miles south-east of Aberystwyth, turned left onto the narrow two-mile dead-end track towards the tiny, isolated old chapel of Soar y Mynydd. In the forestry plantation on Bryn Mawr hill above the chapel, fourteen Provisional I.R.A. men in hiking gear and carrying rucksacks, large holdalls and Adidas sports bags, watched its progress. Dropping their Royal Irish Rangers disguise, they had walked the mile from their helicopter at Carn Saith Wraig and emerged from the forestry plantation as the minibus reached the chapel. They quickly loaded themselves and their gear through its nearside door.

The nine mile drive to Tregaron took eighteen minutes, over steep and winding mountain roads, and it was there that six of the occupants of the minibus transferred to a hired Sherpa van and eight into a hired Ford 7-ton truck, both of which were waiting, unattended, on the car park of the Talbot Hotel, their ignition keys hidden under their front bumpers. At 10.55 a.m., the Sherpa van carrying Tom O'Donnell and his No. 2 group, and the Ford truck carrying *The Soldier* and his No. 1 group, headed out of Tregaron.

* * *

Fifteen minutes after the two Provisional I.R.A. groups had left Tregaron, the Heir to the British throne was walking through Dark Gate Street, waving to enthusiastic crowds and shaking eagerly-proferred hands. At 11.23 a.m. the royal party re-entered its vehicles, and at 11.32, after a slow drive through the remainder of the town, the police motor cycle outrider reached the top of the long climb out of Aberystwyth. He led the convoy around the right-hand bend by the Devil's Bridge turn and down the hill, on the coast road towards Aberaeron. On the landward side of the road flew the shadowing Bell 47 helicopter, its police observer watching that road like a hawk.

The second phase of the royal visit was safely over. The third, the walkabout in Aberaeron, should be reached in about twenty-five minutes.

At that moment, the terrorists' 'Puma' helicopter, with the remaining members of the I.R.A. Active Service Unit, was lifting out of its mountain hollow, eighteen miles to the south-east. At a height of a hundred feet its tricycle undercarriage was retracted and the aircraft swung around to face north-west, dipped its nose and set off on a heading of 322 degrees across Cwm Berwyn, to hover at two thousand feet over Tregaron bog. Now manned by only four—one of whom was *The Soldier*'s second-in-command, Gerry McMahon—it would remain for a while in that area as the terrorists' airborne command post.

The helicopter had already received and acknowledged its first message. James Duggan, commander of the boat team, No. 3 group, had performed his crucial overnight task and his group was taking up its final positions.

Michael Roche's big moment was well and truly at hand.

* * *

11.45 a.m. The royal convoy was four miles south of Aberystwyth and slowing down for a group of about eighty people at the roadside. In Aberaeron, twelve miles further on, in a disused Coastguard look-out building high on its northern edge, two armed police officers scanned the town centre, nearly a quarter of a mile away. One was using the telescopic sight of his 7.62 mm sniper rifle and the other—a Smith and Wesson magnum revolver at his hip—was using powerful binoculars. Their task was to watch the roofs and upper windows all down the main street immediately in front of them, and around the two-acre grassed open space—the park—in the town centre, where the walkabout was scheduled to take place. They were manning one of the three main observation posts which formed a triangle, one side of which was the main street ahead of them, down which the Prince would begin his walk in fourteen minutes time.

The second point of the triangle was the tower of All Saints Church, straight ahead at the far end of the main street, from where another police marksman, also accompanied by a pistol-carrying cover-man with binoculars, used the 'scope of his rifle to survey the town.

The third O.P. in the triangle was on the roof of the police station. There, a small scaffold-mounted deck on the reverse slope of the roof, level with its apex, provided a comfortable observation and firing point for two more marksmen. With telescopic sights and binoculars they looked across the park to the whole length of the main street, which ran across their front. They had the church tower to their half left, 292 metres away, and the coastguard station to their half-right at 293 metres. When the police helicopter arrived, no part of that town would be hidden from police observation.

At 11.45a.m. the U.H.F. radio carried the voice of the police-woman operator in the police station, making her final checks with the observation points: "Oscar Papa One, report please." One of the men in the coastguard station placed his microphone to his lips: "Oscar Papa One, Roger, all clear."

"Oscar Papa Two . . ." said the girl, calling the church tower.

The rest of that call went unheard in the coastguard station. The door crashed open and the two policemen were cut down by a hail of bullets fired into their backs from the terrorists' two silenced Czech-made Skorpion machine pistols.

In seconds, two other members of the P.I.R.A. party were on

the flat roof above, assembling their hugely powerful tripod-mounted Browning M.85 ·5 inch heavy machine gun. Its disintegrating link ammunition belt was threaded across the breach and the cover snapped shut. The machine gunner set his sights at 293 metres exactly and aimed at the police station to his half left. Then he and his number two lay waiting. Alongside them sat a fifth terrorist, holding a SAM-7 rocket launcher, primed with its fifty-one inch, twenty-pound, heat-seeking anti-aircraft missile.

Meanwhile, the sixth gunman on Coastguard Hill was in the Sherpa van, extending its radio antennae and switching on the power of its radio transmitters.

It was 11.48 a.m. Tom O'Donnell, leader of No. 2 group, had achieved his first objective.

*   *   *

At 11.50 a.m., after walking three hundred yards from the harbour where the *Spalpeen*, was moored, No. 3 group leader, James Duggan, led three of his team into the tower of All Saints Church on the south side of the town. The ground floor was empty. Two of the men bounded up the stairs, their rubber-soled training shoes making not the slightest sound. Emerging onto the roof they found one of the policemen leaning on the parapet, his rifle butt tucked into his shoulder, his right eye to his telescopic sight.

The rifleman's companion turned, his binoculars swinging on their neck-strap. In the milli-second that his right hand twitched towards the revolver at his hip, both of them were dead—cut down by silenced Skorpion machine pistols.

The old verger might have died too, but he didn't. Not quite. A burst of shots caught him across the shoulder and neck and he dropped like a stone, a cry stifled on his parted lips.

Passing their comrades on the narrow staircase, the two killers rushed down to stand guard at the tower door, while James Duggan and the girl emerged onto the roof and unzipped their canvas grips. Their six-pound RPG-7 rocket grenade launcher was quickly assembled, loaded and placed on his right shoulder. With sights set at 146 metres, he put his right eye to the soft rubber of the eyepiece and aimed at the brickwork above the first floor windows of the Castle Hotel, at the corner of Market Street and the town's main street.

It was 11.52 a.m. The royal convoy was seven minutes away, approaching Llanon at sixty miles an hour. One more slow-down before Aberaeron. Seven minutes drive away, in the old Coastguard look-out post and on top of the town's All Saints Church tower, the terrorists were answering the policewoman's radio test-calls with a knowledge and precision of which their instructors at the P.L.O.'s Nahar-El-Barad training camp in Libya would have been proud.

* * *

At 11.59 a.m., precisely on schedule, the police motor cyclist outrider came to a halt at the fork where Princess Avenue and the main street diverge at the northern end of Aberaeron, under the noses of the I.R.A. watchers in the Coastguard station. The Bell helicopter moved to its pre-arranged hover position, five hundred feet over the field at the rear of the police station to the east of the town centre. Its police observer had a bird's-eye view of the whole walkabout area.

With the great swell of holidaymakers adding to the large number of local people, it seemed as though not another soul could be squeezed behind the four hundred yards of crush barriers that stretched towards the church. The walk began.

Except for one vehicle—the Rover protection car—the whole convoy had snaked off left and worked its way to the front of the police station, where it parked, ready to move back into the bottom end of the main street and pick up the party at the end of their walk. The stationary vehicles took up nearly the whole length of the street along the pavement's edge. Right on the expected spot, smack in the middle of the M.85 machine gunner's sights, sat the police car carrying the radio control unit that gave the convoy its self-contained car-to-car communications system.

The Rover protection car had taken a different route. It had gone around the block on the opposite side of the main street and come to rest in Castle Lane, a couple of yards from, and facing, the main street, immediately opposite the rest of the convoy. A second motor cyclist outrider waited there. In the event of an attack on the Prince or any threat to him, his task would be to guide the protection car at high speed to a pre-arranged 'safe house', a large country mansion two miles out of town on the road inland. Any incident which threatened the Prince would send the motor cycle and the car hurtling out of Castle Lane to where his personal protection officers would be covering him bodily, and they would whisk him off to the safe house and remain there until the emergency was over.

*   *   *

The watchers on Coastguard Hill, the church tower, the police station, the other O.P.s and in the hovering helicopter—friend and foe—could see every inch of the royal progress. Slowly, the Prince and his entourage walked along the crush barriers. He shook hands, he waved, he quipped with the crowd and he crossed from one side of the street to the other to give everyone a chance. It was a rapturous welcome—a mass of colour like every holiday-time royal progress. Around him, their eyes everywhere, walked his cohort of armed police officers, their field of vision and movement left discreetly clear for several yards around. Yard by yard, the procession crept down North Street and came to Albion Square, where the park opened out on their left.

It was eleven minutes past noon. The royal group had reached a point about ten yards from the far end of the park railings. *And the town centre erupted in a storm of flame, smoke and thunder.*

Almost simultaneously, the M.85 machine gun on Coastguard Hill and the grenade-launcher on the church tower opened up.

At the same instant, one of the Coastguard Hill team activated their radio transmitter and jammed the entire police network— U.H.F. and V.H.F. The royal convoy's own car-to-car system had less than a second's life in it.

His first belt loaded in groups of three rounds—explosive and incendiary—the M.85 machine gunner sent several short bursts of fire across the park. His first caused the police radio car on which his sights had been set to burst into flames and removed the only remaining radio communications in Aberaeron. He then disabled the Rolls and the lead police car in front of it. They burst into flames, immobilising the entire convoy. He switched to his next target, the marksmen on the police station roof to his left. They and the roof around them were shot to pieces. Dipping his sights down

129

the front wall of the police station, he fired more short bursts at a line of police cars parked separately from the royal convoy. Most of the reserve fleet was left burning; all the vehicles holed like sieves.

Firing explosive rounds only, the machine gunner next turned on the upper parts of the town centre buildings to his right, in a line six metres above the pavement, and blasted away at the brickwork. Then a stream of white smoke snaked across the north east of the town from Coastguard Hill. It marked the track of the SAM-7's Strela anti-aircraft missile, fired at the police observation helicopter by one of the machine gunner's comrades. The pilot saw it coming, opened his throttle, banked away to port and tried to put his machine into a sweeping dive. But the missile's infra-red heat-seeking head found its mark unerringly. The aircraft exploded like a sunburst.

Opening fire at the same moment as the Coastguard Hill team, James Duggan, the RPG-7 operator on the church tower, fired twelve grenades in one minute flat. The first shattered the upper corner walls of the hotel. With a deafening roar and a blinding flash, several tons of masonry disintegrated, filled the air and showered onto the street below, stampeding the crowd and effectively blocking the road south.

Then, aiming carefully for the brickwork of the upper floors along the frontage beyond the hotel, he fired his remaining eleven specially-filled grenades at measured distances—smoke, percussion, smoke, percussion and smoke again—and before he was half way through, the packed town centre was shrouded in black smoke, while the blinding flashes and ear-splitting cracks of the percussion grenades stunned and disorientated everyone.

Throughout this assault on the main-street buildings, more than seven hundred explosive and incendiary bullets added their own thunder and flame to the general havoc and chaos. The terrorists' tactic of concentrating the minds of the mass of the people on their own safety and distracting attention from the source of it all was working perfectly.

*   *   *

The explosions of the rocket grenade on the wall of the Castle Hotel and the first incendiary bullets in the police radio car saw the Prince immediately hurled to the ground by his personal detective, who threw himself across his body to protect him. Four other armed police officers with him, knelt, revolvers drawn, ready to fight off any close-quarter attacker. But although dust and debris cascaded through the blanket of smoke around them, there was nothing to shoot at. They were only there for a matter of seconds anyway.

Even before the second grenade streaked from the top of the church tower, the reserve motor cyclist and the Rover protection car hurtled from the mouth of Castle Lane and screamed to a stop by the huddled group near the park railings. Before the fifth grenade had exploded they were off again.

The Prince was smothered by his detective across the rear seat, with one man ready to smash the rear window and shoot at any pursuer and the other ready to take on anyone trying to get in their way. These two had reholstered their revolvers and now held Heckler and Koch MP.5 sub-machine guns hurriedly unclipped from their emergency racks. Loaded with thirty rounds of 9 mm parabellum and firing at the rate of a hundred rounds a minute, the MP.5s would give them more than even chances against anybody.

But there was still nothing to shoot at.

*   *   *

Within two minutes of opening fire, the M.85 machine gun had put more than a thousand rounds into the buildings around the main street, which was enveloped in a dense cloud of black smoke. As it ceased firing and the gunner cleared his weapon, the terrorists' 'Puma' helicopter, which had arrived right on time behind Coastguard Hill, out of view of the town centre, was called in and the I.R.A. men and their weapons tumbled aboard. Then off it went, inland, behind the reverse slope of Coastguard Hill and the cover afforded by the ridge which forms the north side of the Aeron river valley.

The radio-jamming equipment in the Sherpa was still blacking out all police radio communications. The time bomb left inside the van would ensure its destruction as soon as its purpose had been achieved, while the trembler device attached to it would see that this happened if anyone tried to interfere with it in the meantime.

*   *   *

As the Rover and its outrider sped along Albion Street and turned right in their headlong, two-mile dash to the safe house, explosions and chaos engulfed the town behind them. One explosion went almost unnoticed in the uproar: the two-pound charge of Semtex explosive placed twelve hours earlier by James Duggan's boat team exploded in a manhole in a side street at the southern end of the town. Triggered by a small radio transmitter operated by a dark-haired girl standing by the parapet of Lover's Bridge a hundred yards away, it severed the main telephone cable and cut the last remaining communication link between Aberaeron and the outside world.

The girl nonchalantly dropped her control box into the river and walked towards the lane at the rear of the church, from where her four comrades of the grenade-launcher team were already emerging. Their weapons had been abandoned in the church tower and the men's false moustaches and the girl's dark wig stuffed behind a cupboard on the ground floor of the building.

Their luck was holding. The one thing that might have caused them trouble had not materialised: the uniformed policeman standing on point duty on the street corner opposite the church had abandoned his post and run down into the town to help at the scene of destruction there. All the boat team needed now was to keep their cool.

With all attention focussed on the smoke-shrouded town centre, the five walked calmly through the alleyways, across the main street and down the road towards the harbour slipway, where lay the dinghy which would take them the few yards out to the *Spalpeen*, whose engines were already warmed up. It was one hour after high water. In five minutes they were out in the open sea, turning south-west for their dash to Ireland. Once out of sight of Aberaeron Harbour, James Duggan would rip off the false names, and the Fairline Mirage II motor cruiser would rev up to her full twenty-eight-knot speed. They would put as many miles behind them as they could, before slowing down and relaxing. By then their craft would once again bear the name *Slievenamon* of Dungarvan. They would be three happy couples on a sun-baked Irish Sea holiday.

*   *   *

Within a minute of leaving the main street of Aberaeron, the Rover protection car was doing ninety miles an hour on the road inland and passing the last houses of the town, just under a mile from the scene of the attack. One mile to go to the safe house, and the road was clear behind them. Half a minute later, the motor-cyclist outrider signalled a left turn and, gears racing in the change-down, they were in a narrow lane leading over a small hump-backed river bridge to a church and the large Georgian house beyond.

No sooner had they turned off the main road than, out of their sight, a hundred yards behind them, the terrorists' hired 7-ton Ford truck pulled off a lay-by and stopped broadside across the road. Pausing only to set the ninety-second fuse on the explosive charge clamped to its fuel tank, the driver ran to the hump-backed bridge to rejoin his mate, who was already kneeling by the detonator which would blow the bridge and cut off that approach. He joined him in the hedgerow and they covered the approach from the main road with their Kalashnikov AK-47 assault rifles, waiting for the signal to blow the bridge.

At the big house, outrider and police car sent showers of gravel flying as they skidded through the ornate stone entrance into the courtyard. A man leapt forward to greet them. His distinctive blue beret, jumper and holster-belt identified him as a police firearms officer, but the Prince's detective and the three protection officers, guns in hand, rushed their Prince into the house all the same. In their haste, though, they did not keep as close together as they should, and the Prince and his detective were the first through the door. They were attacked by two men. The Prince was thrown aside and a black hood thrust over his head. As his wrists were being secured behind his back by a self-locking nylon strap he heard the sewing-machine-like rip of a machine pistol.

The three policemen coming onto the porch behind them were simultaneously gunned down by bursts of fire from other terrorists and died instantly.

The police motor cyclist who had led the protection car to the safe house threw his hands in the air in surrender, but the uniformed 'Police firearms officer' shot him dead. His body, together with those of the three protection officers and one of the two armed officers originally on duty in the house were locked in

133

the pantry. The old couple who lived there, their gardener, their house-keeper, and the seriously-wounded survivor of the two armed police officers guarding the place, were left bound and gagged behind the locked cellar door.

The Prince, bound like them but black-hooded and with the muzzle of a pistol against the back of his head, sat on the hall floor awaiting his fate.

Outside the house a Verey pistol fired a bright red flare into the sky. The truck across the main road exploded in a ball of fire, the little hump-backed bridge was blown to smithereens, and the terrorists' helicopter, which had been hovering out of sight behind the ridge, rose over the crest of the hill and came in, to drop in the centre of the spacious lawn at the side of the house.

Within three minutes all were aboard. Michael Roche, the Provisional I.R.A.'s legendary *Soldier*, took one last look around him and the helicopter swept up the valley. Seconds later it turned south across the river and flew low, down the valley of the River Mydyr until, just short of the village of Mydroilyn, it turned on a heading of 255 degrees and headed straight for its rendezvous with the *Ghadames*, at a position six degrees west, fifty-two degrees north, eighty-four miles away in the middle of the Irish Sea.

It was twenty-one minutes after noon—just ten minutes since the first shot had been fired in Aberaeron.

CHAPTER SIXTEEN

Abruptly at 12.13 p.m., with the protection car and its outrider on their way to the 'safe house', the shooting stopped in Aberaeron. But the panic and chaos it had generated in those two minutes held the town centre in the grip of a paralysing helplessness for several minutes more.

The flash and bang of machine gun bullets and grenades suddenly gave way to the screams of the crowds fleeing from the shrapnel, fragmented masonry and shards of broken glass that had filled the air inside that dense, choking smoke. The moans of the injured could be heard from the smoke, which hung like a thunder-cloud in the still summer air. Flame flashed like lightning among the blackness where the royal convoy stood crippled and where upper rooms were burning.

The shattered roof of the police station burned around the bodies of the marksmen on the observation point. A lone policewoman sobbed helplessly in the office below, over her useless radio equipment and switchboard.

For three or four irreplaceable minutes, police command and control was virtually non-existent.

Uppermost in the Chief Constable's mind was his responsibility for the safety of the Heir to the Throne. He had instinctively dropped face down, his hands covering the back of his head as debris showered down on him, but now he got to his feet, grabbed the arm of his Divisional Chief Superintendent, groped his way out of the smoke, and sprinted towards the police station at the far side of the park. The sight of burning police cars met him, but, almost incredibly, one of those bullet-riddled cars could be started. Several other police officers, including some of the additional firearms officers who had been deployed around the town, had arrived and somehow he, his chief superintendent and four of the firearms men squeezed into the car, edged it through the chaos, picking up speed as they began to leave the town behind. The Rover protection car had a six minute start on them.

At 12.19 p.m. they were halted by the burning Ford 7-tonner about a hundred yards short of the turning to the big house. They were not the only ones. In the few minutes between the explosion of the truck and their arrival, a long line of vehicles had stacked up on either side of the fiercely-burning wreck and there was chaos there, too.

A minute later they saw the 'British army Puma' helicopter lift off from a point several hundred yards away among the trees where lay the big house, and watched it disappear eastwards around a bend in the river valley.

They were more confused than ever.

Seven or eight more minutes passed before the policemen were able to struggle through the hedgerows and across the narrow stream by the bomb-shattered hump-backed bridge to reach the apparently deserted house. Knowing that they and their four Smith and Wesson revolvers were likely to face some rather more sophisticated weaponry, they had no choice but to approach carefully and very slowly, and to simply cover the place until help could arrive.

*   *   *

In the confusion at Aberaeron, no one had realised that the storm of incendiary and explosive bullets hitting the main street had come from Coastguard Hill, but eventually two police firearms officers were sent up there. They found their two colleagues lying dead in the otherwise deserted look-out station and turned their attention to the terrorists' Sherpa van. As one of them turned the handle and pulled open the rear doors there was a shattering explosion. He, his companion and the van were blown to pieces.

It was 12.29 p.m. The bodies of the two police firearms officers had been found on top of the church tower. Following the destruction of the radio jammer, the first contact was made between Aberaeron and the outside world. Receiving the radio message, the deputy chief constable at police headquarters immediately took control of what he could see was going to escalate very quickly into an incident of major operational and political proportions. While his staff alerted the other emergency services and British Telecom, and sent additional police vehicles and firearms teams to the scene, he unlocked his filing cabinet, withdrew his Counter-Terrorism Contingency Plan folder from a drawer and called the duty officer at the Home Office in London.

From that moment on, in a well-rehearsed sequence, the complex structure designed to deal with terrorist hostage-taking took shape swiftly and—given the serious weakness of the initial absence of a telephone link with the scene—smoothly.

*   *   *

At 12.46 p.m., thirty-five minutes after the first shots had been fired and only seventeen after radio communication had been restored, twenty fully-equipped men of the S.A.S. Regiment's standby Counter-Revolutionary Warfare team took off from their depot in Hereford in an army Puma helicopter for the sixty-nine mile, twenty-six minute flight to the scene. To back them up, a high-speed, six-vehicle convoy of S.A.S. troops, weapons and equipment, escorted by two police motor cycle outriders, with beacons flashing and sirens blaring, set off from Hereford, heading for Brecon and the A.40 road into West Wales.

At R.A.F. Lyneham, a Lockheed C.130 Hercules transport plane, kept warmed up on standby for the S.A.S., was airborne for its hundred and forty mile, twenty-three minute flight to R.A.F. Aberporth, fourteen miles from the scene of the kidnap, in case the team might need to be moved farther afield.

*   *   *

In London, the Cabinet Office Briefing Room (C.O.B.R.) was already alive with activity as civil servants prepared for the arrival of the Home Secretary, a Foreign Office Minister and representatives of other government departments, the security service, the armed forces and the police, who would comprise his advisory team for what was beginning to look like the most demanding of all possible situations—the appalling prospect that the Heir to the British throne was either dead or in the hands of ruthless terrorists.

Here the political decisions would be made, and from here would go the Home Secretary's authority—radioed directly to the S.A.S. Commander on the ground—for the deployment and use of troops. Here the intelligence services would pool their information and expertise in an attempt to determine the attitudes and intentions of their opponents, whoever they might be. From here the chief constable, whose operational responsibility at the scene was paramount, would receive the constant stream of advice,

137

guidance and help that would be indispensable to the proper execution of that unenviable responsibility.

*   *   *

Amongst the confusion and slowly-clearing fog of battle in Aberaeron, few people were more frustrated than the press corps. Still-cameramen photographed furiously and T.V. crews roamed the town under the eye of an equally frustrated police press officer, shooting miles of video-tape that, unless transport could be found, stood little chance of reaching their Cardiff studios in time for any but the latest bulletins.

The T.V. teams should have been ideally placed for the scoop of their lives. Equipped with E.N.G. (electronic news gathering) equipment, they had only to drive the few miles to their transmitter stations and plug in to their land-line terminals to be able to put their material straight through to their Cardiff newsrooms or even straight on to their viewers' T.V. screens. But with uncanny precision the terrorists had anticipated them. Streams of bullets from the Coastguard Hill machine gun had found their vehicles and put them all out of action.

H.T.V.'s unit could still have got its material to Cardiff, but the Bell Jet Ranger helicopter which had detoured for another assignment after leaving Aberystwyth and was to rejoin them for the final stages of the royal progress in Aberaeron, had no sooner landed on the rugby field between the town and the sea than it was commandeered by a police superintendent, over all the pleas and threats of the H.T.V. presenter whose only lifeline it represented.

The pilot of the helicopter was able to give the police some information of the utmost value, however. Coming down the Aeron Valley at 12.20 p.m.—two minutes before landing on the rugby field—he had been startled to see an army Puma coming at speed towards him. Veering to starboard and climbing to avoid it, he saw it make a right-angled turn to the south and, from his own resumed course now several hundred feet above the sides of the valley, he saw it holding a steady course in that direction. "It would have taken him out over the sea at Aberporth," he told the superintendent. But there was no one to whom the superintendent could usefully pass that information, for at the time the Sherpa van

138

on Coastguard Hill was still jamming all radio communications. Its destruction was still seven minutes away.

Some of the radio and newspaper men contrived to get out of Aberaeron and phone in their stories. The news, therefore, broke on B.B.C. radio's one o'clock bulletins. It was known, said the radio reporter down a crackling telephone line from Llanarth, that the Prince had been removed from the scene of the attack by his protection officers and taken in a fast car to a place of safety. What had happened since, he said, was not at all clear, but the opinion expressed by an un-named 'senior police officer' at the scene was that His Royal Highness was safe and unharmed.

The reporter could know nothing about the burning truck near the 'safe house', because a police road block had been placed outside Aberaeron. He did know that the H.T.V. helicopter pilot had seen an army Puma helicopter flying out of the valley and heading west. No doubt, he ventured, this was part of the contingency plan prepared by the authorities for an eventuality such as the attack in Aberaeron. It was safe to assume that the Heir to the Throne was by now safely out of the area.

At the speed of light, that brief but stunning news flashed its way by satellite to all parts of the globe. Within half an hour the world was getting B.B.C. T.V. pictures as well, as its team managed at last to make its transmitter hook-up.

*   *   *

It was 8.30 a.m. local time in Boston, Massachusetts. As the warm morning sun shone down on the terrace overlooking Martin Burke's swimming pool, he, Dan Twomey and Seamus McDonagh sat at their breakfast table, resuming the conversation that had been interrupted when they went to bed at three. On the table lay a copy of the 1916 Proclamation of the Irish Republic, on which six drops of blood spread and merged into one. McDonagh received his two of the six keys needed to gain access to those priceless records. All he needed to do now, they told him, was to have the mark tattooed under his right arm, and, said Burke, ''. . . for you to make a Will along the same lines as ours, which we shall be amending when my attorney gets here later this morning. You see, when I die, the chest of records goes to Dan and when he dies it

139

goes to you, and so on as our deaths lead to the recruitment of others. We have to make sure it keeps 'in the family' and that no other eyes ever see the inside of it.''

Important details to be sure, but the main deed had been done: *An Triúir* was born again.

As the three men drank their breakfast champagne in celebration of the event, Twomey looked at his watch, went over to the T.V. set and switched it on. ''By the way,'' he said, ''you've joined us just in time to witness our latest scoop for the I.R.A., Seamus.''

The T.V. news reader was recounting the B.B.C. radio story of the storm of fire and smoke in Aberaeron, and, though McDonagh had half his attention focussed on it, he showed by his answer that he was still listening to Twomey. ''*Boru*?''

''*Boru*. We made our phone calls.''

''And?''

''And we showed them how to kidnap the next in line to the British Throne. And to-day they did it!''

McDonagh's eyebrows rose in astonishment as what was being said by Twomey suddenly gelled with what was being said by the T.V. presenter. ''How the hell did you do *that*?''

Twomey laughed. ''I went right to the horse's mouth and he gave me the lot, on a plate.''

He and Burke raised their glasses and thrust them towards McDonagh, laughing as they did so. He raised his and touched them. ''*Erin go bragh!*''

''*Erin go bragh* as well,'' said Burke. ''But we can drink another toast, Seamus. Our own.'' He raised his glass and spoke the words of the ancient Irish poet, Cailte, which *An Triúir* had taken for their own: ''*The truth on our tongues . . . the purity in our hearts . . . the strength in our arms!*''

''I'll drink to that,'' said McDonagh, ''but it should be in something more appropriate.'' And almost before the words were out of his mouth, the butler had placed on the table six bottles of Guinness and three glasses.

It looked like being another hard day!

CHAPTER SEVENTEEN

Five minutes after the news broke on the B.B.C.'s one o'clock radio news bulletin, the security officer at the Royal Aircraft Establishment at Aberporth telephoned police headquarters. The radar operators monitoring movements within the rocket-testing range area had tracked an aircraft travelling out to sea. H.M.S. *Manchester*, a Type 42 destroyer on the range for missile trials, had logged a visual sighting and identified it as a British army Puma helicopter.

This sparked off a flurry of activity in C.O.B.R. The Ministry of Defence, having quickly ascertained that the army had not had a Puma in the Welsh mountains that weekend, called in a Nimrod maritime jet from its Atlantic patrol, some hundred and seventy miles north-west of Cape Finisterre. At its maximum 'operational necessity' speed of five hundred knots, it would be in the southern Irish Sea in fifty minutes, so a second Nimrod was ordered up from Cornwall. As further back-up, two R.A.F. Sea King rescue helicopters were scrambled from Brawdy at the tip of the Pembrokeshire peninsula.

The M.O.D. also cancelled H.M.S. *Manchester*'s missile trials and directed her to rendezvous with the aircraft, as they did the County Class destroyer, H.M.S. *Fife*, from just off Falmouth. Both warships were soon on course at their maximum speeds of thirty knots plus.

*   *   *

At 1.30 p.m., eight men of the S.A.S. Counter-revolutionary Warfare team entered the 'safe' house and confirmed that the Prince and his personal detective had been carried off in a helicopter masquerading as British. Where it was now, one hour and ten minutes after take-off, was anybody's guess. No one had a clue who the attackers were, where they had come from or where they could have gone to. No one had yet claimed responsibility and none of the attackers had spoken one word during the whole operation.

The direction taken by the helicopter, assuming it had maintained its original course, suggested Ireland as a destination and the I.R.A. as the culprits, so the Foreign Office Minister in C.O.B.R. was soon in touch with his opposite number across the water, and it was not long before the British and Irish Prime Ministers were deep in conversation on the telephone.

If, as now seemed likely, this *were* an I.R.A. operation and the Prince *had* been abducted rather than killed, he and his abductors could well end up at a hideout somewhere in Ireland. If so, said the British Prime Minister, the British people would expect—no, *demand*—that the S.A.S. should go to his rescue.

Politically impossible, retorted the Irish *Taoiseach* (Prime Minister).

But they were talking about the Heir to the British throne, insisted the Prime Minister. As Her Majesty's chief minister she would demand that the S.A.S. be allowed into the Republic. After all, there were many precedents for one country to pursue hostage-taking terrorists into another.

Given the Irish people's perception of the S.A.S., retorted the *Taoiseach*, and given the fact that the shooting of the three I.R.A. terrorists in Gibraltar was still fresh in the Irish memory, such a move would enrage the opposition in the *Dail* and all the sensitivities of the Republic's population. He would not agree under any circumstances. The *Garda Siochana*'s anti-terrorist task force, along with the Irish army's version of the S.A.S.—the Army Rangers—would do all that was necessary.

The Prime Minister pointed to the Irish Rangers' relative lack of experience in real-life terrorist actions, and reminded the *Taoiseach* of some of the more notable failures of imitators of the British S.A.S., for example the U.S. Delta Force's Iranian fiasco, and the Egyptian Sa'Aqa ('Thunderbolt') Force's catastrophic assault on the hi-jacked airliner at Malta's Luqa airport.

Reminding the Prime Minister of the brilliant success of the Irish police in securing the safe release of banker's wife, Jenny Guinness, the *Taoiseach* remained adamant.

Diplomatic stalemate. The British and Irish Cabinets were called into emergency sessions. In London, there was trouble enough on the agenda, but the British Cabinet members and their Prime Minister had been seated less than five minutes when another item was added to it, in the shape of the second instalment of the Provisional I.R.A.'s West Wales terror package.

*   *   *

Approaching Llandovery from the east, about three miles on the Brecon side, the A.40 road narrows and twists through a series of tight bends in thickly-wooded country which rises precipitously on the left and drops away as steeply on the right to the River Gwydderig. On the tighest of the bends, in a lay-by cut into the rocks, stands a small obelisk known as the 'Mail Coach Pillar', whose memorial plaque bears a warning to heavy-drinking nineteenth century stage-coach drivers; a reminder of the fate of one of their brethren, the driver of the Gloucester-Carmarthen coach, who, on the 19th of December, 1835, took his guard and six other passengers with him over the precipice.

Just over a hundred and fifty years later, that bend took fourteen more lives when 300lbs of Czech Semtex explosive in the back of a van parked on the lay-by was detonated by two men at the end of a wire high up in the woods. A colossal explosion hit the Aberaeron-bound S.A.S. convoy with a hurricane of fire, sweeping the police outriders to their deaths and blasting the shattered and flaming remains of the three S.A.S. Range-Rovers and their occupants through the tops of the trees and into the river, a hundred and twenty feet below. The police car bringing up the rear ran into the ball of fire and followed them down.

Thus did Big Michael Roche keep his promise to deliver a bonus with his kidnap plan. ''What if I told you,'' he had said to his chief, ''that the chances are we'd get some of the bastards who did for McCann, Farrell and Savage in Gibraltar for good measure?'' They would never know, of course, because the British army would never make such things public—not even the fact that it was an S.A.S. convoy—but the Provisional I.R.A. could at least be sure that if they hadn't got the six S.A.S. men they were after, they had killed a dozen of their comrades.

*   *   *

By 3.30 that afternoon, Aberaeron was isolated by police road-blocks and surrounded by huge holiday traffic jams. The centre of

143

the town had been evacuated and sealed off. It was a gigantic 'scene of crime', the exclusive preserve of the forensic scientist, the ballistic, explosive and fingerprint expert, and the Home Office pathologist.

The main telephone cable had been repaired, communications restored, and the police had taken over the town's comprehensive school in South Road, the only place capable of housing an operations base of the size required for an incident of this magnitude. Police, security and military personnel and their weapons and equipment had begun to pour into the school, while miracles were being performed in accommodating fleets of vehicles in the school yard.

British Telecom engineers were installing telephones, telex machines, computer links and facsimile transmission equipment, some of which was already in direct communication with C.O.B.R. in London.

From the town's cottage hospital a fleet of ambulances shuttled the injured to hospitals farther afield. In the town itself the fires had been put out by men and appliances which had begun to arrive within half an hour of the restoration of radio communications. The casualty bureau established at the police station and linked by direct telephone line to the school dealt with relatives' enquiries and hospital and mortuary liaison.

It was now possible to count the cost in human life and suffering. Given the storm of gunfire poured into the town, it had been surprisingly light. The terrorists' tactic of causing terror and confusion by keeping their fire high and creating the maximum amount of smoke, noise and flying debris had kept people's heads down, while at the same time avoiding the risk of hitting their kidnap target.

Two civilians had died. A hundred and seventeen had been injured, only thirteen of them seriously, and those mainly from the area where the stationary convoy had come under fire and the first grenade had blown a hole in the front of the Castle Hotel.

Police deaths numbered fifteen—thirteen of them cold-blooded murders at the three observation posts and at the safe house. Two others had been found dead in the debris-strewn main street.

*   *   *

Things could not have looked blacker in the Cabinet Office Briefing Room in London that Saturday afternoon, but at 3.47 p.m., a glimmer of light appeared, when an officer with the Security Service team received a call from Naval Intelligence: "We received some photos from Milford Haven this morning," said the caller, "and I think we might have something of interest to you. They're photos of a Libyan cargo ship, the *Ghadames*. She put in for repairs at Milford and our photographic interpreter thought there was something odd about her. He's been trying to fathom out what it is and he thinks he might have an answer. You see, the *Ghadames* was formerly the *Thessalonika*, registered at Piraeus in Greece. She was sold to the Libyans a couple of months ago. But her original name was *Francesco Cardinale* and her original port of registration Genoa. She was built in 1972 at the Stettin Shipyard in Poland and was of a type known in the trade as an S-boat. At first, our man thought he was looking at a Super-S, the follow-on to the S-boat, which the Poles began building in 1980. It was only when he came across the name changes that he realised he was really looking at an old S-boat. When he put the two silhouettes together, he realised the *Ghadames'* superstructure had had an extension built on its after end."

"What kind of an extension?"

"We're not altogether sure, but we have a theory. When our man referred back to a report and some photographs from a contact of ours in Malta he realised that the after deck has been fitted with recesses to receive girders, possibly to support a false deck. The Milford photographs show them. It's possible that there's been a helicopter behind a false bulkhead and that the poop deck has been rigged to provide a pad. It's a reasonable hypothesis, given your incident in Cardigan Bay. Especially since we've checked with Liverpool where the *Ghadames* was supposed to load and she's never been anywhere near. Nor was she expected. It looks as if the papers her captain produced to the Customs at Milford were false. St. Anne's Coastguard confirm that she headed north-west after leaving Milford. And what with your Puma heading out into the Irish Sea . . ."

It was enough. Within half an hour one of the Nimrods had located the *Ghadames* and was shadowing her. She was moving south, presumably towards the Bay of Biscay and Libya, at seventeen knots. Her position was 51 degrees 12 minutes north, 6 degrees west, fifty-six miles west of Lundy Island. H.M.S. *Fife* was already on a northerly course and H.M.S. *Manchester* was west of Milford Haven steaming south. Interception by *Fife* should occur at 6.20 p.m. and by *Manchester* twenty minutes later.

Half an hour after the conversation between C.O.B.R. and Naval Intelligence, two Royal Marines Sea King HC Mk.4 Commando helicopters packed with men, weapons, assault boats and other equipment, were airborne at Plymouth and heading for a rendezvous with the destroyers.

The prospect of a battle with a foreign merchant ship on the high seas based on the speculation of a photographic intelligence analyst was just one more diplomatic problem to occupy the minds of the British Cabinet.

*   *   *

H.M.S. *Fife*, her S.B.S. team safely aboard, duly rendezvoused with the *Ghadames*, forty-seven miles north-north-west of Land's End. The navy's challenge to stop met with a flat refusal. "We are in international waters and you have no right to stop us," said her Libyan captain. It seemed that no amount of persuasion would make him heave to.

The message from the Navy to C.O.B.R. raised three simple questions: "Do we force her to stop and board her against opposition? Do we follow her until further orders? Or do we allow her to proceed unmolested?"

It was 6.27 p.m. The Cabinet agonised. Five thousand British nationals working in Libya would be put at the mercy of rioting mobs and an unpredictable president if this turned into a shooting match. There had been agonising before, over the Iranian embassy and over the Lufthansa airliner at Mogadishu, but this time things were radically different. Whereas a normal hostage-taking situation occurs at a fixed location, this one was moving away—*at fifteen miles every hour, three hundred and fifty miles with every day that passed*, further and further away, towards an environment where rescue by storm would be impossible. And the hostage here was the Heir to the British Throne.

While they agonised, a Royal Marines Major of the crack S.B.S.

146

studied *Ghadames* through powerful binoculars. He was already in possession of photographs and detailed plans of a cargo ship of the *Ghadames'* class, and with the assistance of the naval construction specialist on his team he would have studied every detail of the vessel before the signal—whatever it might be—came from London. By the time they had finished, his team would have worked out their every move, including weapons, assault tactics and ship clearance procedures; the assault craft and their manoeuvres would have been decided upon and the use of helicopters for abseil assault or diversion would have been worked out in every detail.

The answer came at 7.53 p.m. They were to stop the *Ghadames* immediately and to board her. If they were likely to be resisted they were to assault the ship under cover of darkness, and in the meantime H.M. Ships *Fife* and *Manchester* would use harassing manoeuvres and a bit of buzzing by their Lynx helicopters to keeps the *Ghadames'* crew guessing. Four Navy Phantom jets would fly from Culdrose in Cornwall in order to keep a substantial amount of airspace around them free of interference, while the Nimrods would help keep shipping out of the area.

The captain of H.M.S. *Fife* would take tactical command of the task force and would be kept informed of further developments.

At 7.55 p.m., by radio and by flashing an international code signal, *Fife*'s captain gave the *Ghadames'* master an order to stop. Again he refused. The twin 4.5 inch guns in *Fife*'s forward turret put two shots across her bows. The cargo ship hove to, but her captain refused to be boarded, saying that he and his crew would fight to the death if any attempt were made to do so. Men armed with sub-machine guns were seen at the ship's rail.

The sun hung red in a cloudless evening sky, and slid into a purple-streaked haze on the western horizon, spreading a fiery carpet across the flat surface of the sea. Two Dell Quay 5.2-metre assault craft carrying armed marines and propelled by 140 h.p. Johnson outboards streaked around the *Ghadames*. A Navy Lynx helicopter kept a watchful eye overhead. On board H.M. Ships *Fife* and *Manchester* there was feverish activity, as boats, helicopters, weapons and equipment were readied, and men donned their battle gear, blacked their faces and received their briefings.

Practised many times over, the tactics evolved by the S.B.S. for assaulting terrorist-manned ships at sea had never yet had to be employed for real. All they needed now to make their bit of maritime history was the personal order of the Prime Minister. It reached the Task Force Commander at 11.21 p.m.

*   *   *

"Noise is what I need," said the S.B.S. Major to the captain of H.M.S. *Fife*. "Noise and lots of light. Off-stage."

And noise and lots of light were what he was given.

The captain and crew of the stationary *Ghadames* had watched with growing interest, not to say apprehension, the lowering of boats and the men scrambling up and down the nets hanging over the sides of the British destroyers some half a mile from their port side. Boarding parties were obviously being assembled for an assault on their ship, and a constant stream of short-wave morse signals from the *Ghadames* kept Tripoli informed of every move.

By now there were at least half a dozen Sea King and four Lynx helicopters dashing about between the warships and hovering over the assault boats that continued to circle the *Ghadames*. Some on board the Libyan ship said there were more, many more, but it was difficult to keep count, so hectic was the activity. Every now and again a rocket would curve up into the night sky from one of the destroyers, leaving a flare hanging there, radiating a bright glare of dazzling whiteness over the whole scene.

By one o'clock in the morning, just when it all seemed to be reaching a climax and Captain al-Maqhur and his crew were bracing themselves to face an assault by the much-feared Royal Marines, everything fell quiet. Darkness suddenly descended. The floodlights which had illuminated the warships like Christmas trees were turned off, as a white flare spluttered and died in the sky. Even the boats which had circled the *Ghadames* continuously for the past six hours suddenly ceased their high-pitched roar.

It had to be a trick, guessed Captain al-Maqhur. He was right. After some four or five eerie minutes, in a silence broken only by the throbbing of his own ship's engines, everything was suddenly switched back on again.

The sky over the *Ghadames*' port side suddenly burst into

something brighter than daylight as a whole host of flares shot up into the sky like a gigantic firework display of blinding flashes and deafening detonations. From the once again brilliantly flood-lit British warships at least eighteen assault boats full of men roared at the Libyans as if they were taking part in a mass-start powerboat race. Even the Libyans' fear was momentarily banished by its sheer brilliance and scale.

But they never did see the end of that power boat race.

There was a loud explosion on the steel roof immediately above their heads, jarring through the brains of the crowd on the *Ghadames'* bridge as if they were locked in a steel drum and someone was striking it with a sledge-hammer. With the explosion ringing in their ears, blinded by the eye-searing brightness of the scene before them, they found themselves being roughly thrown to the floor and pinioned. It was happening all over the ship. Fearsome looking men in black, with Heckler and Koch sub-machine guns at the ready, overpowered every man at the deck rail, seized the bridge and dashed through the ship's accommodation and engine room, dragging men from their bunks or frightening them into yelling surrender.

The Special Boat Squadron Major had got his off-stage noise and light sure enough, and his assault team had come in from the blind side. Having gone out in a wide circle, two Sea King commando helicopters had sped in from starboard and put forty men onto the *Ghadames'* 'monkey island' (the roof of the bridge) and her main deck. Abseiling down from between fifty and a hundred feet, the marines had dropped like avenging angels, cutting with explosive cord the radio aerial at its outlet on the bridge roof.

In an assault of breathtaking *élan*, the S.B.S. had won control of the *Ghadames* in ninety seconds. Without firing a shot.

With a framed linear charge of R.D.X. explosive, they blew a hole in the quarter-inch steel plate of the stern-facing double doors of the suspected helicopter hangar. *All they found was a large empty space.*

Reinforced by sailors from the two warships, they searched the *Ghadames* from stem to stern, finding nothing but the steel box-sockets by the rails of the poop deck to back up the theory that the ship had carried either terrorists or helicopter.

Captain al-Maqhur was outraged. At first the Royal Marines Major could get nothing out of him but abuse. Then he demanded immediate repairs to his radio aerial and immediate release for his ship, his crew and himself. He was in international waters; this was an act of piracy. Yes, he would produce his papers. Here were his instructions from the Libyan General Maritime Transport Organisation to go to Liverpool to collect a cargo. Here was a copy of the radio message telling him that there was, after all, no cargo for him at Liverpool. Here were his orders to proceed to Dunkirk and take on a cargo that really was waiting for him there. He was sure that if the Major would take the trouble to check with Dunkirk, all would be confirmed. Could he please be on his way?

CHAPTER EIGHTEEN

In C.O.B.R., the Home Secretary and the Prime Minister were stunned when the news came through from Naval Command Centre in Northwood. Not only did it put them right back into square one—not knowing if the Prince were alive or dead, or where he could possibly have been taken to—but it presented them with a diplomatic incident of staggering proportions.

To say that there was panic in high places would be to overstate the case. It took, however, an hour and a half for those in charge to decide what further orders to give to the naval commander on the spot. All was not going smoothly in C.O.B.R.

The captain of H.M.S. *Fife* had wanted to know if he should release the *Ghadames*. It was the Prime Minister who gave the answer, which was relayed to him at 04.57 hours that Sunday morning. The captain and crew of the *Ghadames* were to be placed under guard and the navy was to take the vessel into Falmouth. Arrangements would be made for the police, along with officers from the Secret Intelligence Service and officials from the Foreign Office, to interrogate Captain-al-Maqhur and his crew. The ship would be boarded by forensic scientists and fingerprint experts, who would subject it to a thorough examination for clues as to its involvement or otherwise with the helicopter used in the kidnapping. In the meantime the Foreign Office would step further into the diplomatic minefield by informing the Libyan government of what had taken place.

There remained, of course, the question, 'What had happened to the Heir to the Throne if he hadn't been landed aboard the Ghadames?' There seemed to be only two possible answers. Either the terrorists' helicopter had ditched in the Irish Sea before being able to land on the *Ghadames* or it had flown to Ireland. To cover the first possibility a full air-sea rescue operation would be mounted, and to cover the second the British Prime Minister would immediately telephone her opposite number in Ireland.

*   *   *

It is a curious fact, given the extreme sensitivity of the Irish to any suspicion of incursions into their territory by the British military, that the sight of R.A.F. Sea King helicopters sitting on the tarmac at Cork airport is one that arouses little interest and no hostility. There is a good reason for this. In the matter of saving life at sea, all nations are one. The Irish and British lifeboat services are provided and maintained by the Royal National Lifeboat Institution, so the familiar yellow-coloured R.A.F. Sea King air-sea rescue helicopters fly missions and exercises with lifeboats on both sides of the Irish Sea. There is too, the advantage of being able to refuel at Cork or Shannon airports and extend the helicopters' 380 mile range from Brawdy in West Wales far out into the Atlantic. Indeed, still fresh in everyone's minds was the fact that a large number of R.A.F. Sea Kings had operated in and out of Cork in the huge search and recovery operation mounted after the destruction by Sikh terrorists of Air India flight 182 and its three hundred and twenty nine passengers.

A not unfamiliar sight in Cork, then. So when an R.A.F. Sea King landed at eight o'clock on the Sunday morning and taxied to the refuelling bay no one took a bit of notice. Thus, at 8.15 that Sunday morning, did the Irish *Taoiseach*, his Foreign Minister and four aides, accompanied by armed Irish Special Branch protection officers, leave Cork unobserved. They landed at Brawdy at 9.25 a.m. and were quickly taken by a convoy of cars to the conference room in the administration block, where they were greeted by the Prime Minister, her Foreign Secretary and their aides, who had flown from R.A.F. Northolt.

The formalities over, it was down to business—on the one hand, trying to persuade the Irish that were the Prince to turn up on their territory his rescue should be the responsibility of the British S.A.S., and, on the other, trying to make the British understand that for an Irish government to concede that would be electoral suicide. Precedents in international terrorism were cited, agreed, but pronounced irrelevant to the political climate of the Irish Republic.

The feelings of the British people—already abundantly clear from the plethora of T.V. and radio comment and from huge demonstrations in London and provincial cities—were sympathetically understood. But the feelings of the Irish people were plain

152

enough too. It was a truism, said the *Taoiseach*, that there was too much history in Ireland, but it was also true that some of it was too recent and too explosive for him to think of conceding the Prime Minister's point. Why should the British have to rescue their own Prince if—and it was by no means a foregone conclusion—he *was* in Ireland? The Irish had their own *élite* counter-terrorism force.

On almost every other point raised in that wide-ranging and intensive two and a half hour discussion, both sides were one. On that one the deadlock fused solid.

*   *   *

At 4.30, twenty-eight hours after the disappearance of the Heir to the Throne, there was still not the slightest indication of where he had been taken or who had kidnapped him. The abortive raid on the *Ghadames* had deepened the mystery. So the telex message which rattled off the machine in the communications room at the Home Office in Queen Anne's Gate came like a bolt out of the blue:

'The kidnapping of the Heir to the British Throne and the destruction of the S.A.S. convoy going to his aid were carried out by by the Provisional I.R.A., but this message is from another source. I repeat: this message is not from the Provisional I.R.A. and it will be in your best interests to deal with me and not them. The purpose of this telex is to establish my *bona fides*. You can do this by checking the following:

1. The I.R.A. unit which carried out the kidnapping was helicoptered to Map Ref. SN 771528, east of Tregaron in Mid Wales, from the Libyan cargo ship *Ghadames*, now steaming from the Irish Sea towards Dunkirk, France.

2. If your navy boards the *Ghadames* they will find nothing to connect it with the kidnapping. It was a decoy. The helicopter was tipped over the side as soon as it had put its occupants back on board, and the A.S.U., with their hostage, were taken off by boat.

3. The captain of the *Ghadames* is Qasim al-Maqhur of the Libyan Navy, and he will tell your men that he took his ship to Liverpool for orders, but that there was no cargo there and she

153

is now heading for Dunkirk to load a general cargo for Tripoli. He will be able to produce papers to that effect.

4. Check No. 1 hold. Behind the centremost of the forward stanchions, in the recess behind the second crossbar up from the deck, will be found a plastic envelope secured to the inside of the girder by masking tape. It contains a note and a piece torn from the Libyan newspaper Al Fajr Al-Jadid, dated 31st July. The note says '*These pieces of paper will become of crucial importance to you at 4.30 pm on Sunday 13th August. Act quickly. Your Prince will die if you stray one inch from the instructions you will receive.*'

5. At exactly 6 pm to-day, *The Times* newspaper in London will receive a call from the Provisional I.R.A. giving an established P.I.R.A. code. The message will be very brief—that the I.R.A.'s demands must be met in full; no negotiation, no further contact.

6. You can avoid the consequences of failing to obey the P.I.R.A.'s instructions only by co-operating with the sender of this message, who is acting independently.

7. At 7 pm to-day, one hour after the P.I.R.A. makes its demands, you will receive a telephone call from me on 01-213-3000 telling you on what terms I will give your Prince back to you. Message ends.'

The telex message was in the Cabinet Office Briefing Room within ten minutes, and within forty the Prime Minister and Home Secretary were looking at a message from the Royal Navy in Falmouth confirming that the note and the Libyan newspaper fragment had been found where the sender of the telex had said they would be.

Far away, in Nassau, Bahamas, carrying out to the letter the instructions for the operation of her lover's communications equipment, yet completely unaware of what she was really doing, Michael Roche's ravishing Latin-American secretary had successfully launched Phase Two of his elaborate escape plan.

*   *   *

Precisely at six o'clock that Sunday evening, the telephone rang on *The Times* newsdesk. The news editor and a detective superintendent of the Metropolitan Police Special Branch picked up their receivers and pressed their tape-recorder buttons simultaneously. The voice, which gave a code word used in past contacts between Provisional I.R.A. sources and the newspaper, had the distinctive ring of Dublin City: "The Provisional I.R.A. has the Heir to the British Throne as its prisoner. Any attempt to trace this call will cost him his life. The terms for his release are simple and non-negotiable. This message will not be repeated. There will be no further contact. Are you ready?"

"I am," said the news editor.

The detective noted that it was obviously a 'live' call and not a tape.

"Right," said the caller. "The terms for his release are these: By this time next Saturday—six days from now—the British Prime Minister will have made in the British parliament, and the British ambassador to the United Nations will have made to the Security Council, the following declaration of intent: That all British troops and administrators will be withdrawn from the Six Counties within two years, under United Nations supervision and with a U.N. peace-keeping force taking over the role of the R.U.C. and the Ulster Defence Regiment, which will be as quickly disbanded. Thereafter, the U.N. will guide the thirty-two counties of Ireland towards a unified government with a guarantee that organisations now proscribed would play their full part in the process of reconstructing government and law and order in the new Republic. Failure to give this undertaking in the manner prescribed will result in the hostage being killed at 1800 hours B.S.T. on Saturday. But that will not be the end of the matter. Having clearly demonstrated its penetration of the British establishment by its ability to kidnap a well-protected member of the royal family and wipe out an S.A.S. unit being sent to his aid, the Provisional I.R.A. will go one step further. The execution of the British monarch on the steps of Westminster Abbey, or wherever else the funeral took place, would plunge Britain into a constitutional crisis that could be resolved only by the creation of a regency. That is the end of the message. Nothing more will be heard from us unless our demands are met."

The line went dead.

At 6.30 that night, all British and Irish radio and T.V. programmes were interrupted by a news flash which swept rapidly around the world. The Provisional I.R.A. had claimed responsibility for the attack at Aberaeron and the ambush of the army convoy at Llandovery, and had said they were holding the Prince. Certain demands had been made and were being urgently studied by Her Majesty's government. The full text of the P.I.R.A.'s communication would be given in full in the next scheduled news bulletins.

*   *   *

In Northern Ireland, the outrage brought out into the open the long-threatened Protestant backlash, in the form of widespread sectarian killings, a bombing blitz in Londonderry's Catholic Bogside and pitched battles between terrorist gangs in West Belfast, with the security forces holding the ring and sharing the casualties.

On the mainland, public reaction to the news was staggering, given the apathy that normally characterised its reaction to the Irish troubles. In some places it seemed that just about everyone had taken to the streets. Huge crowds filled the Mall and packed the space on and around the Victoria Memorial in a silent vigil outside Buckingham Palace. Thousands demonstrated in Whitehall behind tightly-guarded crush barriers at the end of Downing Street. A riot erupted in Trafalgar Square as 'Troops Out' demonstrators, sensing a climactic moment in their campaign to get the British army out of Northern Ireland, were furiously attacked by those who saw their movement as sympathetic to the I.R.A. Chanting crowds in city centres all over the country demanded 'Death to the I.R.A.', 'Send in the S.A.S.', 'War with Ireland'.

Police and other observers detected a widespread and growing unanimity that Ulster was not worth the candle. Public sentiment was in turmoil, the traditional abhorence for making deals with terrorists assailed by an overwhelming desire to see the Prince returned alive and well . . . and to sink the black North of Ireland into the Atlantic Ocean. The British people were torn between finding a compromise and turning on their attackers and tearing them to pieces.

It was no surprise to anyone in the Cabinet Office Briefing Room when the first reports came in from London's Kilburn district, Liverpool's Bootle, Luton, Reading, Glasgow, Birmingham and Manchester of the burning of Irishmen's homes.

CHAPTER NINETEEN

As seven o'clock approached, the Prime Minister, Home Secretary and a small group of advisers were anxiously waiting for the telephone to ring. The line on 01-213-3000 had been isolated and connected to a red telephone fitted with a tape recorder and loud speaker in the Home Secretary's emergency office. British Telecom technicians had been working furiously to set up the means of tracing the call, but all involved knew just how risky this was. One unwise move could mean death for their Prince. Furthermore, for all the advanced technology available to them, the advent of world-wide auto-dialling, and the existence of computer-linked telex and telephone systems capable of switching calls from one unit to another with bewildering rapidity, made such a task virtually impossible.

The seconds ticked by. Five minutes to seven. In Nassau, Bahamas, Maria Carmina Sanchez was setting her communications system to 'Auto-call' and the timer for 14.00 hours Bahamas time. Two minutes to seven. Tension mounted in C.O.B.R. Was the mysterious informer betraying the Provisional I.R.A. or was he laying a false trail to trap the British?

Ten seconds . . . nine . . . eight . . . seven . . . six . . . five . . . four . . . three. Any second now. Two . . . one . . . seven o'clock! And one second . . . two . . . three . . . four . . . five . . . ten . . . twenty . . . twenty-one . . . twenty-two. The light went on; the telephone rang. A Metropolitan Police Deputy Assistant Commissioner picked up the receiver: "Hello."

It was a recorded voice: "Now listen carefully. I am the one who sent you the telex message earlier to-day. If you try to trace me or in any way trick me, your Prince will be dead. I shall tell you once and once only. You will arrange for ten million pounds Sterling to be deposited in the account of Future Sovereign Holdings (Panama) Incorporated, in the Bank Henneker A.G., in the Bahnhofplatz in Zurich, Switzerland. The deposit is to be made at exactly 14.30 hours B.S.T. tomorrow, Monday 14th August. 14.30 B.S.T. precisely. If any enquiry is made at the bank, or any attempt made to monitor the handling of the deposit there, I shall know about it immediately and the deal will be off. Ten million pounds Sterling. The account of Future Sovereign Holdings (Panama) Incorporated, The Bank Henneker A.G., Zurich, Switzerland. Monday 14th August. 14.30 B.S.T. precisely. Then, if you've done your job properly, you'll get another call from me telling you where to find your Prince. Keep your telex and this telephone line free.''

The line went dead.

The Prime Minister and the Home Secretary had heard it all over the speaker. What were they to do? Surrendering to the Provisional I.R.A. demand that Britain withdraw from Northern Ireland was out of the question. The Queen herself had already said so, whatever the consequences to her son. But this? *Was* it a trick? Or was it worth taking a chance? The caller had shown good faith through his earlier message, which had led to the finding of the documents in the hold of the *Ghadames*. Discussion was animated, opinion divided, and it was beginning to seem as if even this alternative involved such a betrayal of principle that it should be disregarded. *Until one of the advisory team suddenly woke up to the connection.*

The head of M.I.6, motioned to a secretary and whispered in his ear. The secretary left the room. Half an hour later he was back, with Ben Craig, head of M.I.6's Irish agent-running section. ''Oh, Ben,'' said his boss, ''I think we've come up with something more on that affair of Steve Gannon's with . . . what's his name?''

''Roche?''

''Yes, Roche. Listen to this.''

The tape-recorder was played back. ''Good God!'' said Craig. ''Ten million pounds! And the dates are right. Roche instructed him to be ready to board a boat at Nassau and then an aircraft at Norman's Cay, to fly a package to Nicaragua. We knew the Provos were planning a major operation on the mainland and that *The Soldier* was to lead it. Our analysts have been working overtime on it and they're convinced that Michael Roche *is The Soldier*. Whatever it is Gannon has to take to Nicaragua is worth Roche paying him £150,000, and our surveillance on Roche tracked him to the Geneva bank and to several banks in the Bahamas. We were thinking it might be connected with drugs, because although the C.I.A. and the State Department have always denied it, there's a

159

lot of evidence that the Contras in Costa Rica have been running drugs to pay for arms shipments. We thought the I.R.A. might have latched onto this as an additional source to Libya. Then we found that the Irish police have a murder warrant out for Roche and, putting two and two together, thought it was his way of escaping to where there's no extradition. But this looks more like it. The date is exactly right, and the time difference would allow the money to be transferred from Switzerland to the Bahamas and drawn out in cash by an accomplice there in time for the trip to Lake Nicaragua.''

Craig paused to gather his thoughts. "That's it!" he exclaimed. "He's decided to double-cross the I.R.A. and do a ransom deal himself. Why in God's name didn't we make the connection before? *The code name Carlos . . . Spanish for Charles!*''

The Prime Minister slapped her hand on the table. "This *must* be it. We *can* control it. Get Mr. Gannon here at once.''

Craig hesitated. His chief looked at him quizzically. The Prime Minister and the Home Secretary seemed puzzled at his hesitancy. He explained: "Steve Gannon has disappeared. He dashed off to Dublin on Friday to meet an agent who wanted to see him urgently, and we've neither seen nor heard from him since. He should have flown from Heathrow to Nassau this afternoon, but he failed to make the flight. I was about to report to you . . .''

"Disappeared?'' exclaimed the Intelligence chief. "What the devil do you mean, disappeared? How? Where was his back-up?''

Craig shook his head. "There *was* no back-up, sir. He was in Holland and his flight was imminent. He said he couldn't wait while we set it up. He was under pressure with the schedule for the Bahamas trip, so he decided to chance it. I did press the point, but . . . well . . . he's a very experienced operator, and . . .'' His words trailed off.

The politicians were appalled. Was he dead? Had *he* been kidnapped? Had the informant been a double-agent and Gannon walked into a trap? Was the M.I.6 man himself an accomplice in a terrorist act which had obviously been based on information leaked from the very heart of the Establishment? What about Gannon's Bahamas trip and his parachute drop into Lake Nicaragua? What was to be done about that? The two S.B.S. officers who were to drop with him, and the rest of the back-up team, were in the Bahamas, in position, waiting for Gannon, the key to the whole operation.

There was a pause for deep reflection as the gravity of this new development sank in. It could still be done, said the intelligence and military advisers at length, provided that Gannon's disappearance had not meant that Roche had made other arrangements or that Gannon himself was a traitor. This would not be known until an approach was made to the crew of the boat in the Nassau Yacht Basin. There was little choice in any case. This was the only chance of getting a line on the Prince's whereabouts.

The Prime Minister called an emergency Cabinet meeting and quickly gained their unanimous support for her solution. An order went to the Bank of England to transfer ten million pounds Sterling—around sixteen million U.S. dollars—from the government's contingency fund to the Future Sovereign Holdings account in Zurich at precisely 14.30 B.S.T. the next day. This, the Prime Minister reasoned, would simply be the logical follow-through to the operation mounted by M.I.6 against Michael Roche after his approach to Gannon. It was an avenue which had to be explored anyway, independently of the efforts to find and release the Heir to the Throne. If, in the process, the kidnap hideout should happen to be located and the hostage released, so much the better.

If the M.I.6 analysts were right and Michael Roche was the one who was by-passing the Provisional I.R.A. and bargaining for the disclosure of the kidnap hideout, that disclosure would come in another telephone call or telex message after the ransom had been paid into the Swiss bank, transferred to the Bahamas and dropped by parachute into Lake Nicaragua. Everything hinged on whether the boat was in Nassau and the aircraft on the runway at Norman's Cay at the appointed times. They would just have to hope they were, for that would be confirmation that they were on course for freeing the Prince without capitulating to the I.R.A.

Orders were given for a third S.B.S. officer to be assigned to the parachute drop as a replacement for Gannon and for that part of the operation to be carried through with American assistance as planned. Should the boat and air trip from the Bahamas fail to materialise, they would fall back on the R.A.F. in Belize to provide transport to Lake Nicaragua.

Roche's stupendous gamble was starting to pay off. He had hit the British right where he knew it would really hurt them, and he had gauged the measure of their resolution as surely as if he had used a micrometer.

*　　　*　　　*

After the crucial Cabinet meeting, the Home Secretary held his first press conference since the kidnapping, and the world's news media were there to hear what he had to say. It was little enough: no surrender to terrorism . . . the situation far from clear . . . essential to conduct these matters under a strict cloak of secrecy . . . life at stake . . . and so on.

As always when reporters scan their reams of nothingness after coming out of a press-conference, imagination and speculation filled the newspapers and T.V. screens. And the passions of the British public rose in direct proportion to the sensationalism of the fare dished out to them . . . to the detriment of everyone and everything Irish.

Nothing and no-one Irish was immune from the fury on the streets; not even Kilkenny-born Second World War veteran Paddy Conlan and his family, who had lived in Kilburn for more than forty years and whose eldest son was a sergeant major in his father's old regiment, the Irish Guards. Having survived countless brushes with death as a tank commander with the Guards Armoured Division in its drive from Normandy to the North German ports, Paddy Conlan was incinerated in his own home by a rain of petrol bombs which gutted five houses in the street and put eleven people in hospital.

*　　　*　　　*

Monday morning, 14th August. "Are you telling me," asked an incredulous Home Secretary, "that if any one of the people on that list had felt so inclined he could simply have stuck the royal visit operational order in a copying machine?"

"That seems to be it, sir, more or less," said the Metropolitan Police Deputy Assistant Commissioner who had conducted the preliminary investigation. "But, of course," he added hurriedly, "every man on the distribution list, right up the line from the local people to the Palace, is a trusted police officer. Several of them have been positively vetted . . ."

"So was Blunt!" said the Home Secretary icily.

"Well, they've all got so much service . . . and there were civilians and military on the distribution list as well . . . and . . ."

"And one of those sets of plans gets to the I.R.A. and/or the Libyans."

"We don't know *that*, sir . . ."

The Home Secretary was beginning to lose patience. "How else does the I.R.A. or whoever it was know exactly where the police observation posts are located, where the royal convoy is going to park, every move of the royal party, all about the so-called safe house procedure, and even how to isolate the whole damned area from radio and telephone communication? What about the S.A.S. convoy? They must have had the contingency plan as well as the royal visit order."

"They knew every last detail, sir."

"How the hell could they have got hold of *both* documents? How many people are we talking about? How many suspects are there?"

"I'm afraid it's impossible at the moment to estimate how many people would have had access to the contingency plan. It could run into hundreds, what with the army, navy and air force and all the other agencies that would have a copy. At least twenty-four for the royal visit order. One of them is dead and another missing. The Detective Chief Superintendent, Mr. Walsh, was killed in the street, and . . ." He swallowed hard. "And the Prince's personal detective has disappeared."

"Disappeared? May one ask what you mean by that?"

"Well, sir, no one can say what happened when they arrived at the safe house, so we don't know whether he is alive or dead. We just have to assume that they were both carried off in the helicopter. Unless . . ." he swallowed hard again, ". . . unless he was the one who gave them the information in the first place."

The Welsh chief constable looked up at the ceiling and the Metropolitan Police Commissioner stared coldly ahead, for people in both their forces were involved. The chief constable was on the suspect list himself! So was the officer in charge of all Royalty

Protection, his staff, and the detective who had been closest to the Prince when the terrorists had seized him. It was cold comfort to the chief and the commissioner to know that the suspect list also extended to army and civil service personnel. *They* were not having to face a Home Secretary with serious doubts about his own future.

"Good God Almighty!" he said, snatching at his telephone. "Get me the Chief Inspector of Constabulary ... quickly." The telephone rang back in seconds. The Chief H.M.I. was not immediately available. "Tell them to find him ... *now!*"

He turned his attention back to the three police officers and his Parliamentary Private Secretary. "Gentlemen, I can't imagine anything worse at this moment. The I.R.A. has us by the balls. We've lost the Heir to the Throne and if we don't get him back alive the next in line is only seven years old and we face a Regency. We are having to clutch at straws to work out where he might be, the Irish government won't co-operate and the Prime Minister is breathing down my neck because she has to make a statement to the House this afternoon. The Libyans have burned down our embassy and started rounding up ex-patriates, and they're playing hell at the U.N. The world's press is out for blood and you tell me that we've got an I.R.A. man planted right in the middle of our royalty protection organisation. God only knows where else they might be ..."

His telephone rang again. It was the Chief H.M.I. The Home Secretary snapped out his order: appoint a chief constable, gather a team of high-ranking officers with first-class C.I.D. pedigrees, take apart the list of suspects. Quickly. With his eyes on the chief constable and the commissioner, he told the Chief H.M.I. that every police officer, soldier, civil servant or civilian who had had the handling of the Royal Visit Operational Order *and* the counter-terrorism contingency plan must immediately be suspended from duty until a thorough vetting had been done and every movement since that order was first drafted satisfactorily accounted for.

He put down the phone. "With my luck," he said, "the bloody Chief H.M.I. or the man he picks for the job will be one of them ..."

*   *   *

The Prime Minister rose from her seat at two o'clock. The House, recalled from summer recess for a special sitting, was packed to standing room; the news media were there in force. Radio technicians in the control rooms made final adjustments, and commentators announced that this historic broadcast was being transmitted by satellite around the world.

"Mr. Speaker, Sir," she said to a silent chamber. "I come to this house to-day bearing the gravest news it has ever been my sad duty to bring. Wicked men, their hands already stained with the innocent blood of thousands, have struck right at the heart of the British people in the hope that by this foul deed they will finally crush our resolve to fight terrorism without fear, without compromise and without descending to *their* dark depths of lawlessness and barbarity.

"It is but a short time since they attempted to murder the democratically-elected government of this country. And just after noon last Saturday, they carried out an indiscriminate and bloody attack with heavy machine-gun and rocket fire on a crowded town centre at Aberaeron in West Wales, where His Royal Highness was walking through the crowds gathered to do him honour ..."

She recounted the details of the kidnapping and the ambush of the S.A.S., the damage, the casualties and, to a degree, the interception of the *Ghadames*, which, she told the House, now lay in Falmouth under heavy guard. In the interests of keeping the terrorists in ignorance of as many as possible of the activities of the security forces, she could say no more about that at this stage, save that the British government had good grounds for believing there *was* a Libyan involvement. The strongest representations were, of course, being made in Tripoli through the Italian Embassy, which looked after British interests there.

H.M. Government, she said, deeply regretted the plight of its people in Libya who were suffering in the backlash to the inter-ception of the *Ghadames*. Strenuous diplomatic efforts were being made on their behalf. She appealed for calm, for a more reasoned response from Libya than threats of holy war, for an end to attacks on the homes of Irish residents and businesses in Britain and for order to return to the streets of British and Northern Irish cities. None of this made the awful task facing the British nation any easier. It merely played into the hands of the terrorists.

As to the claim of responsibility by the Provisional I.R.A., its demands and its threat to kill His Royal Highness if they were not met, the British stance in the face of terrorist threats and actions was already well known to the world . . .

Her words were punctuated by emotional 'hear-hears', and followed by grave speeches of support from the honourable members opposite who had been at her throat the last time they had met. There were wholehearted pledges of solidarity from all quarters of the House: No compromise with terrorism . . . steadfastness . . . unflinching resolve . . . untiring efforts . . . hunt down with every means at the government's disposal.

The debate was everything a debate on such a momentous topic should be, its gravity and determination increasing in direct proportion to its futility. The real work, the real decisions, were taking place a few streets away—in the Cabinet Office Briefing Room, the nerve centre of the British response to this blow at its heart.

CHAPTER TWENTY

The news that Steve Gannon had disappeared reached the M.I.6 contingent in the Bahamas the day before he and his fellow parachutists were to board the Carillo brothers' boat. The false passports and other documents supplied by Roche had disappeared with him. Fortunately, he had telephoned Ben Craig in London with the map co-ordinates of the drop-zone and other information contained in the Amsterdam bank envelope and, though the loss of the passports was likely to cause problems when they went to board the boat, Craig ordered that they should go ahead and try, using a substitute for Gannon. Should that fail, there was always their 'last resort' plan involving the British forces in the Central American state of Belize.

The operation began just after two o'clock on the afternoon of Monday 14th August, as the Prime Minister was addressing the House of Commons. The launch *Arabella* was where Roche had said she would be, in the East Bay Yacht Basin in Nassau, under observation by M.I.6 and Bahamian Special Branch officers, when a car drew up alongside it. A woman removed two holdalls from the boot and handed them to a member of the crew. She drove away, followed by Bahamian plain clothes officers, who tracked her to a building in Nassau's Shirley Street.

To the surprise of the M.I.6 men she was identified as Roche's secretary, last seen boarding a helicopter with him at Mallow Race Course, twenty-two miles from Cork, nearly a month before. Officers keeping observation on the banks in Nassau had seen her visit eight of them in Charlotte Street, Marlborough Street and Shirley Street, where she had withdrawn nearly sixteen million dollars in hundred dollar bills—undoubtedly the contents of the packages now aboard the *Arabella*. Since the amount withdrawn was the equivalent of ten million pounds Sterling, Roche's connection with the kidnapping was established beyond all doubt.

For now, though, Maria Carmina Sanchez would merely be watched and a tap put on her telephone. It was just possible that she might have a further part to play in the affair, such as telling the British government where to find the Prince after the delivery of the ransom, so that any interference with her could have catastrophic consequences.

Steve Gannon's replacement—an officer of the Royal Marines Special Boat Squadron—arrived at the *Arabella*, as arranged, at 2.30 p.m. and walked up the gangway. A tanned, husky-looking man of Hispanic appearance, wearing a red and white baseball cap and a T-shirt emblazoned with the words 'Save the Whale: Harpoon People', climbed out of the cockpit.

"Mr. Carillo?."

The man ignored the question. "What can I do for you, *señor*?"

"Bentley. Richard Bentley. We have a trip to Norman's Cay and a plane to meet."

The skipper came to the rail and looked him up and down. "I.D.?"

"I have the flight plan, the co-ordinates . . ."

"Get lost," hissed the skipper. "I.D. or get lost."

"But I've got your fifty thousand dollars. Have you got the parachutes and the rest of the gear?"

The skipper, a Cuban, veteran of the Colombia-Bahamas-Florida drugs trail who could smell a narcotics agent a mile away, put his face close to his, looked him straight in the eyes, pressed a menacing finger into his solar plexus and hissed again: "I wouldn't know a Richard Bentley if I saw one, friend. Not unless he had a passport and a photograph. Try one of the other boats. Maybe they deal with Richard Bentleys. Me, I go fishing."

The Englishman pretended to be floundering, so as to allow the police to close in: "But . . ."

"But nothing," said the Cuban, lifting him off his feet, launching him down the gang-plank and leaping up to the bridge to start the engine. At that moment, though, four large black men in civilian clothes came hurtling along the pontoon, jumped aboard the *Arabella*, hustled him off the bridge and switched off the engine.

"I am Detective Superintendent Winston Earl of the Bahamian Police Drugs Squad," said one of them to the handcuffed skipper. "I have a warrant to seize your boat and search it for drugs, and I am taking you and your crew into custody . . ."

The trip in the *Arabella* was off. The plan of last resort would have to be implemented. Instructions were sent to the F.B.I. at

Miami airport for the seizure of the Carillo brothers' plane before it could take off for Norman's Cay and for the arrest of the pilot and co-pilot, who, along with the boat crew arrested in Nassau, would be kept incommunicado while the British forces in Belize took up the task of delivering the S.B.S. free-fall parachute team and the ransom to the waters of Lake Nicaragua.

*   *   *

Tuesday 15th August. In Nassau the time was 5.45 a.m. Maria Carmina Sanchez, still under police surveillance, was in her rented office in Shirley Street in a state of high panic. The telex message from her brother in Costa Rica which was to follow the delivery of the ransom to Lake Nicaragua and give her the go-ahead for the despatch of the final voice message to the Home Office in London, giving the location of the kidnap hide-out, had not arrived.

She had practised and practised. She had no more idea of the content of that audio disc or where it was going than she had had of the others, but she knew the drill backwards. It was all on Roche's instruction card: 'Telex arrives from your brother in Costa Rica—'*Consignment arrived and intact, repeat intact. Signed Carlos*'.' Nothing about a telex *not* arriving. Nor did she know how to contact her brother in such an event. His home, like hers, was in Caracas, Venezuela, and she could get no answer on the telephone there. She had no idea where Roche might be.

Time was slipping by. 06.00 Bahamas time it said on her instruction card, and it was now ten minutes to. Panic-stricken, she watched the hands of the clock and prayed for the telex machine to come to life. The five minute point for setting the 'Auto-call' was passing. Four minutes, three, two, one. The message should go now if it were to go at all and she were to catch her flight to Miami and be on her way to Costa Rica. She clenched her fists until the long, laquered nails drew blood.

Then she made up her mind. She would send the message anyway. She pressed the 'Phone' button and then the 'Eject' button to open the disc magazine. There was a hammering on the door. Her heart missed a beat and the shock caused her to drop the disc, which fell down the back of the desk and into an air-conditioning vent, entirely beyond her reach. She was hysterical

169

and thought she was going to faint. There was more hammering on the door. She staggered across the room, unlocked and opened it.

The grey-haired black man standing in the doorway had the glint of fright in his bulging eyes, and the hand holding the pipe wrench trembled visibly. But his fear evaporated in a huge sigh of relief at the sight of the girl. "Janitor, Mam," he said. "I wasn't expecting anybody at this time of the morning. Thought you was ..."

Maria's relief was even greater than his. She grabbed his forearms and pulled him into the room, telling him as she did so that she had a bit of clearing up to do and an early flight to catch. "The air-conditioner," she gasped. "I've dropped a computer disc and it's fallen through the grille. Help me, please ..."

The old man bent down and shone his torch into the vent. "Gone, Mam," he said, straightening up. "Clear down the shaft, I guess."

She hustled him out of the room and went back to trying to prise the panel from the air-conditioning unit. Half an hour later she was still trying ... *but Michael Roche's message telling the British where to find their Prince was gone for good.*

Trembling, sobbing, helplessly beating the grille with her fists, the girl finally gave up, grabbed her handbag and suitcase and fled downstairs to the waiting taxi.

The telephone tappers had nothing further on her than several attempts to ring a number in Caracas, Venezuela, so the officer in charge of the M.I.6 team in Nassau sought instructions from C.O.B.R. in London. "Leave her," said Ben Craig. "See where she heads for. We can't risk compromising the ransom delivery and we don't know what else she might have to do with it."

Maria Carmina Sanchez, carrying a passport in the name of Victoria Angelica Valdez, was heading for Miami and Venezuela, en route eventually for Costa Rica, to meet her lover and try to explain to him the blow that had befallen her in Nassau. She could not know that fate had already dealt Michael Roche an even more severe blow, and that his daring plan now hung by only the barest of threads.

*   *   *

In a house on the Muirhevna Mor estate in Dundalk, the Provisional I.R.A.'s border stronghold, known to the initiated as *El Paso*, the Chief of Staff was visited by an intelligence officer with a verbal situation report on the kidnapping operation. "Everybody's in place," he told him. "*The Soldier* and No. 1 group have the hostage secured in the hide-out and the other two teams are being kept in quarantine until it's all over, so security's still water-tight and everything's going fine. Except for *The Soldier*'s accident."

"I heard. How's he doing?"

"Broken right femur and both bones broken in his right forearm. Nasty breaks they are and all. The doc's put his arm and leg in plaster. He's still in pain, so he's drugged up to the eyeballs and out of action altogether. He'll be staying in there until Tom O'Donnell and his team go in on the last day to take the lot of them out, but Gerry McMahon suggests you let him go in now and take over. There's really nobody in command there at the moment. We're keeping the doc who treated him in quarantine as well, by the way, with Jimmy Duggan's team."

"Send McMahon in," said the Chief of Staff. "I wanted him in anyway. The Army Council has other orders for him. There's a warrant out for *The Soldier*. The Gards [*Garda Siochana*] are going to charge him with murdering his wife in that chopper crash; he's too big a risk to us now. He must have guessed the chopper was sabotaged, so even if his cover isn't blown by the arrest itself, he knows too much for us to risk his doing a deal with the police. He's got to go. Gerry McMahon is to go in and take over from him, and when they're brought out by O'Donnell at the end of the operation, he's to give *The Soldier* the chop and get rid of his body. There must be no cock-up this time. *The Soldier*'s got to go and that's it!"

CHAPTER TWENTY ONE

Eleven o'clock the mystery caller had said. Pay the ransom money into the Zurich account of Future Sovereign Holdings and keep the phone line free on 01-213-3000. The next call would be at eleven o'clock on Tuesday morning.

It was five past eleven. The red phone in the Cabinet Office Briefing Room remained stubbornly silent. They could not know of the accident that had befallen Roche's audio disc in the Bahamas, nor that Roche had now lost all control over the situation.

"No wonder," said the Home Secretary glumly. "No money, no delivery."

The Prime Minister had just arrived. "I don't quite follow," she said. "What about the R.A.F. and the Marines in Belize?"

The Home Secretary looked at her over his spectacles, his raised eyes and creased forehead emphasising that permanently worried expression of his. "I'm afraid, Prime Minister, that things didn't go as planned. There was a terrible accident."

She looked at him aghast. "Do you mean the ransom money was not delivered?"

"Oh, yes, it was delivered as planned. The Hercules, escorted by two Harriers, took the S.B.S. to Lake Nicaragua. The Lieutenant was dropped with the money and the other two dropped some distance away, near enough to observe through night glasses. The rendezvous was made. A boat came out from the Costa Rican shore and the Lieutenant had just climbed aboard when they were attacked by a Nicaraguan government patrol boat. Shot to pieces. All killed. The latest we have is that the Sandinista government is claiming to have intercepted a C.I.A. arms drop to the Contras and to have seized seventeen million dollars that were to have paid for it. Quite a propaganda *coup* I'm afraid."

The Prime Minister was stunned. "And the other two Marines?"

"They got ashore and the C.I.A. is organising their return to Belize through its own channels." He took off his glasses, wiped

172

them and replaced them. "*What it amounts to is that the ransom has been lost.*"

The faces of everyone around that long oak conference table conveyed the same despondency. Desultory conversation, endless repetition of the problem and the mocking presence of that silent red telephone merely added to the general air of gloom. For half an hour they sat, casting around for ideas as to how and where to deploy the growing air, sea and land force gathered in and around West Wales and the Irish Sea; how to intensify the efforts of M.I.6's network of Irish agents; how best to co-ordinate the Anglo-Irish strategy.

The conference room door opened and a waitress wheeled in a trolley with coffee and biscuits. She was two yards from the Prime Minister when the red telephone rang, with what, in the circumstances, was an ear-splitting shrillness.

"Get out!" shouted the Home Secretary as the Deputy Assistant Commissioner of Police snatched at the handset and an aide pressed the buttons activating the tape-recorder and amplifier. The terrified waitress fled, leaving a trail of biscuits scattered across the crimson carpet.

"Hello," said the police officer.

"I want to speak to your Home Secretary."

"I'm afraid he's not avail . . ."

"Get him!"

"Look . . . the code word . . . give me the code word."

"Screw your code word! This isn't the I.R.A. Get him! Now! If you don't want your Prince's blood on your hands, get him!"

This was no tape-recording. The Home Secretary grabbed the handset. "Home Secretary."

"Right, Home Secretary. Don't waste time trying to talk to me, just listen. Make a note of this. Irish Ordnance Survey, Dingle Bay. Look for Minard Head on the south side of the Dingle Peninsula—co-ordinates 503907. There's a farm just behind the headland and a bungalow a few yards up the track. Your Prince is in that bungalow. There are well-armed men guarding it and some holding the farmer and his family inside the farmhouse. The approaches are well protected and they have watchers as far out as Tralee and Castlemaine in radio communication with the hide-

173

out. They can give up to forty-five minutes warning of any approach from inland. That's it. It's up to you. Do you read me?"

"Now hold on a minute. The code word . . ."

The caller became agitated. "Screw it! I'm not the I.R.A. Do you read me?"

"Yes, but . . ."

The line went dead. The Home Secretary held the receiver away from him, regarding it reproachfully. Then he replaced it, gently.

An aide had already extracted sheet 20 of the Irish Ordnance Survey from the set lying on a table at the end of the room and spread it on the table in front of the Prime Minister. Service officers and civilian advisers crowded around.

If the caller were telling the truth, the Dingle Peninsula was an impressive choice. The narrow strip of land jutting out into the Atlantic at the most westerly point of Ireland could be said to offer the best kind of defensive position for such an enterprise. Thirty miles long and between five and twelve miles wide, it was served by only two roads from the hinterland of County Kerry, one on the northern side, from Tralee, and the other, on the southern side, from Castlemaine. A mountain range rising to nearly three thousand feet ran down between the roads and was crossed by only two passes—the Conair Pass above Dingle town and the road between Anascaul and Tralee. Those approaches could easily be covered for a good distance from the hide-out.

The other defensive advantages of the hiding place would be two-fold: first its proximity to the one hundred foot cliffs at Minard Head, about twelve miles up Dingle Bay from the Atlantic and, second, the fact that it lay two miles from the Castlemaine to Dingle road and the uneven ground between consisted of small fields, high hedges and a maze of narrow, sunken lanes.

It was also well away—two hundred miles away—from all the activity in the southern Irish sea and could explain why the Libyan ship *Ghadames* had been laid on as a diversion, since it had occupied the British for the whole of the time that it would have taken the kidnappers to round the south coast of Ireland.

But was this just another P.I.R.A. diversion? The head of M.I.6 thought it probably was. The Foreign Secretary thought it could be a ploy to bedevil relations with the Irish government by tricking the British into making their own rescue attempt. The Brigadier representing the army was all for sending in the S.A.S. to 'knock over' the place, while the Royal Navy Commander reminded the Prime Minister of the capabilities of the Royal Marines Special Boat Squadron. There was no shortage of advice.

All eyes were on the Prime Minister, whose thoughts seemed unaffected by the Home Secretary's reminder of the absence of an identification feature—either the Provisional I.R.A.'s code-word or any other—from the telephone call. Her eyes narrowed and her lips pursed. Her right index finger roamed idly over the blue on the map representing the waters of Dingle Bay. For a moment it hesitated, and then it shot across to the point marked 'Minard Head'. "It will have to be done," she said. "We have no other information and no likelihood of getting any in time. We have only four days."

C.O.B.R. was suddenly alive again, and a rapid closed-circuit T.V. discussion between the Prime Minister and her service chiefs in the Naval Command Centre at Northwood set in motion *Operation Relay Run* . . . a desperate mission to rescue the Heir to the British Throne.

*   *   *

At five o'clock that Tuesday afternoon, six hours after the call identifying the kidnap hide-out, an R.A.F. maritime reconnaissance Nimrod jet from 42 Squadron in Cornwall began its first eight-mile-high pass down the narrow neck of land, its flight-director system locking in the aircraft's computer and auto-pilot to produce a precise flight path, its counter-radar equipment masking it from the Irish air-traffic control at Shannon.

The Nimrod's Linescan 212 infra-red camera scanned the terrain along its arrow-straight track in an action automatically adjusted to its speed and height. On colour infra-red film it absorbed a sequence of images built up from thermal emissions from the ground—a heat picture on which changes detected over successive flight passes gave indications of crucial importance to an assault team, distinguishing, for example, between living vegetation and recently-uprooted or detached material . . . vegetation that had already begun to die, as when used to camouflage a man or a hiding place.

175

At the same time, the Nimrod's high-level conventional camera was taking minutely-detailed three-dimensional photographs which would provide assault troops with the next best thing to a scale model of their objective and its surroundings. By day, the aircraft's AGI F.126 high-altitude reconnaissance cameras would take conventional black and white pictures, while on its night passes it would employ massive infra-red flashes invisible to the naked eye. The results were the same: three dimensional images capable of being enlarged *seventy times* with definition so sharp that a pinhead-sized object in a photographic frame could be enlarged to something like four inches.

*　　　*　　　*

Midnight, Wednesday 16th August. For the second night in succession, H.M. Submarine *Oracle*, lying submerged twelve miles inside Dingle Bay, put up her periscope and surveyed the cliffs above Minard Head. The night was dark, save for the thin streak of a new moon, and a clear sky full of stars. A Royal Marines S.B.S. Major studying his objective in the bright, sickly-green light of the periscope's electronic image intensifier, saw thickly-hedged fields sloping upwards from the cliff top, up to and beyond the farm, which was situated only yards from the edge. Further up stood a fairly new bungalow and, two or three miles beyond that, the mountains reared up to almost three thousand feet—Slievanea, Slievenagower, Knockanulanane, Beenoske and Stradbally. Rising to three hundred feet in the foreground, half a mile east of the farm, was Glan Mountain, while at an equal distance to the west, rising steeply to seven hundred and sixty feet, lay Sea Hill—both presenting useful observation points for the men he was about to put ashore.

H.M. Submarine *Oracle*, a vessel about the size of some of the larger U-boats of World War Two, was crowded enough with only her own crew of 7 officers and 62 men, with hammocks hanging alongside her torpedoes and in every nook and cranny. In her role as a covert troop-carrier for coastal reconnaissance she became a sardine can. So it was this night, as eight men of the S.B.S. and two officers of the army's S.A.S.—parachuted into the Atlantic with inflatable boats, weapons and equipment—prepared for a further night reconnaissance of the ground around Minard Head.

With the benefit of the photographic material dropped from the Nimrods, they knew to an inch the locations of what appeared to be two manned observation posts, one on Sea Hill and the other on Glan Mountain. They knew, too, that those observation posts were manned only during daylight hours. The aerial photographs had shown armed men in camouflaged clothing moving to and fro between the farmhouse and the bungalow, and had indicated that there was a camouflaged weapons pit, probably containing a machine-gunner, covering the lane leading from the main road.

A physical reconnaissance of the beach had been made by an S.B.S. team the night before, and what they had found there had led to an abrupt change of plan. Their detection equipment had picked up emissions from geophones—small sensors stuck in the ground at irregular intervals, which would have picked up the slightest footfall for many yards around. The beach and cliff were thus unapproachable, so the reconnaissance party would have to land on unguarded beaches on either side and approach the farm indirectly.

Until recently, geophones had been impossible to penetrate, but government scientists had developed a counter-instrument, which the S.B.S. had been evaluating on field trials. It was still on the secret list and the only one available was held at the government research establishment at Aldermaston, so it had been rushed by road to R.A.F. Brawdy in West Wales, brought out by helicopter, and winched down with its operator to the submarine.

Despite this hitch, the first night's physical reconnaissance had combined with the results of the aerial surveillance to give them most of what they needed to know about their objective. What they needed now were the answers to five crucial questions: first, how to open up the Minard Head beach for a frontal approach. This they would be able to do tonight with the geophone de-activator, which would substitute a steady signal on the same wavelength to deceive the monitors and allow the marines to walk through the geophone field unhindered. Next, if this really were the kidnappers' hide-out, how many terrorists were holding the hostage or hostages in the bungalow? How many rooms were there in the building? Which of them were they using? What sentries or other protective measures were they employing to detect intruders during the night, when their O.P.s on the hill-tops were unoccupied?

It was to answer those questions that a full S.B.S. reconnaissance party was about to go ashore.

Their mission would involve lying absolutely motionless and wide-awake in skilfully-camouflaged 'hides', in darkness and in daylight, for days if necessary. During the day they would be watching the watchers on the two hills and noting movements in and around the bungalow and the farm. At night they would emerge to do their reconnaissance. It was the very kind of mission for which they had trained for long, punishing weeks, often in atrocious conditions, in such places as Dartmoor and the cold lochs of the Scottish Highlands, and which they had carried out so superbly in the Falklands war, under the noses of the Argentinians and in advance of the British landing. No one in the world did it better. Which was just as well, because if they were detected, the hostage or hostages would surely die. If they went undetected but still did not get it right, the hostages would die anyway as the S.A.S. assault team attempted to rescue them.

Slowly and with only a quiet hissing sound and a swirl of water, the submarine rose to the surface like a great black whale coming up for air, its deck level with the surface and awash. In a well-practised drill, three five-metre two-man canoes slid from the submarine's deck, each carrying two S.B.S. marines, followed by an inflatable dinghy carrying two others and a load of equipment. As they approached the beach, they scanned it through a variety of optical and other counter-surveillance devices. A light-intensifier showed up the beach and the cliffs as if it were broad daylight; a thermal imager showed that there were no sentries, and their top-secret piece of equipment from Aldermaston neutralised the geophone field.

As they came ashore their metal detectors told them that the terrorists were not relying on trip wires, but when they reached the top of the cliffs their infra-red illuminator alerted them to something they would have to approach very gingerly indeed. It detected a complex criss-cross network of infra-red beams that surrounded the bungalow and extended right down beyond the farm to the very top of one hundred foot cliffs. Known as 'passive infra-red' beams, they radiated outwards to a hundred metres from posts in the ground. The beams—invisible but for the S.B.S. men's illuminators—shone at about knee height, and somewhere in the bungalow or the farmhouse there would be a monitor which would show the exact spot at which a beam was broken. With the aid of the S.B.S. infra-red illuminators, that beam field could now be seen and safely negotiated.

Whether or not it was the kidnap hideout, the marines were certainly dealing with *some* kind of terrorist base, and a very heavily-guarded one at that.

Before daylight four of them were in place on the heights on either side of the farm. The others, having finished exploring and mapping the beach and the cliff paths, had returned to the submarine, which was now submerged, heading out to the south west of the Blasket Islands. Once there she would string an aeriel buoy up to the surface and wait for reports from the shore party.

*　　*　　*

By midnight on Thursday, the picture was sufficiently clear for the S.A.S. colonel aboard H.M. Submarine *Oracle* to select the best time for an assault and put ashore an advance party of his own men to prepare the way for the assault team. They were briefed by the Royal Marines lieutenant in charge of the S.B.S. beach reconnaissance party.

Up to now, he said, everything had gone perfectly for the terrorists. Every movement, every facet of their operation had fallen into place with split-second timing, apparently confounding Clausewitz's dictum that '*No plan survives contact with the enemy.*' They had not made one mistake. But perhaps they had now made the mistake that would be their undoing. Obviously falling for the novelty of electronic gadgetry, they had abandoned virtually all their night-time building perimeter protection to it. There were no night sentries. People emerging after dark came out one or two at a time and at lengthy intervals, probably merely for a breath of air, and it was known that there were two of them permanently in the farmhouse, presumably to keep an eye on the farmer and his family, who could be seen going about their farm work during the day, apparently under guard.

Whatever electronic gadgetry the terrorists had, it evidently did not include portable light-intensifiers, or at least there was no one out at night to use them. They would have night sights fitted to their weapons, but that was not by any means the same as having the ability to scan whole areas, at considerable distances, as if one were in broad daylight. The S.B.S. men watching them from half a mile away did have that ability. They were even able to relay to their submarine live T.V. pictures from infra-red-boosted compact T.V. cameras, through small, portable dish aerials.

The briefing over, the face-blackened, black-suited S.A.S. men were put ashore under cover of darkness and began closing in on the farmhouse and bungalow. The S.B.S. men having already detected and noted the presence and movements of people inside the buildings through their thermal imagers, their S.A.S. comrades were about to add to that knowledge with another electronic aid. Carefully negotiating the infra-red beam field and listening closely through their ear-phones to the cautionary commentaries of those covering them with image-intensifiers further out, they placed tiny sensors at various points around the buildings and retreated.

For the next twenty-four hours, the senior officers aboard the submarine analysed the signals picked up from those sensor-transmitters and relayed to them from the S.B.S. reconnaissance team, and began to work out something of what was happening in there. And there was one outstanding puzzle: all the movement and conversation patterns indicated the presence of *three* people who, given their relative immobility and apparent non-involvement in the activity in the place, might be hostages. Yet only the Prince and his personal detective were missing. Still, said the S.A.S. colonel, they would soon solve that one when they went in, because those two could be expected to drop to the floor out of the line of fire when the shooting started. After all, the S.A.S. had given them enough training in the art of survival in terrorist hostage-taking and S.A.S. siege-breaking.

CHAPTER TWENTY TWO

In the Briefing Room, linked by direct telephone, telex, close-circuit T.V. and facsimile-transmission lines to the Naval Command Centre at Northwood, the plan for rescuing whoever might be held in the terrorists' west of Ireland hideaway was being finalised.

The Director General of M.I.6 reported that his service was orchestrating a systematic deception of the Irish security forces. It was working very successfully and agents were reporting police, army and naval activity exactly in line with the false leads they were planting. There was an immense concentration of Irish police and land forces along the coastline from Wexford to Cape Clear, where all five of the Irish navy's gun-boats were also gathered.

What no one needed to be told was that none of the information the Irish were getting from the British 'plants' was coming back through official channels. For all their protestations of co-operation and co-ordination—normally so honestly and effectively observed —the Irish government was still so fearful of the political consequences of an introduction into the Republic of the hated S.A.S. that they were not taking the slightest chance that the British might decide to go it alone.

And the news from West Kerry? By mid-morning on Friday, the naval commander in Dingle Bay had been able to confirm that the mystery caller seemed to have been spot on. All that was missing was proof that the terrorists were, in fact, holding the Heir to the Throne. The S.A.S. colonel on board *Oracle* had finalised his plans anyway. In his latest message to the Naval Command Centre he was recommending an assault at one o'clock on Saturday morning, seventeen hours in advance of the Provisional I.R.A.'s deadline.

A 'disinformation' operation had also been mounted on the diplomatic front. 'Informed sources' in the Foreign Office were planting rumours among the news media of possible developments in the U.N. in New York, in line with the terrorists' demands, and of the British political will being not quite what it seemed in this most unprecedented of terrorist situations, a suspicion which seemed to be confirmed by a good deal of otherwise unexplained diplomatic activity at the United Nations, and between the Foreign Office and foreign embassies in London. Bargaining for the lives of hostages in a hi-jacked aircraft, where resolution and no compromise were the order of the day, was one thing, said the leaks. Bargaining for the life of the next in line to the British throne was quite another. Speculation was rife; the terrorists scented victory.

The 'disinformation' about the Libyan ship was a two-edged weapon. First, the Provisional I.R.A. must be made to think the British had no clue to what had happened beyond the approach of their helicopter to where the *Ghadames* was proceeding down the Irish Sea. The longer they held on to the vessel, the less they would seem to know about where to turn next. Second, the Libyans must be kept guessing too, so Whitehall-inspired news-media rumour abounded, while a blanket of secrecy lay over the 12,000 ton cargo ship anchored in Falmouth Harbour.

If the British 'activity' at the U.N. was a blind, that of the Libyans was only too real. They were demanding an emergency meeting of the Security Council and mobilising all the rag-bag of third-world ex-colonial wild-cat dictatorships that relished such events. But that was the open face of Libya. Somewhere out there, in his Bedouin tent, Colonel Muammar Gaddafi would once again be calling down the wrath of Allah on the British and activating his well-armed, long-reaching network of terrorists to strike back at them. In spite of all she had on her hands at that moment, Britain must therefore put herself into the highest possible state of alert at ports, airports, British embassies abroad, and in all the thousand-and-one places where terrorism can strike without warning.

*   *   *

At four o'clock in the afternoon, H.M. Submarine *Oracle*'s coded signal setting out the aims, method and recommended timing of the task force's proposed assault plan rattled off the telex terminal in the Naval Command Centre at Northwood and was quickly decoded and relayed through secure telex lines to C.O.B.R. and Downing Street. *Oracle*, it said, had been joined by her sister-ship, *Otter*, which had on board a 20-man S.A.S. assault team. All was ready for a 1 a.m. assault.

The Prime Minister and her crisis management team had about one hour in which to study and approve the plan if the forces on the ground were to complete their preparations and get into position. If they gave the go-ahead they would then have to set the 'Rules of Engagement', defining the circumstances in which the troops involved could open fire and kill. If the S.A.S. experience in Gibraltar were anything to go by, this was probably the nub of their dilemma.

It was the Brigadier advising on behalf of the army—an ex-S.A.S. officer himself—who raised the question: "There are bound to be deaths," he said. "And there is bound to be a coroner's inquest, this time by an *Irish* coroner and an *Irish* jury. It was difficult enough in Gibraltar. In *Ireland* . . ."

"*There will be no inquest!*" snapped the Prime Minister.

The room fell silent. It was evident that she had had all the advice she was going to listen to on that particular point.

The Prime Minister gave her decision at twenty minutes to five: "Whatever the outcome; whatever the diplomatic repercussions; whatever the risk to life and limb of our troops or those they seek to rescue, it must go ahead. We have Her Majesty's authority to act according to our best judgement, and in my judgement we have no alternative." She turned to the Home Secretary: "Please give the order." She handed him a typed sheet of paper. "Here are the Rules of Engagement. Please have them encoded and transmitted. If they are adhered to, there will be no question of a repeat of Gibraltar, *because there will be no inquest.*"

The Home Secretary picked up the telephone labelled 'Naval Command Centre, Northwood'. "Home Secretary," he said. "Will you please make a note of this . . ."

"Go ahead, sir," said the voice on the other end.

The Home Secretary's reply died on his lips as the light on one of the scrambled direct-line telephones on the Prime Minister's desk began to flash and the sound of its buzzer killed every sound and movement in the room. It was the one labelled '*Dublin*'. She picked up the handset: "Prime Minister."

The voice at the other end was instantly recognisable. "*Taoiseach* here, Prime Minister. I think we have good news for you. Or at least we have a big development. The I.R.A. has shown out at last."

The Prime Minister and the Home Secretary, who was listening in over the telephone amplifier, exchanged startled glances. "In what way?" she asked, trying to conceal her alarm at the news.

"In the way of a siege. At a farm in County Waterford, twenty-five miles in from the Irish Sea. We have it surrounded by our Army Rangers and our negotiators are in contact by land-line with those inside. They seem to be holding two hostages and our people are hopeful that they can talk them out."

It was a bombshell!

The Prime Minister interrupted sharply, as the Home Secretary replaced the 'Northwood' telephone handset. "We must get someone over there at once, *Taoiseach*."

"Not soldiers, Prime Minister. I think we've settled that pretty thoroughly. We would welcome a ministerial party, and someone connected with the Palace. We would appreciate some help on the spot in the way of verifying that it is the Prince they are holding."

"At once," said the Prime Minister, waving a hand in the direction of the Home Secretary.

"But no military, please," the *Taoiseach* insisted. "We have everything under control and, please God, we'll get your Prince back safe and sound."

The receiver was replaced, and the Prime Minister and Home Secretary looked at each other with the stunned surprise of a boxer hit right between the eyes as the final bell is sounding. *Two* hideouts. *Two* sieges. One in the east and one in the west. A hundred and forty miles apart! "Up to now," said the Prime Minister, grimly, "we've been playing Russian roulette with only one bullet in the chamber. Now there are two. God help us!"

*   *   *

The Irish authorities were completely ignorant of the activity on the Dingle Peninsula, and, while both sides were going through the motions of total co-operation and co-ordination, the Dublin government had been keeping this dramatic development in County Waterford to itself until it was deemed too late for armed British intervention.

Even as plans for the assault were being finalised on board the British submarines, a team of Irish police officers, sent to

184

investigate suspicious activity at a farm near the village of Ahenny, had challenged the occupants of a car coming out of the farm track and come under fire from automatic weapons. They had fired back and chased two men back into the farmhouse, shooting a third dead in the process.

The concentration of the Irish security forces along its Irish Sea coastline—partly the result of British deception—meant that the police officers were very quickly reinforced and a tight cordon thrown around the farm. That concentration, with its network of road blocks and its helicopter umbrella, also meant that the authorities were able to enforce a total news blackout.

By mid-afternoon, Kilcormac Farm had been surrounded by an inner cordon of army snipers, sub-machine gunners and gas-gunners, with an outer cordon of armed police which excluded from the area all but the police negotiators and Irish Army Rangers assault troops. Beyond the outer cordon lay the forward command post of the army commander and police chief, which was linked by every modern communication system to the government's crisis centre, sixty miles away in Cork City's Collins Barracks.

The terrorists' link with the outside world was a *Garda Siochana* Detective Superintendent who had trained with the New York City Police in the techniques of siege negotiation. Painstakingly dragging out the negotiations, while endeavouring to establish a rapport with the man on the other end of the field telephone, he was testing out a range of psychological ploys in an attempt to achieve the release of the hostages—of whom, according to the I.R.A. man he was speaking to, there were two—without further bloodshed.

It was not a new experience for the detective, but this time the stakes were so high that he had become an extension of the will of the *Taoiseach*, who had taken personal control from his Dublin office.

All day the negotiations followed the familiar ebb and flow between imminent surrender and defiance, between moderate language and hysterical tirade. They reached nail-biting peaks when a wrong word could have been catastrophic, and they descended to almost incredibly light-hearted banter as the adversaries established that unique bond between terrorist and negotiator which only a psychiatrist can begin to explain.

The crisis came at just after midnight, at the very moment when, unknown to those surrounding Kilcormac Farm, the S.A.S. were closing in for the kill on the cliffs above Dingle Bay, a hundred and forty miles westward.

During negotiations over the supply of food and drink, an Irish army sniper, eyes glued to his night sight, gently moved his body to ease his stiffness and accidentally squeezed the trigger. The crack of the rifle shot split the silence of the night as the bullet swished through heather and hedge, to be answered by a whole fusillade of shots from the floodlit farmhouse. Over the field telephone the I.R.A. man's voice shrieked obscenities. The watchers saw a window open to reveal two men inside, and they witnessed an execution, as one of the men put a pistol to the other's head, shot him and pitched him out.

"Bastards," screamed the voice. "If youse don't all get out of here you can have the other one and we'll come out shooting."

But he himself had only seconds to live.

The Army Rangers captain and his team up front heard their colonel's order over their radio earphones—"Go! Go! Go!"—and four stun grenades exploded almost simultaneously inside the house, blinding and deafening everyone in it for the vital eight seconds that the Rangers needed to storm the building and kill or secure its occupants.

Doors and windows caved in and fearsome-looking figures, clad from head to foot in black, hurtled through the apertures, firing bursts from snub-nosed Uzi sub-machine guns at anything looking remotely hostile, and throwing everyone out, terrorist and hostage alike, to be spreadeagled on the ground and pinioned by the assault squad's back-up men.

The phosphorous-based stun grenades set the building ablaze, adding another dimension of fury to the devastating fire-fight which broke the siege of Kilcormac Farm.

At a signal from the Rangers captain in the house, two ambulances raced up the rough track to the farmhouse, followed by two fire engines. It took a few minutes to distinguish hostage from terrorist and to count the dead and wounded. Of the I.R.A. men—there were seven of them—six had died and one was unconscious and looked as if he did not have long to live. Of the two hostages, one was, of course, already dead. The other was found to have been shot and to be in a very serious condition, his life seemingly ebbing fast with the blood that pumped from his four bullet wounds.

The dead hostage had been shot through the back of the head with a high velocity round which had blown away his face. He was unrecognisable. His companion, unconscious, covered in blood and with no means of identification about him, was equally unidentifiable, for the moment at least.

The priority was to get the surviving hostage to the Regional Hospital in Cork and he was quickly airborne in an army helicopter, attended by members of an army para-medic team which had been standing by. Was he the Heir to the British Throne, or was he the protection officer kidnapped with him? Only the party of British government and palace officials, now on their way from London to Cork, could answer that.

The *Taoiseach* was already back on the telephone to the Prime Minister, giving the sketchy details that were available from the confused aftermath of the firefight and the hectic activity in and around the intensive care unit at the Cork Regional Hospital. Even as he spoke, the count-down for the assault on the Dingle Peninsula was in its final stage. There were only seconds to go. It was now unstoppable.

CHAPTER TWENT THREE

Five minutes to one on Saturday morning, 19th August. The S.A.S. assault troops have crossed the infra-red beam field and stand against the walls of the bungalow and the farmhouse above Minard Head. They know there are four men in a bedroom in the bungalow and six in the living-room, one or more of whom could be hostages. For the moment, one of the six is in the bathroom, urinating, and all the indications from conversations going on inside indicate that the hostage or hostages are awake, perhaps disturbed by the man going to the bathroom. That is good news— they will be able to get down out of the cross-fire if they are able to react quickly enough.

Minutes pass. The one who had gone to the bathroom has returned to the living room. Ninety seconds to go . . . eighty-five . . . eighty. One of the men in the living room is asking for a drink. One of the others goes to the kitchen. Sixty seconds . . . fifty-five. The commentary coming over the S.A.S. men's earphones from their commander drones on: "The man in the kitchen is putting on the kettle."

Forty seconds . . . thirty-five . . . the commentary shows a trace of excitement: "Something has broken a beam . . . one of them is coming out." Sure enough, alerted by the movement of a goat straying across the front path, one of the terrorists carefully opens the kitchen door and emerges into the darkness. He is the first to pay the price of substituting electronic novelties for real, live sentries. For a second or two, his sub-machine gun cocked and at the ready, he pauses to allow his eyes to get used to the darkness. To the man standing a yard behind him he is only too visible. A hand over the mouth and a nine-inch blade plunged deftly into the heart despatches him instantly and silently.

Seven seconds to go . . . six, five, four . . . three, two, one, zero . . . *CRASH*!

Simultaneously, three stun grenades are hurled through the windows and explode inside the bungalow with deafening cracks and blinding white flashes; two four-foot diameter holes are blasted through the breeze-block walls—one in the unwindowed east wall of the living room and one into the bedroom in which the off-duty terrorists are sleeping. Two S.A.S. men dive through, firing as they go. Four others burst through the doors into the other rooms, spraying them with fire. "Down, down, down!" they yell. Seven Irish terrorists die instantly in a hail of bullets. Two men running out of the nearby farmhouse with guns in their hands are dead before they have covered two yards, and the one manning the M.60 machine gun in the hedgerow weapons-pit never hears a thing before he receives his burst in the back.

*   *   *

It was just gone three in the morning when the telephone rang in the police station at Castlemaine, the old harbour town at the head of Dingle Bay. *Garda Siochana* Sergeant Kevin O'Leary put down his mug of tea and answered it: "Gards, Castlemaine."

"Operator here. I've got a fellow in a coin box who hasn't any coins on him and he's asking for the police. He sounds a bit desperate to me. Here you are, caller . . ."

A click and a buzz. "Who am I speaking to?" asked a voice in a distinctly un-Irish accent.

"Sergeant O'Leary. Who is that?"

"Detective Chief Inspector Alan Robertson of the Metropolitan Police. I'm the Prince's personal detective and he and I have just escaped. We don't know where the hell we are and we need help, quickly. Would you send someone to pick us up?"

A long pause. Then: "Kelleher! If that's you . . ."

"Please, sergeant, this is serious. There are dead men where we've come from and if we don't get to a safe place quickly we'll be dead too."

Another pause. "Where are you?"

"I'm in a phone box near a beach. There's a pub opposite. Foley's Bar it's called. And a graveyard behind me."

Yet another pause. "It's Inch Strand you are. Now wait a minute . . ." He was thinking. "Get out of that box at once and jump over the wall into the graveyard and both of you stay there until you see the police car draw up. Don't move until you see us. You never know what the buggers are up to if they brought you all the way down to Kerry. Hold on a second . . ."

The detective waited. The sergeant came back: "How do I know this isn't some kind of a joke . . . or a trick . . . an ambush? I need some positive identification . . . something I can make a quick check on. It wouldn't be the first time the I.R.A.'s led us into traps."

"Of course. Write down this number. It's the private line to the Police Office at Buckingham Palace and you can dial it direct. It's manned twenty-four hours a day. Ask to speak to the Duty Protection Officer and tell him to look on the annual leave list and confirm for you that I've been dropped from the rota for duty at Balmoral and have changed my annual leave, to begin on the 23rd of August so that I can be with my wife when she has our second child. Now for God's sake please be quick about it."

The call was, of course, expected at the Palace and it took only seven or eight minutes for Sergeant O'Leary to ring back to the telephone box. "We'll be with you in less than twenty minutes, sir," he said. "There's a car at Milltown and he'll pick me up on his way through. Another is coming up from Dingle, so we should both arrive at about the same time. They're both marked patrol cars and there'll be five of us, all in uniform. Now get out of that box as quick as you can, and don't move a muscle until you see us stop the cars and flash the headlights three times."

"O.K. We'll do that. But after you've given the signal I want all of you except the drivers to get out of the cars and stand in the headlights and *we'll* come to *you*."

The detective left the telephone box and joined the Prince behind the stone wall separating the graveyard from the Dingle road. A few feet away, behind a plinth supporting a large marble angel, two figures, their black faces and clothing making them invisible in the darkness, sat and watched, covering them with sub-machine guns. Two others lurked by the wall of Foley's Bar opposite. They were men of the Royal Marines Special Boat Squadron.

Fourteen minutes passed. A car could be heard roaring up from the direction of Castlemaine, its high headlamp beams bouncing like searchlights in the dark sky as it sped along the dead-straight but undulating road. It had already passed through the hamlet of Caheracruttera three miles away, and an I.R.A. observer in a roadside cottage there was trying in vain to make a radio report to

190

the Minard Head hideaway. The police car arrived at the telephone box and, with the engine still running, the sergeant and two constables got out and stood in the glare of the headlights. As they did so, the second car came hurtling down the steep hill from the direction of Dingle and its crew identified themselves in the same way.

The Prince's detective emerged from his hiding place and ran to the sergeant's car, his S.B.S. escort covering his every movement, weapons cocked and ready. The Prince followed at his detective's signal.

Having picked up its passengers, the police car turned back towards Castlemaine and sped away, closely followed by its escort. Three minutes later they were going past the I.R.A. observer at Caheracruttera again. Relieved that they seemed to be regular patrol cars on the prowl, he stopped calling Minard Head and cursed quietly. If it wasn't the bloody mountains interfering with his radio it was the freak weather conditions. Sod the high pressure area. He had kept telling them they should have put him further up the mountain . . .

The Police cars gone, the four marines sprinted back to Inch Strand, pushed their inflatable through the slight breakers, leapt into it, started up their sixty horse-power Johnson outboard, and streaked off down the bay to the waiting submarine.

*   *   *

"Be Christ, it *is* yourself!" Sergeant O'Leary had said as the blood-stained, unshaven Prince climbed into the back seat beside him. "What happened, sir? Where did they have you?"

The Prince's detective, well-rehearsed on his way down the bay, answered for him: "I don't know where we were. Somewhere near the top of a cliff I would guess. Wouldn't have the slightest idea how to find the place again. I knew we were in a farm building. We were hooded most of the time. I heard animals and chickens. The people holding us started quarrelling over something or other. They'd been quarrelling for a day or two, on and off. It got pretty heated eventually, somebody fired a shot and then there was firing all over the place. Don't ask me how we got out. All I know is that I whipped off my hood, spied a gap between me and an open door, grabbed the Prince, and we were away. I could hear the shooting for a few minutes after we left. There were explosions as well. I don't know for how long. We just kept running.''

"Well, you're all right now, gents. This is John Kelleher and this is Paddy Culhane. We're all armed and once we get you back to the station there'll be others with us very soon. You'll be ready for a mug of tea, I'm sure. By the way,'' said the sergeant to the detective, ''how come you've got a gun?''

Robertson held out his right hand to show a semi-automatic pistol. "I grabbed it from the floor as I dropped below the firing.''

"Well, I think you ought to give it to me, sir.''

"Not on your bloody life, sergeant. Not 'til you get us to a place of safety. I've been without a gun for nearly a week and I'm not letting go of this one. Not just yet anyway.''

Sergeant O'Leary nodded assent and picked up his radio mike. "Kilo one three to control . . . kilo one three to control.''

"Go ahead, kilo one three.''

"E.T.A. Castlemaine ten minutes . . .''

"Kilo one three, you are to go straight on to Killarney. Kilo one seven is coming down from Castleisland to join you at Castlemaine and Kilo one nine will come in from Killarney to meet you at about Listry Bridge.''

"Roger. Kilo one three out.''

"There you are,'' said O'Leary to the Prince. "It looks as if we'll have you back with the missus and kids in no time . . .''

"Thank you, gentlemen. I'll find some better way later, but you will never know how I feel at this moment.''

*　　　*　　　*

The *Garda* convoy arrived at the heavily-guarded police station in Killarney at five minutes after four o'clock, and the Prince and his detective were hustled inside in the midst of a tight bodyguard of uniformed *Gardai*. In an office on the ground floor they were greeted with warm handshakes by two senior *Garda* officers, to whom the detective handed his pistol. Detective Superintendent Cooney ejected the magazine, cleared the weapon and examined it. "Czech,'' he said. "CZ.75, nine mil. Where'd you get it?''

"I told Sergeant O'Leary. When the shooting started and I

192

dropped to the floor it fell near me and I grabbed it. I let go a couple of shots as we were getting out of the place.''

''We've found any number of these in I.R.A. arms caches. The Libyans are supplying them.''

''Well, you're welcome to it now,'' laughed the detective as he took a mug of steaming tea from a policewoman.

Chief Superintendent Kilmichael explained that they would have to delay their progress towards Cork for just a little while in order to get from them whatever help they could give in the way of directions to the place from which they had escaped. The maps spread on the table were of little use, save to show that it must be somewhere on the southern edge of the Dingle Peninsula within a distance of four or five miles west of Inch Strand. Unfortunately, the chief superintendent explained, a large body of his men had been drafted east to check the harbours around Cork, but strenuous efforts were being made at that very moment to give him a large force of *Gardai*, soldiers, transport and helicopters by mid-morning. If they would be good enough to tell Detective Superintendent Cooney all they could remember about the people who had held them and how they had got away . . .

''I'm afraid it's very little,'' the Prince replied. ''I was hooded and no-one spoke to me for . . . how many days?''

''Six, nearly seven, since they kidnapped you.''

As the Prince had so rightly said, there was little enough he could give them. Mercifully, though, neither he nor his detective had been badly injured, though the dried blood on their clothing, face and hands, looked alarming. A glancing bullet had left an ugly red wheal on the detective's left temple, while the Prince had a gash on the back of his head which could have been caused by a flying splinter. Little enough to show for their ordeal.

After many strong, friendly handshakes, they boarded an Irish army Alouette helicopter, and were at Collins Barracks in Cork City by about half past five that morning. There they were greeted by the *Taoiseach* and the Foreign Minister, and also by people from their own side of the Irish Sea. They left Collins Barracks by helicopter for a massively-guarded Cork airport, where the Prince said his farewells before boarding an aircraft of the Queen's Flight for R.A.F. Northolt.

He walked along the line-up of dignitaries at the foot of the aircraft steps. He shook hands with the *Taoiseach* and expressed his deep gratitude for all that had been done for him. Then, with a twinkle in his eye, unable to resist a joke in even the most difficult of times, he remarked to the Irish Prime Minister: "Well, *Taoiseach*, so ends the first royal visit to Cork since my great-great-great-grandmother came in the 1840s. *And she had a twenty-one gun salute, too!*"

The *Taoiseach* laughed. The Prince climbed the aircraft steps, turned at the door to wave, and five minutes later was heading back across the Irish Sea for home.

*   *   *

Despite all attempts by the British and Irish governments to maintain a news media blackout while operations continued on the Irish side, the news leaked out. Picking up the story from *Radiotelefís Eirrean*, the British T.V. channels and radio networks carried news-flashes reporting rumours that the Prince had been rescued by the Irish security forces . . . no official confirmation . . . unnamed police sources quoted as saying . . . seems certain that His Royal Highness was unharmed . . . terrible ordeal . . .

The nation was electrified. The Prince arrived at Buckingham Palace to a tumultuous welcome from hundreds of thousands of cheering, flag-waving people, many of whom had camped there for days waiting for news.

The announcement from the Palace came at four o'clock in the afternoon: "It is with great joy and relief that Her Majesty the Queen has welcomed her son after his safe deliverance to his family and his people from terrorist hands. The prayers of the British people have been answered . . . grateful thanks to the Irish government and members of its security forces who have brought him to safety."

At about the same time, the Prime Minister made a statement to a packed House of Commons. Relief mingled with defiance as, in ringing tones, she spelled out once again the determination of the British people, their Royal Family and their government never to treat with terrorists, and to hunt down terrorism with every means in their power and every ounce of their strength.

The House responded as one, and many an angry voice was raised when one member, well known for his persistence in a certain 'naval matter' left over from the Falklands War, asked how and by whom the Prince had been rescued.

The Prime Minister poured ice on him. "Mr. Deputy Speaker, sir. His Royal Highness's imprisonment and release took place on *Irish* soil and the most intensive investigation and activity are now taking place there with a view to clarifying the situation and bringing to book those responsible for this outrage. Within the well-established framework of co-operation between the security forces on both sides of the Irish Sea through the Anglo-Irish Agreement, there will be the utmost co-ordination of effort. At the appropriate time the House will be given the fullest possible account of the affair. As full, that is, as will be consistent with considerations of security . . ." She flashed a look of contempt at her questioner, ". . . *on both sides of the Irish Sea*. In the meantime, I am sure that the rest of the House will join me in expressing the thanks of the nation to all concerned in the safe deliverance of the Heir to the British Throne."

CHAPTER TWENTY FOUR

The Provisional I.R.A. reached Minard Head before the *Garda Siochana*. At four o'clock, as dawn began to brush the eastern sky with faint streaks of light, a Ford Transit van made its way slowly down the narrow lanes from Anascaul. It contained five men, the relief for the Prince's captors.

The first sign that things were not as they should be came when their headlamp recognition signal was not met with a torch-flash from the machine-gun post at the top of the farm track. The approach from then on was that of men suspecting an ambush.

The gun pit was empty, except for an unfired M.60 machine gun.

The terrorists, weapons cocked, spread out and moved slowly inwards from cover to cover. The bungalow doors were open. Every window was smashed. A four-foot rectangular hole had been blown in the living room wall and one in a bedroom. The place was empty. Its inside walls were riddled with bullet holes and sprayed with blood. But there was not a single body in the place.

At the farm, the farmer and his family were huddled in terror behind locked doors. They had seen nothing. They had heard shooting and a loud explosion. The two gunmen who had been standing guard over them had run outside and they had not seen them since. Their own curiosity had been stifled when two black-masked men carrying sub-machine guns had kicked open the front door, searched the house, and warned them that if they came out, or if they did not lock all their doors and draw their curtains, they would be killed. There had been silence since. Since when? Since sometime after one.

That was enough. The terrorists made a quick check over the ground and the farm's outbuildings and ascertained that there were no bodies there either. Then their Transit van hurtled up the farm track, through the winding lanes and up over the mountain road past Anascaul, heading for Tralee.

But they were trapped. By the time they reached Curraheen, four miles short of Tralee, the *Garda Siochana*, alerted by the Prince's arrival at Inch Strand to the fact that he had been held on the Dingle Peninsula, had put up road blocks. There was one at Tonevane cross-roads, and there was no way back.

The I.R.A. driver changed down, rammed the accelerator to the floor and headed straight for the policemen standing in the road ahead. There was a furious burst of fire from the roadside as the Transit swerved around the two blocking vans and scattered the policemen. It struck one of the vans a glancing blow and careered up the bank. It almost heeled over. The windscreen went as the police sprayed it with Uzi sub-machine gun fire. The driver fought with his steering wheel while blood and brains from his passenger's exploding head flew around him. Volunteer Thomas O'Donnell, leader of the Coastguard Hill team in the ill-fated kidnap mission, was the first to die.

In the back, three men lay prone as bullets punctured the walls of the van and crashed and whined above them. But the van was through. There was a *Gardai* chase-car on its tail, but now they could fight back. A rear window was poked out by the muzzle of a Kalashnikov assault rifle and a hundred-round-a-minute stream of 7.62 mm bullets went through the police car's bonnet and windscreen, ripped apart both its front tyres, and sent it out of control. Its rear end slewed around and it rolled over and over, sideways, coming to rest on its flattened roof, its wheels spinning and its occupants dead.

The battered van sped on, only to run into the third element of the well-planned police road block—its 'long-stop' on the bridge at Blennerville, a mile further on. This time they stood no chance. Carefully-sited police marksmen killed the driver, punctured a tyre and sent the Transit crashing through a gap in the end of the three-foot thick stone parapet, into Tralee Bay. Holed like a sieve, its windows shot to smithereens, it sank like a stone. If any of its occupants had survived the torrent of gunfire, they drowned in the muddy waters a mile and a half out of Tralee.

*   *   *

In the late afternoon of that memorable Saturday, the Police Incident Control Centre in the school at Aberaeron received a telephone call from the *Garda Siochana* in Killarney. ''Hello, sir,'' said Detective Superintendent Cooney to Deputy Assistant Commissioner Manston.

"Hello to you, Mr. Cooney. Congratulations on getting our Prince back for us."

"Arragh, ye can thank the Provos mainly, Mr. Manston. They made a desperate hash of it in the end."

"So they did. And how do things stand now?"

"Well, sir, you know we got five of them coming away from the place—killed at the Tralee road block. Now we've found the farm as well, down on a headland on Dingle Bay."

"Excellent."

"And there's a hell of a mess there. There's been a lot of shooting and there's a hell of a lot of blood about, but no bodies at all. Not a one. Somebody *must* have been killed there, because all them that we got on the road block at Tralee were unwounded before we hit them. I imagine they'd be the ones doing the shooting there. It's hard to tell yet, and . . ." he laughed again, ". . . they're not saying anything. God knows what's happened to them who was killed at the farm, but we've got the army out there with us now and we have a big search going on."

"What about the farm itself?" asked Manston, who was as much in the dark as his Irish counterpart. "There'll be plenty of spent ammo I expect. What about weapons?"

"Oh, yes, there's weapons. Czech M.60 Skorpion sub-machine guns, Czech-made pump-action shotguns and several Czech-made pistols. Plenty of ballistics and forensic evidence—Russian nine mil parabellum, Czech-made Semtex explosive. All the kind of stuff ye found at Aberaeron. It's all of a piece with the stuff we've been recovering from the Libyan shipments. The action here and yours in Wales look as if they completely tie up as far as weapons and ammunition go. It's like your Prince and his man said: they've obviously fought among themselves. Are ye sending somebody over?"

"Yes. I'll lay it on with our lab. liaison and their people can go over with my own lads. We might as well tidy up all the loose ends. And you'll be preparing your report for the Coroner anyway . . . for the Inquest . . . so we might be able to help each other."

"Oh, there'll be no inquest," said Cooney. "Not unless we come up with some bodies. Our law's the same as yours. No body, no inquest. There'll be a full investigation, of course, and we could have a murder trial without a body, so if we can identify the gunmen we might be able to put a case together. But, no body, no inquest. Try and come over all the same. Don't forget, sir, we have a lot to celebrate, so make a bit of time to come over yourself, for a conference. We could meet in Cork and paint the town a bit. Bring some of your boys with ye.''

''A fine idea. I'll look forward to it. Keep in touch.''

At Killarney police station, Detective Superintendent Cooney put down his telephone with a thoughtful frown, quietly repeating his words to Deputy Assistant Commissioner Manston: ''*No bodies, no inquest.*'' He turned to his Cork City detective inspector. ''I wonder, Pat. I wonder if they did come over and fetch 'em out themselves.''

Pat Muldoon was obviously thinking along the same lines. ''Possible. But then why wouldn't they take them with them once they'd got them, instead of leaving them loose in hostile territory?'' He stopped and waited for an answer. None came.

Cooney was smiling.

A look of incredulity spread over Muldoon's face. ''They wouldn't, would they?''

Cooney smiled even more broadly.

''Would they?'' asked the D.I. as if something were gradually dawning on him.

''Devious bastards, the Brits,'' said Cooney. ''But clever with it. If they did, they did us a bloody good turn anyway, so they've earned a few drinks off us.''

Muldoon saw the joke, and laughed loud and long with his boss.

One man who could have helped them solve the mystery was the Quartermaster of the S.A.S. Regiment's Foreign Weapons Section. Even as they laughed, he was on his way to Northern Ireland to replenish his stocks from another, recently-discovered, Libyan-supplied arms cache, somewhere near Crossmaglen.

*   *   *

If the Irish government entertained doubts about how things had managed to work out so well, it kept them to itself. Public opinion in Ireland seemed to be mainly concerned with the smoking ruins of Irishmen's houses and cars in Kilburn, Bootle, Luton, Reading, Glasgow, Birmingham and Manchester, wondering what good the

199

Provisional I.R.A. had done *them* with its bloody assault on Aberaeron. *They* were in no mood to swallow I.R.A. propaganda.

* * *

In the Cabinet Office Briefing Room, the first item on the agenda at the de-briefing was an official press statement issued by the Dublin government. It brought sly smiles to the faces of the contingent from the Secret Intelligence Service.

'The Justice Ministry has received what it believes is reliable information from well-placed sources within the Provisional I.R.A. which indicates that the gun battle at the farm on Minard Head which gave His Royal Highness his opportunity to escape, was the result of a long-running internal power struggle in the organisation. It is assumed, therefore, that the Provisionals have buried their own dead and are putting out misleading claims in furtherance of their cover-up of the truth of this matter.'

"Well," said the Service's Director General, "it shows our Irish agent network is still alive and kicking, despite what happened to Major Gannon."

"Can you be sure?" asked the Prime Minister. "How *is* the major? Will he be all right?"

"They knocked him about quite a bit and he had four bullets in him. He's still in intensive care in the hospital in Cork and it's rather touch and go, but the doctors say he should pull through. He's a very fit man. It will be some time before he'll be well enough to go through a full de-briefing, but we've had the chance of a few words with him and he's convinced they never penetrated his cover. It wasn't for the want of trying. Both he and Hurley were tortured while they were held at Kilcormac Farm, but it seems pretty clear they didn't get anything out of them. What he does say, though, is that some of the things they put to Hurley while interrogating him showed that they had been feeding him false information to test him, and that the arrests and searches that were made as a result showed that he really had passed it on to us. The important thing is that they didn't make the link between Colclough, the writer, and Gannon, the agent-runner. His cover doesn't seem to have been broken."

200

"What isn't clear to me," said the Prime Minister, "is why this man Hurley should have subjected himself to such appalling risks. He must have had a very powerful motive."

The M.I.6 Director said he was afraid he did not have the answer to that. "But this kind of thing is not all that uncommon. I suppose that, in such a complex weave of politics, religion, hatred and violence as we have in Northern Ireland, a man can have a hundred different reasons, and informers often come and go without us ever being able to work out anything about them but their honesty of purpose. Hurley was just another such case. It certainly wasn't money alone. He and Gannon seemed to hit it off in some special way, and we sometimes find that that is all there is to it anyway. We can count ourselves lucky that Major Gannon's cover and our organisation weren't exposed in the process. We feel sure that the I.R.A.'s own press statement on the affair confirms this."

"What do they say about it?"

The Director pushed a sheet of paper over to the Prime Minister, and then read from his own copy for the benefit of the others:

"It was put out in Dublin by Provisional Sinn Fein, the I.R.A.'s political wing, and it says this:

'In a spectacular cover-up, which is a disgrace to the Irish Nation, the Irish government has connived with the British to allow the S.A.S. to enter the Republic and storm the farmhouse at Minard Head, where an Active Service Unit of the Provisional I.R.A. was holding the Heir to the British throne. Eleven Republican Volunteers were brutally murdered and their bodies removed for secret disposal. This was not only a further confirmation that the British government operates a "Shoot to Kill" policy in Ireland, but also further evidence that the cover-up disclosed in the Stalker Affair is still in operation. The source of the leak which alerted the British to the kidnap operation was Michael Hurley, who was executed by the I.R.A. during the siege of Kilcormac Farm. His link with the British Secret Service was Gordon Colclough, a writer living at Skerries, who is known to be a paid informer for the British government. Although the Irish security forces rescued him, he will never find a safe hiding place. The murder of the eleven Irishmen at Minard Head will surely be avenged.'

"But the best thing about it, Prime Minister," said the M.I.6 Director, "is the total disarray it has caused in the Provisional I.R.A. in their search for a traitor in their own ranks. There have been several killings and a number of their men have gone on the run from their own people. It couldn't have come at a better time. They were already in the middle of one of their power struggles and this has blown the organisation wide open. But it was a very close shave and we are going to have to remove Gannon from the Irish scene and kill off 'Gordon Colclough'. As it happens, we already had plans for him. We had him lined up for a vacancy at the British Embassy in Washington. Cultural Attaché.''

The Prime Minister raised her eyebrows and the Director laughed. "A cover, Prime Minister. It's an operational post. He will be liaising with the F.B.I., to investigate the activities of Irish-American I.R.A. sympathisers ... Noraid and all that. Major Gannon and his wife will be resident in Washington and his civil service cover will be maintained by the fact that the post is ostensibly a Central Office of Information secondment.''

"Is the major happy about that?''

"Absolutely, Prime Minister. We discussed it with him earlier in the year when we knew the vacancy was going to arise. It suits all our purposes now.''

She turned to the Home Secretary. "Would you bring me up to date on the investigations into how the I.R.A. knew so much about the royal visit to Wales and the route taken by the S.A.S. convoy? They had an incredible amount of detail to work on, didn't they?''

He opened a bound file and turned several pages. "I have a preliminary report, Prime Minister, and its conclusion so far is that everyone on the distribution list for the operational order can be vouched for. Or very nearly. The problem is that two of them are dead, and while a thorough and satisfactory enquiry has been made into their background and activities, it will never be confirmed by personal interviews. One was the head of the local C.I.D., whose job it was to prepare for the security of the visit in co-operation with the Royalty Protection Squad. He was killed in the street, either by a ricochet or a splinter. We can't be sure until we get the *post mortem* report.''

"And the other? I presume you mean the Scotland Yard man.''

"Yes. That's rather a difficult case. As you know, the Assistant

Commissioner was responsible for all V.I.P. protection, including royalty protection, but, while he would have had access to the operational order, there was that other matter . . .''

"You mean the male prostitution investigation."

"Yes, Prime Minister. He was under investigation at the time he went with his male friend on holiday to Australia. Whether that had any bearing on his death there . . . and it *was* two months before the kidnapping . . . the Australian police can't tell, and our own Metropolitan Police Officers haven't been able to take it any further. Whether he drowned himself deliberately because of the scandal, or whether it was an accident, I'm afraid we'll never know. When they found him he could only be identified by his dental records. Decomposition and bite injuries from sharks saw to that. So I'm afraid we'll never know. All we do know is that he was in possession of all the information on the royal visit and our planned response to it.

"And Major Gannon? I seem to remember that when he disappeared in Dublin the day before the kidnapping there was some speculation here that he might be the traitor."

"No, Prime Minister, we can definitely rule him out. It was something quite outside his sphere of operation and we can prove conclusively that he had no contact with anyone remotely connected with the matter . . . either the royal visit itself or the S.A.S. response. And, of course, the I.R.A. tortured him at Kilcormac Farm."

"You may take it from me," said Her Majesty's Chief Inspector of Constabulary, "that Major Gannon is absolutely in the clear. Unfortunately the field is still wide open, apart from the fact that two of the people in the frame are dead. The investigation of the leak is still very much alive and we shall just have to hope that it will eventually come up with some kind of answer. We have the very best men working on it."

"Do we know who gave us the location of the kidnap hideout?" she asked.

The Home Secretary consulted his file again. "No, we don't, Prime Minister. But we do know this. The intelligence analysts were correct when they deduced that Michael Roche was *The Soldier* and that he was in the process of betraying the I.R.A. by making a ransom demand of his own. Our intelligence sources tell us that he sustained leg and arm injuries in a fall down the cliff at Minard Head when they were landing with the Prince, and that he was completely out of action thereafter. He was lying on a bed, encased in plaster and under sedation, when the S.A.S. stormed the place.''

''But who could have made that last call if it wasn't Roche? It couldn't have been the I.R.A.''

''It certainly couldn't, but I'm afraid that's all we know, except that we do know that Roche had laid it on with his secretary for her to make such a call from Nassau—by using a pre-recorded audio disc—and that she failed to do so.''

''How do we know that?''

''From a search of the office they had rented in Nassau. The janitor said that the woman told him she had dropped a disc down the air conditioning duct. So far as she was concerned it had gone for good and she abandoned any attempt to send the message, even if—and we doubt it very much—she knew what it said. Our people retrieved the disc and confirmed that it contained a message telling us where the hideout was located. Presumably it should have been despatched after the delivery of the ransom. Perhaps that was why it wasn't. So, Roche didn't tell us, the I.R.A. didn't tell us, and we haven't a clue who did. Like the leak, Prime Minister, we may never know.''

The Prime Minister sat back and began to gather up her papers, a clear indication that the work of the Cabinet Office Briefing Room had come to an end. ''Ladies and Gentlemen,'' she said. ''I thank you most sincerely for all your help in this dreadful crisis. And may I say how delighted I am at the outcome. I'm afraid that, for obvious reasons, the work that has been done during the past ten days or so will never feature in any Honours List, but I'm sure that the gratitude of the British Nation is reward enough.''

*   *   *

As the Prime Minister and her crisis-management team began to disperse, the Home Secretary took a last look at one file which had remained in front of him after all the others had been removed. It was to receive different treatment from the rest, in that he would be the last person to read it for the next hundred years, for it was destined to disappear at once into the limbo reserved for a government's most sensitive files. On its cover were the words *'Operation Relay Run'*, and its contents included the only surviving copies of the telex messages which had passed between C.O.B.R. and the tactical commander of the Task Force which had rescued the hostages from Minard Head. All other copies had been shredded.

The reason for the file's sensitivity lay in its disclosure that the words of Dan Twomey at the meeting held to reconstitute *An Triúir* after the Boston funeral had come only too true. There *had* been a breaking point in the British resolve . . . not, as he had thought, in their resolve to stand firm against terrorism, but in their resolve to fight according to the rules. As the Prime Minister had said, ''A unique situation calls for a unique set of 'Rules of Engagement'.''

A civil servant was already preparing the sealing wax as the Home Secretary read the final batch of messages, the first of which began with the words *'Penultimate stage of Operation Relay Run completed. Baton handed to next runner'*, a reference to the landing of the Prince and his detective on Inch Strand and the picking up of the pair by Sergeant O'Reilly and his fellow *Garda Siochana* officers.

It was the very last of those messages—despatched thirty hours after the S.A.S. assault on the hide-out, when H.M. Submarine *Oracle* had risen again from the depths of the Atlantic Ocean—that held the clue to why there would never be an Irish Coroner's Inquest into the deaths of the I.R.A. terrorists. Headed *'Operation Relay Run completed. Score eleven nil'*, it gave an account of the fate of Big Michael Roche—*The Soldier*—and the ten other I.R.A. men who had fallen into the hands of the S.A.S. on Minard Head.

His pain subdued by morphine and his senses dulled by intra-muscular injections of Valium, Roche had been out of the game from the moment he fell down the cliff. The command of the operation, and of the group holed up with its hostage at the farm there, had thereafter devolved upon Gerry McMahon, who had orders to kill him and dispose of his body when it was all over.

In the event, the British saved him the trouble, when, far to the south-west of the Dingle Peninsula, out in the Atlantic, way beyond Irish territorial waters, H.M. Submarine *Oracle* rose again from the depths. The sea was calm, the sky a clear blue and the horizon empty. Hatches were opened, and, with all the sailors confined below, a group of S.B.S. men hauled out onto *Oracle's* deck eleven large bags made of heavy-duty polythene and tightly bound with polypropylene ropes. They heaved them one by one over the side, where they sank at once into three hundred and fifty fathoms, the heavy weights of metal and stone stowed inside ensuring that they would lie on the ocean bed until Doomsday.

"I'll bet that big bugger with the casts on his arm and leg will stay down for sure," joked one marine. "That plaster must weigh a bloody ton."

"God Bless Ireland," said another. "Eleven more for Stalker!"

It had not worked out exactly in the way he had intended, but Big Michael Roche's plan *had* worked, after all. He really *had* found a new way out of the Provisional I.R.A. He really *had* got out without a coffin. A heavy-duty polythene sack, yes. But not a coffin!

CHAPTER TWENTY FIVE

Daniel Joseph Twomey had never missed a Venetian Night. He had never failed to witness the climax of Chicago's summertime Air and Water Show, which—centred on its Lake Michigan frontage—brings together the very best of outdoor spectacle in the two elements which give the show its name. Nor had he ever failed to end his evening in the Emerald Isle Bar on East Pearson Street, where he and his fellow ex-patriates could wallow in nostalgia, Irish songs and Guinness and turn the clock back to times sad, happy and heroic. He always arrived smack on seven o'clock, a piece of timekeeping he would *never* have observed back in the embattled days of the Black and Tans and the Irish Civil War nearly seventy years before. Such time-keeping then could have notoriously fatal consequences. So it did on the evening of Thursday 24th August, when his chauffeur-driven Cadillac glided to a halt by the crowded sidewalk on Lake Shore Drive.

As his chauffeur opened the rear door and Twomey began to emerge, a hand holding a revolver was thrust over the chauffeur's left shoulder from behind, and two .357 Magnum bullets smashed through the Irishman's right temple. He dropped like a stunned cow. His chauffeur instinctively dropped to his knees over him and the crowd stampeded in a confusion of shouts and screams, in the midst of which the gunman simply disappeared. Daniel Joseph Twomey died instantly.

Nine hundred miles east, in Boston, Massachusetts, it was six o'clock Eastern Standard Time. Also a stickler for time, Martin Neil Burke, Twomey's long-time partner in *An Triúir*, was leaving the prestigious Hancock Building on Clarendon Street, which contained the headquarters of his giant Burtec Corporation. He had taken only a few steps across the broad sidewalk when a powerful motor cycle roared into life fifty yards away. Its rear tyre smoking, it sped across the paving and paused alongside Burke and his escorting chauffeur just long enough for its pillion passener to put into his head, chest and back four short bursts of fire from an Ingram sub-machine gun. Then it roared away and was lost in Boston's evening rush hour.

The newest, and now the only surviving, member of *An Triúir*, Philadelphia banker Seamus McDonagh, was on a business trip to Europe when he learned of the deaths of Twomey and Burke. He read the news in Saturday's European edition of the *New York Herald Tribune*, delivered to him with his breakfast in his hotel room near Belleville-sur-Mer, on France's Atlantic coast. He also had a copy of the London *Times*, in which he read an obituary: 'Sir Daniel James Morant, K.C.M.G., C.V.O., D.S.O. Death in Tragic Circumstances'. It went on to describe the man's life and career, from his birth in Manchester, through his education at Manchester Grammar School and Oxford University, his wartime service as an officer of the Manchester Regiment, and his subsequent career in the Home Civil Service, which included key posts with the Northern Ireland Office and a two-year spell at the heart of government, as an Assistant Secretary to the Cabinet Office. He had retired from the Civil Service as a Deputy Under Secretary of State.

'Seconded in October, 1941, to Combined Operations,' the obituary continued, 'Sir Daniel became a Staff Officer to its Director, Lord Louis Mountbatten, and was involved in the planning of the large-scale amphibious raid on Dieppe, an operation which, though it involved heavy losses, was regarded as carrying important lessons for the planning of the invasion of Europe which followed two years later. Upon the appointment of General Montgomery to the command of the 8th Army in the Western Desert in July, 1942, Sir Daniel left Combined Operations and accompanied him to Egypt to join his staff there, with promotion to Lieutenant Colonel . . .'

The final paragraph told how he had died: 'The death of Sir Daniel James Morant occurred yesterday on the London Underground at Piccadilly Station, when he accidentally slipped from the platform and fell under a moving train.'

After breakfast, McDonagh walked from his hotel to the top of the gleaming white chalk cliffs. Digging his hands into the pockets of his windcheater, he looked down to where the slight westerly wind was creasing the calm blue sea into narrow streaks of white at the edge of the beach two hundred feet below. The sun, rising above and behind him, shone down on golden sands, and the cries of children and the laughter of their parents rang faintly through the morning air. Seamus McDonagh stood deep in thought, for the last time he had seen that beach he had been as near as any man could be to hell.

His thoughts were floating out over the sea, back over the forty-seven years that had passed since the time when, as a fighting-fit, twenty year old U.S. army P.F.C. (Private 1st Class), he had marched down a troopship gangway and stepped once again onto his native Irish soil. A World War Two conscript, McDonagh had landed in Londonderry with the first contingent of U.S. troops to be sent to Europe, in the spring of 1942, and, in June of that year, had become one of the very first U.S. Army Rangers—a troop of forty-five men who, under small, ebullient Captain Roy Murray, had laid foundations of military skill and courage on which a legend would be built.

For McDonagh, though, a man with a fiercely Irish republican background, his first Ranger posting—to Achnacarry, at the eastern end of Scotland's Loch Arkaig—had come as a shock, *for the embryo U.S. Rangers were taken under the wing of the British army*! The shock was short-lived, though, for they were to train with the British Commandos, the world's experts in amphibious warfare, of whom they were to become blood brothers. It was from them that they learned their trade, under the British Acting Vice-Admiral Lord Louis Mountbatten, newly-appointed Chief of Combined Operations, a man the Yanks came to worship every bit as much as did their British comrades-in-arms.

A hard grind their training had been. Long night marches in full battle order, punishing assaults on precipitous cliffs and mountains, exhausting beach landings under fiery umbrellas of live ammunition. Vivid memories flooded back to him, but none of them as vivid as that of the night when they had first done it for real.

He remembered the fine August evening when No. 3 British Commando, with its American Ranger component, had moved out of Newhaven harbour in twenty-five wooden landing craft, to rendezvous with their Royal Navy destroyer escort in the English Channel. And he remembered the bombshell that came at precisely 3.47 a.m., when, out of the darkness ahead, streaking and roaring through the flock of L.C.P.s and pouring a storm of twenty milimetre cannon fire into the frail, scantily-armed craft, German E-boats smashed what should have been the left flank cover for the main landing. What few boats were not shot to pieces and sunk had dispersed in confusion, and when 3 Commando hit the beach below the sheer cliffs of Belleville-sur-Mer where he now stood, only seven of its twenty-five L.C.P.s had made it.

The withering fire of the German defences had done the rest. In broad daylight the commandos and rangers were cut to pieces. McDonagh shuddered as he looked down on the happy holiday-makers below. He was hearing the deafening gunfire, seeing the showers of sand and stones as the beach had exploded around him, hearing the screams of the wounded. Lieutenant Loustalot dying alongside him as a burst of machine-gun fire smashed his head and shoulder . . . the first American soldier to be killed on the mainland of Europe in World War Two. The others—dead and wounded— were left behind as the survivors scrambled through a hail of bullets and mortar fire back down to the beach to where their two remaining L.C.P.s lay far out on the ebbing tide. Only a handful had left that beach alive.

The Dieppe raid, the brain-child of Lord Louis Mountbatten, had ended in disaster, with three and a half thousand casualties out of the five thousand troops—most of them Canadian—put ashore on that August morning, forty-seven years ago, almost to the day.

The war had taken Seamus McDonagh to other beaches—Arzeu in North Africa, Sicily, Salerno, Anzio, and to the Normandy invasion, where, with the 2nd Ranger Battalion, he had scaled the sheer hundred foot cliff at Pointe du Hoc under a storm of machine gun and mortar fire which had carried off two thirds of his comrades. He had survived, but he had never forgotten how the Germans had been waiting for them that night, out at sea and in and around Dieppe, and he had made it his business after the war to find out why. A post-war secondment to the Allied War Crimes Commission in Germany, gave him access to top secret *Abwehr* files where he found his first clues. The source of the tip-off, it seemed, was Irish-American, with a *Clann na Gael* connection, and the story of the 'accidental' encounter between the Allied landing force and a small German coastal convoy had been a smokescreen.

Yet that was only part of the answer, and many more years of expensive and dedicated investigation were to follow before Martin Burke tapped him on the shoulder in Boston's Catholic cemetery and put into his hands the documents that had given him the final key.

McDonagh's next stop was a lay by on the N.27 road, just south of Dieppe, where it forks for Paris. He parked his car on the lay by and walked the quarter of a mile along the footpath to the village of Nautot-sur-Mer and the Military Cemetery, where he walked among the rows of gleaming white stones which mark the graves of those who had fallen alongside him in the terrible battle on the Dieppe beaches nearly half a century before; the graves of Canadians, British and French, of men from other German-occupied European countries. And of a small number of Americans, in a corner of the cemetery, where he found the grave he was looking for. Like the ones alongside it—white stone crosses— it bore the bald eagle and shield of the United States, and tears welled in McDonagh's eyes as he read its inscription.

He knelt, put his lips close to the gravestone and whispered the secret of how his long search for those who had betrayed them to the Germans had come to an end, and how he had, at last, exacted vengeance for the man who lay in that grave and for the seven hundred and fifty-five others around him.

"*An Triúir* did it, Pad. Those two bastards Twomey and Burke set us up. They did for you, Pad, they did for the rest of the guys, and they damn near did for me. Then they did for our chief, Mountbatten. But I got 'em, Pad. I blew their plans to kill Mountbatten's nephew, and *then* I got *them*. I was too late to get that bastard, Brennan, but I sure as hell got the other two sons of bitches. *And* Morant, the guy who gave them the plans for Dieppe." He took his cigar from his mouth, spat, and then smiled. "'We've only to say the word,' they told me, 'and the I.R.A. will kill. No questions, no nothing. We give the order and they just kill.' And you know, Pad . . . they were dead right!"

He gently kissed the cold grave stone, placed his left hand on it, and helped himself to his feet. Taking a pace backwards, he stood to attention and saluted. His eyes misted over as he took a last, lingering look at the inscription on the stone:

'U.S. Rangers.
Ranger McDonagh, P.J.
Killed in action. Dieppe, 19th August, 1942.
Aged 19 years'.

211

He made the sign of the cross, said a last goodbye to his young brother, clamped the cigar back in his mouth and walked slowly away.

*   *   *

Seamus McDonagh was a trustee of the Philadelphia Orchestra and a patron of the Philadelphia Academy of Fine Arts. So he had no difficulty in contriving a meeting with the newly-appointed Cultural Attaché at the British Embassy in Washington—Steven Gannon. They met first at a reception after the Philadelphia Orchestra's New Year concert, and again at a reception hosted by the British Embassy in Washington to welcome the Royal Ballet on its tour of North America. The fact that the two men hit it off so well owed as much to Gannon's interest in McDonagh's involvement in Noraid fund-raising as to the other's interest in him, but hit it off they did, and it was not long before Gannon, whose wife had not yet joined him in America, found himself invited to the Irishman's palatial Philadelphia home for a weekend.

In fact, it was the weekend which included Gannon's birthday, and it was as their two champagne glasses touched in an after-dinner birthday toast that Seamus McDonagh delivered his bombshell. ''Happy Birthday,'' he said. ''And now hold on to your hat, Steve. I've got a birthday present for you that's going to be the biggest surprise of your life.'' He paused, put down his glass, and held his arms apart. ''Meet your long-lost brother!''

''Brother?''

''Brother! I never knew until some documents came my way recently. I never knew until then that our ma and pa had had two other sons after Pad and I had been sent over here as kids when the going got tough back home in Ireland. It seems you were born just before Pa died and then fostered out to a family in England. As soon as I found out I set about tracking you down. But of course you were hospitalised after the shooting and I couldn't fix a get-together until now . . .'' He held up his hands. ''Don't worry,'' he laughed, ''I know the score. My F.B.I. contacts are as strong as yours. I'm on *your* side.''

Gannon stood open-mouthed for a few seconds. He threw back his glass of champagne. ''Are you serious?''

212

"As serious as you can get, Steve. The evidence is in my strong-room. I'll show you. I have a feeling you'll be very interested. It should suit your line of work to a T."

Gannon could hardly speak. Even the pointed references to McDonagh's knowledge that he was a British Secret Service agent seemed not to penetrate his spinning brain. "My brother? And I have others?"

"There's only two of us now, Steve. Pad was killed when we landed with the Rangers at Dieppe in '42. I was alongside him when he died. A mortar bomb. Only nineteen he was. Funny you should go on to become a commando too. Well, 'Rangers' they called us—'U.S. Rangers'. It was your Lord Mountbatten who thought up the name, just before he sent us on the Dieppe landing. Not many Yanks know that. I never knew the other boy. He was fostered to England like you . . . to a family named Farrell in Liverpool . . . and he died a year ago. Automobile accident. He was a soldier too. Airborne. Finished up as a brigadier. I've got the file on him as well, *and* a lot more."

Gannon was speechless.

"Take it from me, little brother," said McDonagh, putting his hands on the 'Englishman's' shoulders, "This is going to be the biggest thing that ever happened to us." He refilled their glasses. "A toast, Steve. A toast to something else we have in common."

Gannon raised his glass in a daze. McDonagh's clinked against it. "Our toast, Steve. *'The truth on our tongues . . . the purity in our hearts . . . the strength in our arms!'"*

*   *   *

"All I heard," the butler-bodyguard told the detective, "was a great yell . . . well a loud, piercing scream really, and then two shots. I was bringing in the brandy and I just dropped the tray, drew my gun and dashed in. Mr. Gannon was standing by the fireplace, right there, holding Mr. McDonagh by the throat with his left hand. The muzzle of his revolver was still against his forehead, right between the eyes. The whole wall was covered with blood and brains . . ."

"And then?"

"And then Mr. Gannon let go and Mr. McDonagh fell to the floor. All the back of his head was gone. Mr. Gannon turned around and stood staring at me for, maybe, a couple of seconds. A wild, staring look he had, and sweat pouring from his face . . . like somebody demented. Then he began screaming out words I couldn't make any sense of . . . something about purity, and strength, and truth. I knew as soon as he started raising his revolver that he was going to kill me. So I shot him . . . twice."

*   *   *

The killings caused a sensation, but they soon faded from the headlines following the verdict of the Philadelphia Coroner that Gannon had killed McDonagh while suffering some kind of brainstorm, and that the butler had killed Gannon in self-defence.

What had triggered off the brainstorm, or what else might have driven Gannon to kill a man he hardly knew, remained a mystery, said the Coroner.

A search of the house had proved negative, though had the investigating officer thought of digging up the strongroom floor it would have been a very different story. For there lay the steel chest containing *An Triúir*'s only records, protected by a self-destruct device that would have incinerated those records had anyone but McDonagh attempted to gain entry.

So *An Triúir* died as it had lived . . . unknown, unrecognised, unheard of, except by a select number of those it had helped in their work of terror. Its small army of British 'sleepers' lived on, though, each unaware of the existence of the others; aware of nothing but the code-name *Boru* . . . and a legacy of demons, which would pursue them to their graves.